D1002179

HELL BAY

Also by Will Thomas

HELL BAY

WILL THOMAS

MINOTAUR BOOKS ❦ NEW YORK

This is a work of fiction. All of the characters, organizations, and events portrayed in this novel are either products of the author's imagination or are used fictitiously.

HELL BAY. Copyright © 2016 by Will Thomas. All rights reserved. Printed in the United States of America. For information, address St. Martin's Press, 175 Fifth Avenue, New York, N.Y. 10010.

www.minotaurbooks.com

Library of Congress Cataloging-in-Publication Data

Names: Thomas, Will, 1958– author.
Title: Hell Bay : a Barker & Llewelyn novel / Will Thomas.
Description: First edition. | New York : Minotaur Books, 2016.
Identifiers: LCCN 2016021608 | ISBN 978-1-250-07795-0 (hardcover) |
    ISBN 978-1-4668-9028-2 (e-book)
Subjects: LCSH: Barker, Cyrus (Fictitious character)—Fiction. | Private
    investigators—England—London—Fiction. | Great Britain—History—
Victoria, 1837–1901—Fiction. | Murder—Investigation—Fiction. | BISAC:
    FICTION / Mystery & Detective / Traditional British. | FICTION / Mystery
    & Detective / Historical. | GSAFD: Historical fiction. | Mystery fiction.
Classification: LCC PS3620.H644 H44 2016 | DDC 813/.6—dc23
LC record available at https://lccn.loc.gov/2016021608

Our books may be purchased in bulk for promotional, educational, or business use. Please contact your local bookseller or the Macmillan Corporate and Premium Sales Department at 1-800-221-7945, extension 5442, or by e-mail at MacmillanSpecialMarkets@macmillan.com.

First Edition: October 2016

10 9 8 7 6 5 4 3 2 1

To my sisters,
Sherry and Denise,
who enjoy mysteries
as much as I do

ACKNOWLEDGMENTS

First, I would like to thank my agent, Maria Carvainis, whose guiding hand through the years means so much to me.

I have a fabulous team at Minotaur that I would like to thank: my terrific editor, Keith Kahla; Hannah Braaten, Hector DeJean, and so many others who worked on the fabulous cover and all of the many jobs that made it possible to see *Hell Bay* in print.

To the many librarians who helped me assemble the research for this novel, and to the family and friends who encourage me along the way, I extend my thanks.

And to my family, Julia, Caitlin, David, and Heather, who encourage me daily as I create the world of Barker and Llewelyn. My deepest thanks for your love and support.

HELL BAY

PROLOGUE

Harold Throgmorton's face was florid. He had exerted himself too much for a man approaching seventy. He'd reached that age at which a man should sit back and take his ease in life, and even consider an end to work entirely, with a modest pension. And yet, there were a few pleasures here at the Bromley Boarding School he would miss; one of them was caning a child who had dared to be willful at his school. He had collected a number of tools for the work over the years—hickory, oak, malacca—and even made his own improvements upon them, testing them on the backsides of a generation of unruly boys. He had just finished with one, a boy who had deliberately spat on the stairs.

The headmaster reached to the sideboard and poured himself a tumbler of water, willing his hand to stop shaking and his heart to slow to its proper beat. He believed, most of all, in self-discipline. If his students actually took his messages seriously, they could have derived great benefit as they matured and made their way into the world. But no, most if not all of the boys who came through his school lacked any real moral fiber, and each class was worse than the last. They were slack, lazy, and degenerate. All his words of wisdom were no more to them than pearls before swine. Perhaps in his twilight years he should consider putting them down in a book. There might yet be someone in the world who could appreciate such razor-sharp foresight.

He should have gone to London, he told himself. Far better than flogging his life away here in far-off Cornwall. He could have been a headmaster at Eton or Rugby by now. Had he taken the easy way through life? Positions were always open, but hard-won. He had talent; he should have tested it against the best and brightest England had to offer. He could even have taught in Europe at a university, Heidelberg or Berlin. Yes, perhaps he had allowed himself to take an easy route, running a choice boy's school on the west coast for forty years. Once he'd been the youngest headmaster he knew. Now he was the oldest.

There was a knock at the door.

"Come in!" he called.

The door opened and a dried old trout of a fellow entered.

"What is it, Walpole?"

"The tomatoes, sir," the bursar said. "From the grocer. They were bad. The entire bushel. The cook will have to change the menu."

"So, let him get on with it," Throgmorton sputtered.

"We'll have to announce the change."

"Who in bloody hell cares if we do or do not have grilled tomatoes with our supper?"

The old fellow visibly kept from heaving a sigh. Even the bursars were not a patch on the ones that had come before.

"I'll inform everyone if you'd prefer not to do so, sir," the man answered.

"Do it," Throgmorton growled. "I've got more important things to do with my time, thank you."

"Very well," Walpole said, backing toward the door. "I'll see that everyone is told."

When he was gone, the headmaster sat down in his chair and poured himself a second glass. Chaos. Everything was falling into chaos everywhere. Standards were no longer being met, and so they lowered the standards, rather than getting at the root of the problem, which was lazy boys. Boys needed to be disciplined hard and often if they were to make anything of themselves, and only one in a hundred had natural discipline. It requires a man with the knowledge of how much punishment a boy's body could take in order to break their spirits and make them ready for instruction. Once they received it, there was no end to how high they could soar.

There was a sound outside, which came to Harold Throgmorton's attention through a half-open window, raised due to the heat of the day. He crossed to the window, threw up the sash, and looked out upon the knoll the school used for recess after lunch. As usual, the students were skylarking, getting into trouble when there was a perfectly good cricket game in progress toward the back of the green. Throgmorton had the pitch put in himself, to combat indolence. The headmaster's attention focused on two boys nearby, who were engaged in a wrestling match while still standing, one with an arm tight around the other's neck. The aggressor was Toler, a bully if there ever was one. He'd warmed the headmaster's paddle many times. The boy he was picking on was a spindly specimen by the name of Wilkins, thin as a rail and bespectacled.

"Toler!" he bellowed. "What do you think you're about? Leave off tormenting Wilkins before I haul you in here and give you stripes like a tiger!"

Everyone stopped and stared, Toler in particular. He pulled his arm from around the smaller boy's neck and attempted to look innocent, while Wilkins lay in the grass, coughing.

"You think that's funny, do you, Toler? Perhaps we need to call your father in for a conference about your attitude."

The boy's eyes went large. If there was a bigger bully in England than Toler Junior it was Toler Senior. He ran a manufacturing business with an iron thumb, and would not appreciate having to come to the school during office hours to deal with an unruly son. Once junior came in with a blackened eye after being sent home from school the day before.

"Sorry, sir! Wilkins and I were just playing, weren't we, Wilkins?"

Breaking their spirit, that's what it was all about. It was the same with horses. You break their pride by showing there was someone higher up they needed to obey. You do that and they become ready to learn. If they learn their lessons, soon they will be ready to lead. If it was good enough for kings, it was more than good enough for this lot.

From his window, Throgmorton began scrutinizing each and every child in the play yard for infractions. His standards were exacting.

"Barnaby, straighten your tie!"

"Yes, Headmaster."

"Quilby, you know gaiters are not part of the school uniform!"

"Yes, sir! Sorry, sir!"

"Henning, you—"

No one would ever know what infraction he had assigned to Henning, because just at that moment a bullet struck Headmaster Harold Throgmorton square between the eyes. It shattered the pince-nez he was wearing and killed him instantly. Quite probably, he died feeling no pain whatsoever, which, considering how much he had inflicted on others during his many years, doesn't exactly seem fair.

All the young men from fourteen to eighteen who were playing or standing in the yard watched him fall. One of them later claimed that Toler gave a kind of cheer, but no one could verify the claim. All of the witnesses agreed the shot came from the woods that surrounded the school on three sides, but no one actually saw the shooter or any sign of a rifle. There had been no visitors to the school that day, there were no gypsies in the area, and the nearby town of Roxton had little trouble with poachers.

An examination of the woods that afternoon by the local constabulary revealed no trace of an assailant, such as footfalls, cigarette ends lying about, or broken limbs scattered among the bushes. In short, some person or persons unknown had willfully murdered the headmaster and gotten away with it free and clear. So the coroner's jury ruled in the Royal George Inn the following week.

They say in the afterlife all things shall become illuminated. If so, perhaps Throgmorton would find some irony in the fact that the bullet that ended his life came by way of the one student in his generation who took the headmaster's lessons to heart.

CHAPTER ONE

We all make mistakes, of course, even the best of us. Some of us are famous for them. We make big ones, small ones, messy ones, boneheaded ones, spectacular ones, and occasionally deadly ones. Take the fellow in a hurry, who steps off the curb into the path of an approaching omnibus. Something had happened that morning to throw off his schedule, and one by one, events had toppled like standing dominoes until he took the fatal step, which had seemed perfectly reasoned at the time. In one instant, his life became encapsulated in a brief article in *The Times*.

Even those who have a reputation for not making mistakes make them all the same, just not as often or as visibly, but when they do, they can be real crackers. One can fool Mother Nature only so long before she must have her due, and she can be a contentious old biddy when she wants to be.

"What's the name of this place again?" I asked Cyrus Barker as I trotted south beside him in Whitehall Street. The Houses of Parliament and Westminster Abbey were ahead of us, and across the street lay the Colonial Office, just past the Horse Guards who were passing in their shiny helmets. Sometimes I forget what an important street I am fortunate enough to work in.

"The Royal United Service Institution," he supplied in his raspy voice. "Are you having trouble assimilating the name?"

"I am. It sounds like a thousand similar departments in the area. What sets it apart from the others?"

"It was founded by the Duke of Wellington himself in 1831. Its purpose is to monitor other nations both politically and militarily, and suggest policy to the government. Their recommendations are taken very seriously."

"What sort of policy?" I asked, as Barker's long strides ate up the pavement.

"Suppose the Russians start building their navy and begin maneuvers in the North Sea. The Royal United would keep track of their movements and suggest a diplomatic warning and patrols of our own in the region."

"I see," I said.

"The organization is made up of diplomats, historians, and military strategists. They include some of the top minds in the country."

"Then why have I not heard of it before now?"

"You're not supposed to. They don't call attention to themselves."

"How do you know so much about it, then?"

"I try to keep abreast of the various agencies in the immediate vicinity, in case we might be of some use to them."

"Which, apparently, we are."

A telegram had arrived in our chamber that morning requesting our presence. It wasn't the kind of request one refused.

"That is it, there. The White Building."

I stopped and pointed. "That building? Sir, that's the Royal Banqueting Hall. It was built by King Henry VIII as part of the Palace of Whitehall. Are you sure that's the one?"

"Aye, it is. Now, come along."

We're like that, Cyrus Barker and I: chalk and cheese. If something interests one of us, it probably won't interest the other. Somehow, between us, we manage to know an awful lot of information that the general public has never heard of. I began walking again.

"You do know that Charles I was beheaded here. That's why the statue beside our offices faces this way."

"I hadn't," the Guv said, sounding about as bored as I did when he described the purpose of the Royal United Whatever-it-was.

"How did a palace sink to the level of being used as a mere government office?"

"You should consider it fortunate the building is standing at all. Space is at a premium in Whitehall. Shall we step inside?"

We did. I removed my bowler and looked about at what was left of Henry VIII's dream of the "greatest palace in Christendom." I found a once breathtaking building in poor repair, and crowded with modern furniture that in no way matched the décor. At least I could take in the magnificent ceiling.

"Rubens painted that," I said. "Peter Paul Rubens. Inigo Jones brought him here all the way from Antwerp, with the offer of a knighthood. Now look at it!"

The ceiling was decidedly sooty, probably the result of tobacco smoke. Everyone I saw in the bustling offices seemed to have a pipe, cigar, or cigarette in his mouth. The pantheon of gods overhead looked down wearily, as if contemplating a move to a healthier clime.

"We're here to see Lord Hargrave," Barker said to a guard, handing him the card we'd been sent.

The guard clapped a small bell sitting on his desk and an aged porter came along and led us up a staircase built for royalty to the first floor. The few doors that were open revealed either shelves containing books and files, or walls full of maps. People seemed to be lounging about. One fellow was actually seated on his desk rather than at it. Every desk had a full ashtray and a cup of tea on it, or the dregs of one. Men were talking, even gossiping, but no one looked particularly occupied. I still had trouble working out what they did here. They came to conclusions and made recommendations on matters of security. Based on what? Innumerable cigarettes and map reading, it would appear.

We came up to a door which the porter entered without a by-your-leave. There was a desk in this room, a substantial one, but it shared space with more shelves, books, boxes, and maps. Behind the desk was a gentleman approaching his sixtieth year, but doing so with squared shoulders and an authoritative manner. His hair was crisp and iron gray, and he had the kind of mustache that military men favor. When he looked at us, I saw a twinkle in his eye, as if there were a private joke to which we were not privy. He rose slowly but gracefully enough, and offered a hand, which Barker took. Meanwhile, the porter slunk out without comment or introduction.

"Mr. Barker," our host said.

"Lord Hargrave. This is my assistant, Thomas Llewelyn."

He shook my hand. His was dry and callused enough to crack a walnut with. He gestured for us to sit in the two chairs in front of his desk and lowered himself into his own.

"Gentlemen, are you aware of what we do here?" he asked.

"We are," Barker rumbled.

"There is an event which shall occur at my estate tomorrow, a private but important meeting with the French ambassador, Henri Gascoigne. Our purpose is to dictate policy between our governments. You may be aware there has been some friction between our colonies in Africa. It is hoped by our government that a treaty might be brokered between us. Henri is an old friend of mine, and we've both been entrusted with concessions if an agreement can be reached. You understand that I am taking you into my closest confidence. Even the Prince of Wales has not been informed of this meeting."

"How may we be of service, your lordship?"

"You have been recommended to me for security."

Barker held up his large hands, palms upward. "Alas, sir, you are looking at my entire operation. If challenged, I could extend it to five or six men, but not a sufficient number to cover such an event."

Lord Hargrave sat back in his chair, unfazed by Barker's refusal. "There is a second element to the negotiations. As I intimated, they are completely clandestine. In fact, they will be shrouded by another event at our estate, a house party. So far, none of my children have wed, and my wife has devised an event which she hopes may kindle a spark or two in that direction. It is hoped the talks may occur informally during the party."

"Which came first, sir?" I asked. "The plan or the party?"

"They both evolved concurrently, but it was I who put them together. You see, Henri and his wife are godparents to my daughter. It would be suspicious if he made a diplomatic mission here to London, and would raise questions at home. Attending a party at my estate would be another matter."

"May I assume that our presence there as security agents would be sub rosa?" Barker asked.

"Precisely. As long as you are not needed, we shall let the guests believe you are one of them."

Barker's brow curled in perplexity. "I don't think the lad here has much in his favor to suit Her Ladyship as a possible son-in-law. How are we to explain our presence?"

Hargrave chuckled. "As it happens, you are both already on the guest list," he said.

"I? How so?"

"You will be accompanying Mrs. Philippa Ashleigh. She is my wife, Celia's, closest friend, and she is helping to coordinate events. The invitations are already in the post. So you see, your presence is completely plausible, since you are already invited."

Barker crossed his arms and frowned, considering the matter. Of all the services he offered, security work was his least favorite. Too many unexpected things could happen. His Lordship had finessed that rather well, the old diplomat. Philippa, Barker's companion ever since I'd known him, had tried unsuccessfully for years to trap him into one of these week-long house parties, but he was as difficult to corner as a wounded badger. I wondered if the French alliance were a ruse merely to get the Guv into his evening kit at a social function, and at her side for an entire week.

Barker turned his head, studying me suspiciously from behind his dark-lensed spectacles, as if determining whether I was somehow part of this conspiracy. I took the opportunity to scrutinize a painting over the fireplace.

"She has not informed me that I would be accompanying her," he went on, mustering some sangfroid. "Pray tell me more about the party. Where shall it be?"

"On the Isles of Scilly. Ours is called Godolphin Island, after the family house. It is about one kilometer square. There is a jetty at the north end and a lighthouse at the other. Beyond that there is the house, a few outbuildings, and an old cannon left over from old Boney. It's secluded, but we prefer it that way. A launch brings supplies and visitors to the isle. Once it leaves, we will be alone with only each other for company."

"How is the launch summoned when needed? Is there a telephone cable?"

"Oh, dear me, no. Nothing as modern as that. There is a pole by the jetty. We run a red flag up it and the first boat that spies it and docks knows they will receive a gold sovereign for their labor."

"How many guests shall be there?"

In answer, His Lordship reached into the inside pocket of his jacket and handed a folded slip of paper to my employer. I leaned toward him and glanced over his shoulder at the list of names. There were at least a dozen of them there.

"This is quite a houseful. Have you any reason to suspect something might occur?"

"No, nothing at all. There have been minor border disputes between our countries in Africa, but I suspect the enmity between us since the Hundred Years War is finally at an end. We have mutual enemies in Russia and Germany. I would deny that they are our enemies in public, of course, but I want us to understand one another."

Barker crossed his arms, then raked his nails under his chin, a gesture he often made when he was thinking.

"What sort of staff is on the island?"

"There are the usual lot of servants in the house, plus a gardener. There is also a lighthouse keeper named Noah Flannen, but he rarely comes to our side of the island. He prefers his own company. A man of few words, but a good keeper. That's the lot."

"How many servants altogether, would you say?"

"Fifteen at most."

"That is almost two dozen people who might have reason to want the house party to fail. If I might make a recommendation to you, it would be to hire a full detail of guards, even if they are not needed. There is too much that could go wrong."

"The French ambassador insists upon privacy. He wishes to come and see how his favorite goddaughter is doing, and has no desire to see the island full of British men in uniforms."

"How astute is he? Would he notice a few extra footmen or undergardeners?"

"Too astute to trick so easily."

"What are my duties, precisely? To protect M. Gascoigne, he and you together, or the entire party? Each addition becomes progressively difficult."

"I'm concerned with Henri alone, of course, but if something were to occur to someone else and you can help without jeopardizing his safety, I hope you would consider lending your skills. I had considered doing without security entirely, but my natural inclination toward safety made me look for a few men I could trust. I have been told you are those men."

"I won't ask who provided the recommendation."

"That is good, because I will not give it. Do you accept the assignment or not?"

"I am caught in a snare of my own making, but I need not trouble you about that. Mr. Llewelyn and I accept the assignment."

His Lordship beamed a smile at us both. "Good man. Philippa, that is, Mrs. Ashleigh, has all the details. You're to be at the ferry in Land's End tomorrow at eleven. From there, you'll board a launch that will bring you to the island."

"The event will take a full week?"

"Six days and seven nights, yes. But the talk will take only a few days."

"Very well," Barker said. "Have you a sovereign?"

Lord Hargrave fished in his pocket for the required coin and put it in the Guv's hand with a questioning look.

"Thomas," my employer said, handing it to me. "This is a retainer for our services. Pray write up a contract and run it over here for a signature."

"Yes, sir."

Barker stood and nodded at His Lordship. "We won't take up any more of your time, sir. Come, Thomas, we have plans to make. Sir, if I have any further questions, will you be in Whitehall to answer them?"

"I fear not, I'm leaving within the hour."

"Good day, then."

Barker bowed and I clapped my bowler on my head, then we returned to the ground floor. I got another look at the Rubens. Who knew when I'd see it again?

"Damn and blast," Barker rumbled. "Philippa has trussed me like a Christmas goose."

"Surely it's not as bad as all that. It's only a party."

"A party lasts a few hours. It has a beginning, a middle, and an end. This kind of event goes on for days. Everyone gets to know everyone else. One cannot go anywhere without being questioned about everything. One is asked about one's relatives, one's political views, private history, and personal references. One engages in small talk. Do I look like the sort of person who enjoys engaging in small talk?"

"No, sir. I know you don't. But why did you accept the assignment, then?"

"I put off Philippa's last request. I cannot turn down another. Come to think of it, she took my refusal rather easily. I wonder if I've been tricked."

"Oh, no, sir. I'm certain Mrs. Ashleigh would never do such a thing."

We reached Craig's Court just as the old bell in the tower of the Houses of Parliament rang nine times. Barker opened the door, stepped inside, and jammed his walking stick into the stand as if he were a matador performing the *estocada* upon a hapless bull.

Filling a pipe from his cabinet, he was soon puffing angry plumes of smoke toward the ceiling.

"This had better be worth my while," he said. "If I have to endure a week of sweetmeats and polite conversation, I'm liable to set back Anglo-French relations all by myself."

CHAPTER TWO

We were up early the next morning to finish our packing. If I knew our butler, Jacob Maccabee, he was trying to convince the Guv that he was the better candidate to go with him, for while I could not do his work as perfectly as he could, he most certainly could do mine at least as well, if not better. Whether or not it was true, Barker had chosen me for the work and he would be difficult to convince. Rather than wait for a change of mind, I shaved, dressed, finished my packing, and had coffee and a bun for breakfast. We had a train to meet at Paddington Station shortly after ten that morning.

Mac was not the only one displeased by our leave-taking. Harm, Barker's prized Pekingese, trotted in circles by the front door, whining at our presumption in not taking his feelings into account. Whose lap would he sit in at night, and whose bed would he lie at the foot of? Not Mac's, that's for certain. The two barely tolerated each other. I bent to pat his head, but he scooted out from under as if my hand were a hot poker. He would not be mollified as long as we held the ridiculous notion of leaving without him. But then, I knew him well enough to understand he wouldn't go willingly, either. Someone must watch over the garden and keep out the foxes and stray cats or the country would go to ruin.

When we met Mrs. Ashleigh on the platform, the porters were attempting to load her mountain of cases into the luggage van. Save for my bay mare, Juno, all that I owned could fit into a single steamer trunk with room left over. Cyrus Barker owned many things, being a wealthy man, but he always packed sparingly. I'll never understand why women require so many cases of potions and perfumes and foundation garments, not to mention hats, muffs, and so on, but I suspect their difference from us in that regard is part of their charm. If a third of the items they bring along are never worn, well, what is the harm in that? That is, as long as I'm not doing the carrying.

Mrs. Ashleigh was immaculate in a traveling suit of light tweed in a color she would probably call aubergine. Her hat was a small spray of purple flowers and fruit, covered by a stiff veil that just reached the tip of her nose. She looked the most composed person on the platform. The Guv hailed her with his stick, and when they met they took each other's hands, and she patted him on the arm. They are not demonstrative in public. They smiled at each other and, with nary a word between them, entered the first-class coach.

Before we embarked, I left them to their private conversation and stepped out onto the platform. I like engines and keep a guide in my pocket to check off every kind I see. This one was a Great Western Railway Rover Class, a 4-2-2, liveried in GWR Brunswick green and named *Dragon*. She would be taking us from Isambard Kingdom Brunel's masterpiece, Paddington Station, all the way to the west coast. My favorite line is the Brighton, but I must admit the Dragon was a beauty, down to her pert copper chimney cap. I dared lean in close to the footplate and engaged the engine driver and footman in conversation about her. How much coal was she carrying? How fast would she go? What landmarks should I keep an eye open for between here and the coast? I slipped them half a crown before I left, for putting up with my questions. My work is important to me, but if by some miracle they offered me a permanent place on the footplate, I'd have been sorely tempted.

It occurred to me as I sat down in our compartment that this would be the closest I would come to my home and family in many years. A lot had happened to me since I had left Gwent five years before: university, marriage, imprisonment, widowhood, destitution, and finally employment with one of the most unusual men in London. At his insistence, I had finally written to them and begun sending back money regularly to meet the demands of a large family, but so far I had not returned to what I considered my disgrace. But my employer and Mrs. Ashleigh were talking and there I was, off in my own thoughts.

"I've known her for ages," she was saying. "She helped me through my mother's final days when I was a youth and attended my wedding. When I returned years later from China a widow, she made a trip to Sussex especially to see me. We've been friends ever since."

"Is she of like age to her husband?" the Guv asked.

"No, she is nearly a decade younger than Lord Hargrave. They are each from a distinguished family but they are very close. It is considered one of the best matches in society. The house is hers and the money is his. Normally, it is the other way around. She didn't want to leave her ancestral seat, and he agreed. They've been blessed with two sons and a daughter."

"Has he been working in Whitehall long?" Barker asked.

"Four or five years, I think. Before that, he was the ambassador to France under Gladstone. He's considered one of the most knowledgeable men on French affairs, but to tell you the truth, I don't know what his current position is, if he has one. I was surprised to hear he had called upon you."

Barker crossed his arms and sat back against the seat of our carriage. "I was under the impression that you and Lady Hargrave had hatched this between you."

"Oh, no, I rather think this is your fault, not mine," Philippa replied, touching his sleeve again with a gloved hand.

"How so?"

"You have successfully managed to avoid meeting Celia at several events. She may have put forward your name in order to finally make your acquaintance."

Cyrus Barker did his best not to look glum. He finds first-class carriages cramped, however, so after a decent interval, he and I availed ourselves of the smoking car. There he spread out on the bench, filled his traveling meerschaum, and seized a handful of newspapers. I opened a window and took up the least dull-looking of the journals available, an issue of *Blackwood's*. After a few minutes, my employer grunted.

I've become an expert on Barker's grunts. He has several to display irritation, inquisitiveness, confirmation, or even triumph. This one was to show interest. I looked up in enquiry.

"Unusual murder, or perhaps a mere hunting accident. The headmaster of the Bromley Boarding School in Roxton opens a chamber window to call to some of his charges and is shot dead."

"A stray bullet from a poacher, perhaps?" I asked.

"The headmaster, Harold Throgmorton, was known as a strict disciplinarian, but had no known enemies. A search was made of the woods nearby, but no tramps or gypsies were found."

I chuckled and put down my magazine. "The most likely suspects, I'm sure, only neither is likely to have a rifle accurate over twenty feet."

"Precisely. And listen to this."

Local Woman Found Dead
The body of Mrs. Yolanda Tisher was found this morning
outside of her retirement cottage in St. Ives. She was sixty-nine.
Her neck was broken, according to the medical examiner, and
there were signs of a struggle. Mrs. Tisher had run a successful
boarding school for infants for many years, having retired after
three decades. Inspector Whiteburn of the local constabulary
asks that anyone with pertinent information in this case
come forward.

"Boarding school for infants," I said. "I suppose you mean a baby farm for illegitimate children. Where was the first murder?"

"Redruth."

"I've been there once. It's a distance of about twenty miles between them, at least. One's a schoolmaster and the other a schoolmistress of sorts. You think there is a connection?"

"I think two murders in a week in this part of the country exceedingly rare, but the murder methods are dissimilar. If one has a good rifle, why attack a woman in the street? Women of that profession tend to be hardened old crones."

"It sounds as if she put up a struggle."

"No doubt."

"Inspector Whiteburn has his hands full, but then so do we. I suppose when our duties on the Scilly Isles are finished, if the murders are still unsolved, we might look in, if you have a mind to do so."

Barker grunted again. I took it to mean "perhaps."

Back in the first-class carriage, we found Mrs. Ashleigh engaged in conversation with an older gentleman and his wife. It was her way. She was of such a gentle yet vivacious character that people could not help but be drawn to her side. Babies cooed at her, children engaged her in secret-telling, and even gruff elderly men could not help but converse with her. Barker could sit next to a passenger from Brighton to John o' Groat's and not think to ask him a question, even if it were to open a window.

We were introduced, rather against Barker's will, I suspect. The gentleman was Colonel Ross Fraser of the Coldstream Guard, retired. I could have told he was military from across the carriage. There was a crease in his tweed trousers. He had a regulation mustache, and even a regulation wife, reminding me of a bouquet of faded roses, dried and preserved. I know that's not a valid description of either of them, of course, but that was the impression they left with me.

"The Colonel and Mrs. Fraser are coming to Godolphin House," Philippa explained.

"Ah."

"What do you do for a living, Mr. Barker?" the colonel asked, putting out a strong but spotty hand.

"I run an agency in Whitehall. This is my assistant, Thomas Llewelyn."

"I'm pleased to meet you, sir," I said, being polite.

"Hulloa, young fella-m'lad. Have either of you been to Godolphin House before?"

We both admitted that we hadn't. I looked out the window and watched the trees and telegraph poles go by, thinking we would soon be in Wales. Home.

"It's amazing what they have managed to build on what is essentially a barren rock. They have a marvelous gardener. He's practically a miracle worker to grow anything there besides coral and sponges."

"Have you known Lord Hargrave long?"

"Oh, a dog's years at least. He was my aide-de-camp, don't you know. The man's certainly come up in the world since then, but he would have even if he hadn't inherited the family fortune. A first-class brain, Richard has. One has to in order to do what he does."

"Which is?"

"He anticipates the next bad business our enemies intend to pull off, in order to throw a spanner into it. Take the French, for example. They can't dispute our borders in eastern Africa if we've just signed a treaty with them, now can they?"

The colonel smiled, revealing a full set of ivory teeth that had looked better on the elephant. I was trying to decide if his appearance as a bluff, average old soldier was genuine, or whether he was holding cards up his sleeve alongside his regulation handkerchief. If there is one thing I've learned from Barker, it is not to reveal too much about myself in casual conversation. It was the most difficult thing for me to learn. Five minutes' conversation and normally you'll know my hat size. Now, thanks to the Guv, I've learned the art of turning a conversation back on itself.

"I suppose not," I agreed. "How far is the island from Land's End?"

"Expecting a touch of mal de mer, young fella? My wife gets that. It takes her a full day to get her legs under her again. It's about thirty miles. It is the most southeasterly of the Scilly Isles. Quite a distance from London, but you know, he goes home once a fortnight just to see Celia. Never misses one, no matter what the crisis."

"You sound quite proud of him," I said.

"Always knew he would go far."

We grew silent and listened to the two women discussing various topics for a good hour at least. From time to time I joined in to hold up the side, but I don't mind confessing it was rough seas. As soon as I came up with something pithy or worth saying, they had already moved on to another topic of conversation.

It was a long ride to Cornwall, however. Words eventually ran out, and people turned to books and newspapers. The colonel napped in the corner while his wife knitted. Barker and Mrs. Ashleigh seemed to silently commune in each other's company, while I stared out the window through a light rain, watching the faintly familiar countryside for some sign of recognition. It was a struggle not to join the colonel in Slumberland, but I was able to stay awake. My thoughts turned to the newspaper accounts Barker had mentioned. Who, I wondered, would shoot a schoolmaster? I mean, they are never on one's list of personal favorites, but I've never heard of anyone killing one.

In this new century with its innovations and its large companies gobbling up smaller ones like fish in a pond, the newly christened Cornish Riviera Limited can travel from London to Penzance in five hours, but in 1889, it took nearly twice that. We were of sturdier stock then, however, when Victoria was on the throne, and if it took ten hours to get somewhere, that's how long it took. One mustn't grumble. Or if one did, Barker wouldn't listen, which is much of a kind.

It was near teatime as we approached the Cornish coast, and the top windows of the compartment were open or it would be stultifying. I could smell the sharp tang of sea air, which always sounds better than it really is, a mixture of salt, seaweed, and dead fish. As I felt the brakes being applied, I noted that the gaslights were already lit. There was no through line to Land's End, so we would stop for the night here and take an omnibus coach to the coast in the morning. Dragon deposited its cargo of sore, tired, and ravenous passengers upon an unsuspecting Penzance.

CHAPTER THREE

We had reservations at the Union Hotel in Penzance, a solid, traditional old inn of good size. It wasn't Claridge's, but we were sore and tired after our journey and it would do. We dined on halibut and afterward I took a walk about the town. I hadn't been out of London in a while and the place seemed rural and provincial by moonlight and yet it made me think of home again. I stopped in at a pub and had a half pint of bitter, then returned to the hotel and fell into bed. Barker came up a half hour later. The last thing I recall hearing was the clunk of his final shoe on the floor, the last thought that we had just come three hundred miles and I hoped the journey would be worth our effort.

In the morning we had kippered herring and crumpets with our eggs and tea. Mrs. Ashleigh came down in a suit of blue-gray heather which set off the russet in her hair. Barker and I rose as she entered and sat after her.

"Did you see anyone from our party, my dear?" he asked.

"Aside from the colonel and his wife, there is Lady Alicia and the Honorable Algernon Kerry."

"I see."

"Oh, and there is a Dr. Anstruther and his two daughters, Gwendolyn and Bella."

I did no more than look across the dining room at the family, enough to notice that one was dark-haired and the other more fair, but Philippa slapped my hand.

"Those girls are being trotted out for the family's inspection, not yours, Thomas Llewelyn. I won't have you derailing Celia's carefully laid plans."

"I wasn't doing anything," I insisted. "I glanced their way out of curiosity."

"No more glancing! Eat your kipper!"

There are some arguments one has no hope of winning. I ate my kipper. The bone in my throat did not come from any sort of fish at all. It was a bone of contention.

Within half an hour the lobby was full of luggage, ready to be loaded into a caravan of vehicles taking the party to Land's End and our private ferry. Getting to this baleful island was proving to be something of a nuisance. Out of Philippa's line of vision, I regarded the two young women I was warned against, and found them a trifle wanting. One had decidedly beetling brows, while the other looked rather willful. But then, my heart belonged to another, and every woman in comparison with Rebecca Mocatta came out second-rate.

I had met Miss Mocatta during my first case with Barker, then lost touch until I encountered her the year before during the infamous Whitechapel case. She was then married, but became a widow shortly after. We met and decided to start seeing each other after a proper period of mourning. There were decisions to make and family members to face, but there was time, and we would face them together. I had kissed her to seal the pact. Now, after years of chatting up each girl I met to learn if she was the one with whom I wanted to spend my life, I knew who it was and had no wish to chat up anyone else. It was a great relief, I promise you.

We climbed into a brougham, but it was so tight a fit I joined the jarvey up on the box. As it turned out, it was a glorious day and there was no better way to spend it than atop a horse-drawn coach. The countryside approached idyllic, like a scene from Constable, and we made good progress, reaching Land's End in time.

There was no squad of porters waiting to see Mrs. Ashleigh's trunks off the vehicle and onto the ferryboat, and since Barker was attending her, I had reached the valet portion of the case. One by one, I lifted the heavy luggage and carried it up the gangplank. At least I was not alone: a swarthy but pleasant-looking fellow in pince-nez spectacles was matching me case for case.

"*Bum jia,*" he said.

"Morning. Do you speak English?"

"I do. I am a trifle rusty. That is the word, isn't it?"

"It is. I'm Thomas Llewelyn."

"Cesar Rojas. Pleased to meet you. Which one do you work for?"

"The chap with the dark glasses there."

"Is that his wife?"

"Not yet. Which one is yours?"

"The young gentleman in the panama hat," he said.

I regarded the one he indicated. He was a youngish fellow in a colonial suit, but already I could see the signs of either ill humor or dissatisfaction on his face.

"What kind of master is he?" I muttered.

"A tartar," he said, carrying a heavy suitcase over to the boat. "Yours?"

"Oh, he has his moments."

The young master growled some caustic remark to his servant in what I assumed was Portuguese. Though he was tan, the speaker was obviously an Englishman. The valet made some sort of agreeable response to him and redoubled his efforts. I was thankful for the situation I was in. There were hundreds in London that wished they had my situation.

"I'll speak with you later," I said.

"*Adeus.*"

Philippa Ashleigh had found another circle of people to speak to, I noticed, and Barker was doing his best to impersonate someone interested in their conversation. My position was still flexible so far. Barker had told me that at the latest possible moment he would decide what my role might be. If a mere valet, I could be privy to conversations in the kitchen with the house staff. As an assistant, however, I might be included in the main room during important moments.

I don't care for security work. It is much easier to track a killer that has killed already than to protect someone from any number of attacks. So far, I had done it only two or three times, and in most cases, no attempt was made to harm anyone. Sometimes I forget, dealing as I do with death now and then, how rare murder actually is in England.

"The French ambassador?" Mrs. Fraser asked with a note of excitement in her voice. "How exciting! But what brings him to Godolphin House?"

"He is an old friend of Lord Hargrave's, and expressed an interest in seeing him again," Philippa explained. "I suspect Celia invited him because her husband will be so bored with the party. He's an old diplomat and if I know him he won't care two figs whom his children marry."

"You can't leave these matters in men's hands," the woman responded. "They have no head for such things. They'll come up with the most unsuitable persons for their own children."

Mrs. Ashleigh agreed, but even I suspected she was being diplomatic. We had all moved aboard the hired ferry, and after a few minutes it gave a whistle and I could hear the roar of the boiler gathering steam. Many times I had built steam in Barker's own vessel, the *Osprey,* a lorcha out of Macau that he had won, oddly enough, in a fan-tan game, of all things. But, I digress.

The moorings were cast off and we pulled out of the harbor on a beautiful day, warm and fine, with just enough wind to freshen everything. I had been a child the last time I was in Cornwall, and hadn't noticed how beautiful it was. I'd never been to the Scilly Isles, and wondered precisely what our destination would be like. I assumed the house would be grand, but how remote would the island actually be? It seemed to be the kind of place where everything had to be ferried in.

The ferry carried twenty of us, servants included, but it jiggled about in the choppy seas like a cork in a bathtub. I hoped that the ride would be short, or the colonel would be correct about my mal de mer. Everyone on deck was clutching the railing, trying to look cheerful. Still, the vessel left the harbor under full steam, heading bravely into what looked like an empty Channel. In theory, there was nothing between us and the Azores.

Just then, I recalled some old legends my grandfather once told me about the Scilly Isles. It was said that this was the very northernmost tip of Atlantis, and where King Arthur's body was taken upon his death. Grandfather claimed that Lyonnesse was here, the kingdom where the faerie folk abandoned England, never to return. It was a place of magic and tragedy. So many legends for a small bracelet of islands in the middle of nowhere.

The boat tossed and our stomachs turned, but we continued to make progress. Like Lot's wife, I looked back over my shoulder until Land's End was no longer visible. There was nothing but water then, and the ferry, which now seemed very small as we bobbed in a mighty sea. In fact, we had left the Channel now for the Atlantic Ocean. Was the first land I was facing the so-called New World?

"Welcome to Hell Bay," the captain called to us. "For what it's worth."

There was a ragged cheer and some finger-pointing half an hour later when small islands began to appear ahead of us. Regretfully, we passed them one by one, but they gave us much-needed courage that land still existed. Beside me, Barker was looking particularly elemental, as if hewn from granite, while beside him, Philippa looked fragile, like a bluebell growing in the cleft of a rock, sheltering in its lee.

"Land ho!" one of the sailors cried, and we all stood and searched for it, as if to prove it wasn't a prank. A bit of black rock stood up from the ocean ahead of us, but one could not tell if it was a few feet across nearby, or a mountain rising from the sea far away. At that point, we didn't care how big it was. We gathered our possessions about us and prepared to get off the blasted vessel.

As we neared, my eyes made out a jetty ahead of us, made of rock and stout timbers. Eventually, I noticed there were people milling about, looking like ants on an anthill. Lovely little ants, proof that we were not alone in our existence in the universe. There was a lone pier hewn from native rock and at the end of it there stood a person. No; two people, clasped as one. It was our host and hostess. Our journey, which had begun the morning before, was finally coming to an end. As we neared, Lord Hargrave raised an arm in greeting. Adam and Eve were ordered to "be fruitful and multiply," but really, I thought, some places might not be worth the trouble to colonize.

We slowed as we entered, shooting along briskly beside the jetty until finally the steam valve was shut off and we floated to a stop. Ropes were thrown from aboard and fastened tightly in elaborate knots. My feet ached to step onto land, but so did everyone else's. Chivalry demanded the women disembark first, as if the ferry were sinking. Besides, I was still in that nebulous position between upstairs and down. A secretary or assistant was perfectly respectable, but the valet ate in the kitchen. Not that it particularly mattered. I would go wherever Barker needed me. For now, I was one of the last to leave the boat. Oh, blessed, blessed land that while spinning through the heavens at a fantastic rate gives the wonderful impression of standing still. I stood on the dock by the luggage and communed with the rock through the soles of my shoes.

"Mr. Barker, sir," our host called, after speaking with other parties ahead of us. "And my dear Philippa! So good to see you both. Welcome to Godolphin Island."

"Philippa!" Lady Hargrave cried, embracing Mrs. Ashleigh. She was a pleasant-looking woman in her early fifties, still retaining much of the beauty of her youth. She was blond-haired and blue-eyed, and her face was freshened by the breeze and freckled by the sun. By her very presence I began to suspect that perhaps we would all have a good time here.

Barker, on the other hand, was still adamantine. He did not care for house parties, nor bodyguard work. While Philippa and Lady Hargrave chattered together over a thousand different subjects, the two men cudgeled their brains for just one.

"I hear Grace hit for the century this week," His Lordship said.

"Century?" Barker asked, as if he might have misheard him.

"Cricket, sir," I said in his ear.

"I don't keep up with cricket," Barker stated.

"Ah."

"Would it be possible, once everyone is settled, to have one of your groomsmen or gardeners show me about the island?"

That was Cyrus Barker for you, all business at hand. He was there for a purpose, and he would fulfill it. One would as soon discuss the cricket scores with a plow horse.

"Of course, sir. He's generally about somewhere. Come along, Celia! There is much to be done."

A stony staircase led to the top of the cliffs and the island proper. I turned and regarded the pile of luggage and the steamer trunks being unloaded, then regarded the stone steps I was to carry them up and over. A hand tapped me on the shoulder. It was the friendly Cesar.

"They won't move themselves," he said, pointing to the luggage. "You have to carry them, you know."

"Oh, really? Thank you for the tip. What do you say? One at a time, or all at once?"

"No more than two at a time. The *capitán* there says there is a dogcart at the top to take the luggage to the castle."

"Is it a castle?" I asked. "I thought it was just a house."

"I don't know. I haven't seen it yet. House or castle, it doesn't matter much. We're not ever likely to afford either."

We carried the luggage up the stairs to the cart. It took several trips. Cesar helped me with the trunks, which were too unwieldy for one man to lift. The guests had either walked or ridden to the main building. When the dray cart was full, we walked beside it down the drive. We passed through a screen of trees and caught our first glimpse of what would be our home for the next week.

It was a castle, indeed, I told myself. That is, when it was built centuries ago, I'm sure, that was what they intended. It might be small by modern standards, but improvements had been added, like windows and gardens. So this was Godolphin House, a crenellated castle of dark gray stone set in an ambitious garden. It was charming. One felt it was cared for and looked after rather than slaved over. People might actually enjoy working here. In fact, whoever worked here must realize how lucky they were.

I'd have to ask my employer what his first impressions were. He wasn't about to venture any opinion unbidden. Cesar was not so reticent. He whistled.

"Very nice, *senhor*," he said. "One could get used to this."

"Get your master to propose to the daughter of the house and you'll come here more often."

"Let us just see if we can get through this first time, shall we?" Cesar suggested.

CHAPTER FOUR

The decision as to whether I was to remain upstairs or go downstairs had not yet been decided, but I followed the cart around the outside of the house and entered through the back entrance, on the safe side of a wall where I could hear pounding surf. Once inside the kitchen, I set down my own single piece of luggage and looked about. There were a dozen people in the near passages and all of them were talking at once. I debated who most looked like they knew what they were about and finally fixed upon a fellow coming down the passage in a short beard and a swallowtail suit coat. I buttonholed him as he passed.

"Who's in charge of this place?" I asked.

"Who's asking?"

"I'm Mr. Barker's man."

"You'll need the housekeeper, then, Mrs. Tregowith. She's down the hall there. She'll sort you out."

"Right. Thanks. Come along, Cesar."

"Look there!" the Brazilian said, pointing to a wooden case as we passed.

"What is it?" I asked.

"Renaudin Bollinger, 1879. Only the best champagne in the world. Someone shall be eating well this week."

"I doubt it will be us."

We found the housekeeper in the kitchen. Mrs. Tregowith was a severe-looking woman, which I suppose must be an admirable quality in housekeepers as I've never seen one that wasn't. She glared at us as if we were already in trouble for being in her domain.

"And who might you two gentlemen be?"

"I'm Mr. Barker's assistant, Thomas Llewelyn, ma'am. This is Mr. Kerry's valet, Cesar."

The woman pulled a clipboard seemingly from out of the air and consulted it like some kind of oracle.

"You are in room seven with Colonel Fraser's man, and you, Mr. Rojas, are in room nine."

"Is there a chance we could—" I began, but the woman gave me such a thunderous look that I changed tack. "Be of any service to you or your staff?"

"Thank you. I shall keep that in mind. For now, tend to your masters' needs and try not to get underfoot."

"Yes, ma'am," we both said. She reminded me of an early teacher of mine.

We began first with Kerry's luggage. I never knew a man to have so many cases. We carried them upstairs to his rooms and apparently burst in upon him. The tanned Englishman looked furtive, although he appeared to be merely in the act of putting on a cuff link. He gave it to us with both barrels.

"What in hell are you two idiots doing, blundering in like this?"

"We're just bringing in your luggage, sir," Cesar said, not in the least offended by his attitude.

"It's about time, too. Well, be quick about it and get out."

"*Si, senhor.*"

"It's 'Yes, sir,' here, Cesar. We're in England now."

We deposited all the bags we were carrying and went back to the back hall for more. When we were finally done, we prepared to go and get the luggage I was responsible for, but apparently his master had other ideas.

"He can find someone else to help him with his trunks. You've still got to put my things away. Hurry, man, or it will be dinner before you are finished! I want to make a good impression on the family."

Cesar looked at me and shrugged his shoulders. I could tell he felt terrible to be leaving me in the lurch like this, but he wasn't joking when he called his master a tartar.

"It's all right, Cesar," I murmured. "I'm sure I'll find someone else."

I patted his shoulder and went on my way. As it happened, a footman came along and helped me with the heavier steamer trunks, and I carried the other luggage up to the first floor myself. After that, I too began to unpack.

"Will you need help getting ready for lunch, sir?"

Barker looked at me with a furrowed brow. "I think I can manage to dress myself, lad. What a question!"

"What about Mrs. Ashleigh, sir? Does she have a lady's maid with her?"

"Lady Hargrave is lending her one, I understand. There will be a place for you at dinner tonight, by the way. I insisted upon it. I don't anticipate trouble, but I want more than one pair of eyes taking in impressions. Also, I'm perfectly capable of putting away my own garments, so kindly take your hands off my shirts!"

"Yes, sir."

"What was downstairs like?" he asked, as he took the aforementioned shirts from me and began putting them in the wardrobe.

"Rather large, sir, and packed with servants. There are two corridors, one that appears to be for the men, and the other for the women, and a good-sized kitchen between them. I passed a pantry and a dining room for the staff, and any number of doors I cannot account for."

"You will be sleeping in the men's corridor. Have you been assigned a room yet?"

"Yes, sir, I'm bunking with Colonel Fraser's man, I understand. I haven't met him yet. I hope he doesn't snore."

Barker's room was not exactly opulent, but I'm sure it was

worlds better than mine would be. The Guv was a stoic and probably wouldn't notice what amenities the room might contain for his pleasure.

"What impressions have you gained so far, Thomas?" he asked, looking through the curtain onto the lawn.

"Well, sir, the island is certainly remote. I can't believe how far it is from the dock to the top of the cliff. Do you suppose that's the only entrance?"

"A proper question. Let us find out. I believe a tour of the island is in order. Are you ready?"

"Ready, sir."

"Come along, then," he replied.

He walked down the hall with me behind as his tender. We went down the large marble staircase and there encountered the butler, a sturdy man in his sixties.

"Partridge, I'm Cyrus. Barker and this is Thomas Llewelyn. I assume you have been told of our purpose on the island."

"Yes, sir," the man said.

"I'll try not to get in your way. If Lord Hargrave asks, we are circling the island and assessing any dangers we find. Has anything occurred recently to which you might draw my attention? I need as many facts as I can find."

"Nothing of any import has occurred, sir. The guests are settling comfortably into their rooms."

"Very good. Pray keep me informed. We'll be back shortly."

The weather was holding up nicely. There was a breeze, but it was offset by a strong August sun. I was almost hot in my suit. Just south of the great house were several outbuildings, including a stable. Imagine, a horse who spends all its life on an island the size of a thumbnail.

"When is the French ambassador due to arrive?" I asked, as we crossed a well-manicured lawn.

"He is due imminently. That's why we are making a tour of the island. I'm hoping to spot his arrival from the top of the cliff. My word!"

"What?" I asked. He was regarding an old cannon.

"I suspect this was brought here at great expense a century ago to secure the islands from an invasion by Bonaparte."

"It appears to have worked, since we are signing a treaty."

Barker made no remark, being proof against my facetiousness. From the cannon I could see a structure to the south, standing black against the pale sky. It was a lighthouse built of native stone, with a small building attached. Barker nodded to himself as we crossed the lawn to it. The island was being kept in a manner that pleased him. Above all, he appreciates order. We opened the lighthouse door and stepped inside. Barker went across to the staircase and called, using a voice that had been trained on the sea.

"Ahoy!"

"I'll be down in a moment, sir!" a voice called back.

In a moment, a small man with a wizened face and thick sidewhiskers came trotting down to us with the surefootedness of a mountain goat.

"Sirs," he said, pulling off his cap.

Barker introduced us and told him our purpose for being on the island.

"The name's Flannan, sirs. Noah Flannan. Been running His Lordship's lighthouse for nigh on twenty year. What can I do for you?"

"Keep a sharp eye out for vessels. Have you got a foghorn?"

The old man nodded.

"Good," Barker continued. "Give a short blast when the French ambassador hoves into sight, to warn us all. Two blasts if you spy something suspicious, such as a boat circling the island. Do people occasionally land on the island?"

"Almost niver, sir," the old salt said. "Has something happened?"

"Not a thing, Mr. Flannan. We hope it stays that way."

"So do I, Mr. Barker. So, you're one o' them detective fellers?"

"Aye. Before that, I ran a merchant ship in the China Seas."

Flannan's heavy-lidded eyes popped open at the news that he was speaking to a fellow sailor. "I was first mate aboard a steam packet in the Indian Ocean," he said.

The two fell into a conversation about boats and passages that went on for a few minutes. I willed myself not to yawn, but it was a difficult struggle. Fortunately, there was no ale in the lighthouse, or the tales might have continued an hour or more. Finally, the conversation ran down on its own, and with a nod to the lighthouse keeper, we went on our way.

A three-foot wall of native stone encircled the island. It was of indeterminate age and was dotted with lichen and moss. It masked the sight of the waves crashing against the shore below, but not the sound. From time to time a fine spray and even a plume of water shot up into the air.

"Rugged coast," the Guv remarked. "Only a determined man could get out here on his own."

"I don't suppose someone could swim," I said.

Barker shook his head. "Too rough and too far."

"Is there a beach?"

Barker leaned over the wall and looked below. I did the same. It was thirty feet or more to a rocky shoreline. Anyone trying to land there would likely be dashed against the rocks.

I bent and picked up a rock. Holding it out, I dropped it over the side. It bounced once, twice, three times. Barker nodded.

"Let us hurry."

We walked along the low wall for a hundred yards or more. We passed a tall hedge for part of the way, and when we reached an opening, we realized it was a maze. I took two steps into it, but my employer waved me back.

"We cannot afford to blunder about inside for our own amusement. Perhaps in a day or two. For now, let us skirt it and head on."

We came to a copse of stunted trees and Barker stepped inside them. They were nearly impenetrable, but he pushed his way through them. We looked for any sign of a camp, but there was none to be found. It was slow going without some sort of blade to hack our way through. I was winded when we reached the other side.

"Are you well, Mr. Llewelyn?" Barker asked. Aside from when we were with company, he employed only my last name when I was not performing to expectations, such as being winded after a brief stroll in the woods.

"Never better, sir."

"You've got a bit of branch on your lapel."

I picked it off. Mustn't look any less than one's best, not when Cyrus Barker was about.

"We've seen the harbor. If need be, we can examine it more thoroughly later. Let us return to the house."

"I don't know if this is pertinent or not, sir, but when I was helping Cesar carry the luggage to Mr. Kerry's room, we disturbed him doing something. He was acting strangely, as if he had something to hide."

"What were his actions, precisely?" Barker asked, clearly interested.

"He was pinching his nose with his hands, but quickly reverted to adjusting his cuff link. Then he yelled at his valet for intruding on him without warning."

"A charming fellow."

"Yes. If Lord Hargrave's daughter chooses him as a suitor, she may live to regret it."

We returned to the house across another length of manicured lawn. I don't know as much about gardening as I should—Barker will attest to that—but this one seemed to be growing despite adverse conditions. I wondered if there was a well or whether they were dependent on rainwater for these lawns. As we came closer to the house I saw a kitchen garden with some cold frames by a potting shed. As we approached, the gardener stepped out of it. We introduced ourselves and fell into conversation. It is an art form to question someone without their knowing they are being pumped for information.

Andy Corvin was a solidly built fellow, clean shaven, with a tweed cap. He had a strong Cornish accent and appeared uncomfortable talking to outsiders, even if we were hired especially. He was the sort of outdoor servant that tugged on his cap after every sentence, as if hoping each one would be the last.

"This is quite a garden," Barker said. "Do you manage it all alone?"

"Sometimes one of the footmen or the houseboy lends a hand, but for the most part, I do it all."

"Where do you get your water?" I asked.

"We keep barrels of rainwater. When it rains here, it comes on fast. I have installed guttering on all the outbuildings, and when a barrel gets full, I switch it out for an empty one."

"That cannot be easy for you."

"We do what needs must," he replied.

"This is an idyllic spot, if I may say it, and much of it is due to you. Do you ever have unwanted visitors?"

The gardener looked at us with a saturnine brow as if to say he was dealing with two at that very moment.

"Nay. We have posted signs among the rocks: 'Private Property, No Trespassing.' One can only land safely at the dock, and the very few that have arrived unbidden have been given short shrift, and a boot in the posterior if 'tis called for."

"How is your relationship with the neighboring islands?" Barker asked.

"Good. We're seen as a local industry, so to speak. They provide everything for us from beer to flowers, but only upon request."

"How do you get word to them? I see no sign of a telegraph wire."

Barker and I already knew the answer to this, but he tried to confirm each fact a second time, if possible.

"At night we can change the pattern of our lighthouse signal. In the day, there is a flagpole on the north side of the island. We run a red flag up it and a passing boat usually sees it within a couple of hours."

"Not a very efficient system," the Guv observed.

The gardener shrugged his burly shoulders. "It's worked for the last hundred years."

We had accidentally criticized an island tradition, but then, my employer is not famous for his tact.

"We'll leave you to your work, then," the Guv said.

I was ready to return to the house, but Barker poked his blunt nose into every outbuilding that wasn't locked. There was a bunkhouse for the young male staff, a chicken coop, and a stone stable for the horse that had pulled our cart. All of it was hard-won, carried across the sea from Land's End, bit by bit, over the centuries.

We returned to the house. Partridge stood in the hall, awaiting our arrival, as if we were young masters larking about on the lawn.

"Lunch will be served in ten minutes, gentlemen."

I was suddenly famished.

CHAPTER FIVE

We hurried to change, both because this was the sort of place where one changed often, and because we had just been traipsing all over the island. As if by common consent, we both chose tweeds. Mine was a sober gray, but Barker looked like a squire in a brown Norfolk jacket and plus fours. When we found Mrs. Ashleigh, she was wearing a yellow dress with large leg-o'-mutton sleeves. On some women it would have looked wrong, but with her beauty and sweetness, she carried it off, I thought. We went down to lunch.

To my mind, nothing said that we were staying in an actual castle more than the fact that the dining table seated twenty. It was not a number of tables put together, or even two smaller ones abutted, but one table, whose top was planed from a single giant trunk. There were place cards set beside the beautiful and ancient service, and like the others, I searched for my name. I found it between the two young and attractive women Mrs. Ashleigh had warned me about. They were similar looking enough to make me wonder if they were twins, though one had brown hair and the other a coppery red that made Philippa's look pale by comparison.

Bella was the brunette and Gwendolyn the redhead. I introduced myself to Gwendolyn, who seemed willing to talk with a lowly assistant who had narrowly missed being assigned to the servants' table.

"Our father is at the other end of the table, talking with that man in the tinted spectacles," Bella, the dark-haired one, told me.

"That is my employer, Mr. Barker."

"Who is the fashionably dressed woman beside me? I adore her dress."

"That's Mrs. Ashleigh. She's a friend of Lady Celia's."

"My father's a doctor. His Lordship's doctor, actually. They are old friends, as well. I suppose you've heard the purpose of this little house party. I don't mind being shown off like a prize Hereford, but I wish the playing field were more even. There's a girl at the other end who is a duchess."

"Oh, I don't know. I suspect you can hold your own."

"Gallant," she said, smiling. "I like that."

I looked over and caught Mrs. Ashleigh's eye. She gave me a look that could chill water. I turned to the other sister.

"Hello. My name is Thomas Llewelyn."

"So I assumed from your place card. Tell me, are you animal, vegetable, or mineral?"

"In what sense?"

"Were you brought here for matrimonial purposes, or the other?"

"What other?"

She adjusted her serviette on her lap. "The French ambassador doesn't generally arrive to give his benediction on mating rituals. So, which are you?"

"The 'other,' I'm afraid."

"That means you're off the shelf. Gwendolyn will be pleased."

The two girls could not be less alike. Gwendolyn was flirtatious and vivacious, while Bella was dry and ironic. I suspected she was also nearsighted. When not under marital scrutiny, she must wear spectacles. How did she know about the "other"? I would have to inform Barker that the word was out.

Were I to describe every dish as it arrived this book would

become a doorstop like one of Mr. James's novels. Nothing particular occurred, save that the people there became better acquainted. I worked out that Miss Anstruther was correct. We were at the unfashionable end of the table. The real contenders in the race to the altar were on the other end. Perhaps the good doctor and his daughters were brought in at the last moment to fill every chair.

A few hours later, the lighthouse keeper, Flannan, alerted us to the arrival of the French ambassador. A small bell was mounted outside the lighthouse and he rang it loud enough for the island to hear. A good portion of the island's inhabitants went down to see him disembark.

We were in charge of security, if none but us knew it, and so were on hand and in the crowd when he arrived. He was a disappointment, unfortunately. I don't know what I was expecting—Napoleon, perhaps—but not this ordinary-looking, middle-aged man. Henri Gascoigne sported an imperial mustache and curling hair, but he had bulbous eyes and looked a trifle seasick.

"Henri!" His Lordship cried, shaking the man's hand like it was a pump handle. "So glad you could come!"

"It is good to see you again, old friend."

Lord Hargrave introduced him to many of the people present as we climbed the steps up to the cliff level. One of them was Cyrus Barker.

"M'sieur Barker, I should like to speak with you after we are settled."

"I'm at your service, sir," Barker rumbled in that deep, chiseled way of his.

We returned in some disorder. Apparently, at least some of the guests did not know about a foreign celebrity coming to the island. Left to their own devices, the party spread out across the castle in groups of two or three, or singly, the women and the men gossiping about the new arrival.

My heart finally belonged to someone, but my eyes noted that the duchess, Lady Alicia, was young and presentable and a fine choice to be cast in front of the heir and his younger brother. I presumed Cesar's master had been brought here to dangle in front of Miss Burrell. If so, I could not say much for the family's taste in suitable mates, old family friend though Kerry might be.

All the party was suitably impressed by the ambassador, who was an old hand at talking to people in a social setting. He flattered the women, and treated the men as if they were valued companions. What's more, he quickly learned the names of everyone in the room.

I was talked into a game of billiards with the youngest son, Percy, after which I watched another between the two brothers. It has always amazed me the differences in personality between brothers who grow up together. The eldest, Paul, was a good-looking fellow in his early thirties, and seemed quite capable to eventually step into his father's shoes. He bullied his brother during the game but no more than I have received at my own brother's hand.

"Is that the best you can do, Percy?" he demanded. "You know, you'll never get good at this game until you practice."

Percy was affable, and unformed, as is often the case with youngest sons. Eventually, he would choose the army or the church, or would choose a private life of his own away from the estate and its concerns. He was a baby-faced fellow with flaxen hair, and still had some seasoning to go through before he became who or what he was going to be.

This was part of my work, to get to know people by observation and brief conversations, and to develop fast judgments to present to my employer, who was working on larger, more important matters. Of course, my impressions were not always accurate, but I assumed they would be taken with a proverbial grain of salt. If I learned any facts that altered my opinion, I was quick to pass these along, as well. Meanwhile, the Guv carried all these facts and opinions around in his head and posited theories and gathered facts until eventually he answered whatever question he came for.

"What do you think, Thomas?" Mrs. Ashleigh said at my elbow.

"Regarding what, ma'am?"

"Will it be a successful house party?"

"Not if these fellows continue to play billiards instead of meeting these lovely girls. They are too diffident by half."

"Not every fellow has your pointerlike interest in the fairer sex."

"That is an unfair assessment of my healthy interest in women my age, and actually, that part of my life is now coming to an end. I have reached an understanding with a certain person."

"Are you referring to Mrs. Cowan?"

"You know her?"

"We don't generally travel in the same circles. I know of her. I'd like to meet her."

"I hardly think a man of twenty-five years and a widow need someone to stand in loco parentis."

"Don't be precious. What kind of woman is she?"

"A perfect one, in my opinion."

"She'd better be, Thomas. I have high expectations for your happiness in life."

"Thank you," I said.

"So I need not worry you'll be on the prowl this week?"

"'On the prowl'? I'm not some old tomcat."

"Oh, no? Your mother named you, not I. As far as the feminine population is concerned, the sooner we marry you off, the better."

"I'm doing my best, but she has a rigid mourning period to endure. Also, I haven't broached the subject with Mr. Barker. He might not care for the thought of having a married man working for him."

"If he says the slightest word, I shall give him a talking-to he shan't forget for many a year. I plan to escort him down the aisle myself one day. Yours is not the only happiness with which I am concerned."

I wasn't certain whether she was indicating her own or that of Cyrus Barker, but I wasn't about to enquire. I felt like one of the servants, who set out the hors d'oeuvres but are not allowed to sample one. Luckily, I had no interest, and that was not sour grapes. The trick was to convince Mrs. Ashleigh.

The Guv stepped into the room and nodded at me, before leaving again. I followed after him quickly.

"What's going on?" I asked at his heels.

"The ambassador wants to see us."

We hurried up the staircase and through a doorway with the kind of tall door one can only find in large estates. The room was actually a ballroom, a clear space encircled with chairs, but the French ambassador and His Lordship were seated at the far corner. Apparently, I was the topic of discussion.

"He is a rather small person, and young. Is he up to the task?"

"He is," Barker said, which was about as close to a compliment as one could ever expect from him. "He has a knack for survival and he heals quickly."

If I knew my interviewers better, I'd have remarked that my manners were impeccable.

"My man is still on the boat, Richard," Gascoigne assured His Lordship. "I could bring him on land and even press my sailors into service. This is too large an island to be watched over by just two men."

"Give them a chance, Henri. They have just arrived."

The Frenchman chuckled. "Very well. I shall give them that: one single, solitary chance. Do not disappointment me, gentlemen."

Barker cleared his throat. "Who is your man, Your Excellency, if I may ask?"

"You may," came the reply. "He is Monsieur Delacroix. I can introduce the two of you if you wish."

"He is formerly of the Sûreté, is he not? I recall the name. A good fellow."

"He said the same of you, save that there were some questions about your past."

Barker made no response. He didn't seem willing to answer it at the moment. Finally, he spoke.

"He cannot have come all this way merely to sit in the harbor. By all means, he should come and see that you are safely settled."

The atmosphere, so recently charged, seemed to suddenly relax. Both His Lordship and the ambassador had obviously wanted Delacroix to come up but were not sure whether my employer would approve of another bodyguard intruding on his domain.

"Lad, you are fleet of foot. Run down to the harbor and invite Mr. Delacroix up to the house."

"Yes, sir," I said, and undertook the duty.

Of course, I was curious to see Delacroix of the Sûreté, not that I had heard the name before. It hadn't occurred to me that the Guv's name might be known on the Continent in certain circles. I picked my way down the rock-hewn stairs again, then ran along the docks to the sleek-looking steam vessel waiting there.

"Pardon! Capitaine! J'ai un message pour Monsieur Delacroix!"

I waited while the message was passed on and admired the trim vessel before me. She was a steam launch out of Marseilles, and a corker she was, too, in powder blue above the waterline, and gleaming with gold trim.

Finally, Delacroix stepped onto the deck and came forward. He was a brawny-looking fellow with a shaved head and a yellow mustache. His neck looked as thick as my waist, though he was not as tall as the Guv. He looked at me with suspicion.

"What is it?"

"I've come to get you. I am Mr. Barker's assistant. He wishes to invite you to visit the castle and see that the ambassador is safe and comfortable."

The fellow readily agreed, and jumped onto the deck from the rail. He took in the view of the modern English enquiry agent with a slight air of skepticism, but kept his opinion to himself. He followed me up the sheer cliff, step by step, at my heels, as if wishing to overtake my position. Meanwhile, he peppered me with questions.

"How many are on the island?"

"Between thirty and forty, I should say, m'sieur."

"How are the ambassador's spirits?"

"He seemed well enough and bemused by the matchmaking which is going on around him."

"How is Mr. Barker? Is he disturbed by my presence?"

"Not at all, sir. It would take more than that to upset his equilibrium."

"Equilibrium. I like that word."

He continued with the questions. How many guests were there? How many servants? They were the same subjects that Barker had answered for himself. Part of our occupation involves answering questions which anyone could ask. The other part involves out-thinking even the cleverest of criminals trying to hide evidence of their guilt.

Inside the house, the two detectives met with a shaking of hands that would have crushed mine to sawdust. The meeting was in the library, a large, masculine affair, full of faded leather chairs, wood shelving, and books going back over a century or more. I could have whiled away a month there just reading, but though I've been in several large libraries like the one at Godolphin House, I'm generally in the middle of a case, and therefore unable to read anything. The other three men in the room seemed to not even notice the books. We might as well have been in the ballroom again.

Barker and Delacroix talked for half an hour, and then the Guv led him out onto the lawn, and pointed at the various structures and features of the island.

"Are you staying for dinner?" Barker asked. "I'd like to hear about your work at the Sûreté. I understand you worked with Alfred Bertillon himself."

"I did, but I cannot accept the offer," Delacroix said. "English food does not agree with me, and the cook aboard the *Eugénie* is preparing a sea bass, using a sauce we have created together. Food is a hobby of mine and I promised I would help him. Perhaps we can discuss it tomorrow."

"Of course," Barker said. Though he had a French chef of his own, he had no more interest in food than a dog has in catnip. It made no sense to him that one sort of food would be preferred over another.

"*À tout à l'heure, m'sieur*," Delacroix cried, and we watched him cross the lawn in the direction of the harbor.

"He's got a good reputation, then?"

"Very good. He solved several important cases, including a theft at the Louvre."

"We'd better change for dinner, sir," I said. "I'm afraid it shall be bib shirts and tails for the rest of the evening."

His mustache bowed in distaste. I take back the remark I made about him regarding books. He would much prefer a corner of the library and a good book to chatting with a group of strangers.

At dinner, I discovered that Lord Hargrave's cook, Mrs. Albans, was not especially imaginative. I suppose she had learned her craft from *Mrs. Beaton's Everyday Cookery,* and she didn't attempt the ones there that looked too complicated. Dinner was one of those meals where aspic was present in almost every dish. It wasn't bad, but it wasn't particularly wonderful, either. I wished I were with M. Delacroix aboard the *Eugénie.*

The seating was rearranged since lunch. I was placed with the disagreeable Mr. Kerry to my left, and Lady Alicia Travers, the aforementioned duchess. Kerry looked as if the island air did not agree with him, or he was getting a cold. He spent the meal sniffing and keeping his own counsel. Lady Alicia spoke the very minimum to me allowed by good society, while chatting volubly with the eligible eldest son.

At the conclusion, the women did not withdraw, according to Godolphin House custom, but since the day was fine and the sun was just beginning to set, we men stepped out to a circle of iron chairs in the garden for cigars. Each of us guillotined the tip of our cigar with a device brought out for the purpose. There weren't enough chairs for all of us, but it was companionable enough lounging about in pea gravel, especially when Cesar approached with a tray full of small snifters of A. de Fussigny, and began distributing them about.

A fine cigar, a balloon glass full of cognac, a sun setting red as a ball on the western horizon. What more could one want?

There was a short, popping sound from somewhere and a cry

of surprise from poor Cesar. He turned and I saw his face and shirtfront sprayed with blood. It wasn't his blood, however. Out of the corner of my eye, I saw His Lordship's cigar roll to a stop upon the gravel.

CHAPTER SIX

own!" Barker bellowed. "Everyone, stay low! Make your way to the house!"

It was the kind of voice that one obeyed without question, authoritative and harsh. It saved someone's life, for the next we knew, one of the windows shattered behind us. I seized Cesar's arm, since he was too dazed to duck his head, and pulled him inside, through the French doors. There was a crush as everyone tried to enter at once. The women inside were shrieking and the men pushing their way in and cursing, and there was complete chaos for a few moments until the Guv took charge again.

"Ladies and gentlemen, please step away from the windows. His Lordship's killer may yet kill again."

Now that I looked closer at Cesar, it wasn't merely blood on his suit. Pink matter and bone lay in the folds of his clothing.

"It is some kind of expanding bullet," Barker vouchsafed. "Guard the door, lad. No one is to go outside."

"What about His Lordship's body, sir?"

"It must stay where it lies for now, Thomas. Our duty is to the living."

Lady Hargrave was wailing in Mrs. Ashleigh's arms, having suddenly and inexplicably become a widow. Others were crying as well, out of fear, fear that in this case was perfectly justified. Did any of us believe Lord Hargrave was the only intended victim and his killer would now disappear from this remote island as fast as he had come? That did not seem very likely.

Barker murmured in my ear, but his voice carries rather far. "Go downstairs and inform the staff that their master is dead."

"That should be my duty, sir," the butler said, materializing before us. "I shall relay His Lordship's tragic death below stairs."

Partridge made his way down the hall with as much dignity as his frame could bear. This was a dark day for the family. I passed the eldest boy, who had collapsed in a chair looking stunned. The youngest was being comforted ineffectually by one of the doctor's daughters. Some of the women were hysterical over seeing Lord Hargrave killed, and being afraid they might be next.

A footman arrived with a wheeled cart containing bottles of Scotch, Irish whiskey, and medicinal brandy. A good number of the party indulged. I'd have thought the need to keep a clear head would have overruled the brain's need for oblivion, but I was wrong.

"Would you clean this fellow up!" I said to the footman, still holding Cesar by the sleeve.

Blood was beading on his pince-nez spectacles. The footman who had brought the drinks cart led him away. I made my way over to Cyrus Barker, who was speaking with the French ambassador in a low voice. Apparently the latter was still trying to convince him to turn the case over to Delacroix.

"I had no qualms with His Lordship bringing you in, but now that my old friend is gone, I would prefer to have my own bodyguard with me, particularly if there is a madman on the loose. Have you any idea who it is?"

"No, sir," Barker said. "We circled the island looking for signs of habitation other than Godolphin House or the lighthouse, but we found none."

"Delacroix will smoke him out. It is meat and drink to him. He has been with the Sûreté most of his life. Were you a police officer before you became a detective, sir?"

"I was a ship's captain."

"Well, there you are, then."

One thing Barker never does is to blow his own trumpet. I wanted to tell the Frenchman that the Guv was the premier enquiry agent in London, that the royal family had used his services, that he was an expert in Chinese boxing and pistolry, that he could track as well as an American Apache, outthink the smartest of criminals, and that he was absolutely without fear when it came to stepping into a situation such as this. The ambassador would not know this, of course, but Barker was not about to tell him, either, which left them at an impasse.

"I have no objection to Delacroix protecting you, Your Excellency, but how are we to summon him? We are under fire, but the noise of the gun would not have carried as far as the harbor. I doubt he is aware anything is amiss."

"Send this young fellow out to get him again. He is small and he can scamper behind the rocks until he reaches the *Eugénie*."

If I had any sympathy for the ambassador before, it evaporated quickly. Scamper? That was his second remark about my size.

"I need him here. We are two protecting about thirty people. He needs to be at the back of the house when I am at the front."

"I'm sure there are enough men to guard the doors while he is gone."

"If you can gather the men to guard the doors, Llewelyn and I shall both go. We need to secure that boat. It is our only lifeline to the mainland."

"Get Delacroix in here," Gascoigne insisted. "He'll know what to do."

"Thomas, go get your pistol."

I hurried downstairs to my room, unlocked my case and filled my Webley Mark III with .44 rounds. Then I went upstairs again, feeling at least a little better for being armed.

The curtains had all been drawn across the front of the building, and Barker and Partridge stood by the front door. The butler had a stout timber to secure the front door with. I noted it looked dusty. Until this very minute, I'm sure the island's remoteness had been its chief form of security.

"Ready, sir," I said. "How do you propose we make our way to the cliff again? There's a tree about twenty yards away, and a large rock ten yards beyond that. If we move one at a time—"

"We'll take the cart out again," Barker stated.

This was why he was in charge and not I. Of course, if we lay low the cart would get us there safely, at least as long as the man out there with a rifle did not shoot the horse. We made our way out the back door and through the cluster of outbuildings to the stable. The horse had been put in its stall and was munching on hay, but at the Guv's insistence, was put into harness again. It was a good-sized gray Percheron and I for one would not like to see it shot, but we had to warn Delacroix and secure the boat.

"Come help me, lad," Barker said.

With my aid he lifted an empty barrel and placed it beside the driver's board. He could sit beside it, while I lay in the back of the cart. The wood might protect us from a normal shot, but I was not fooling myself. The kind of round that had killed His Lordship would pass through wood, and us, too. I jumped in and with a flick of the reins we rolled out into the drive.

It was a pleasant evening and the visibility was excellent. Too excellent by half, actually. I'd have preferred a nice fog rolling in from the ocean. I lay in the dogcart, looking up into a cloudless sky, occasionally raising my head to look into the copse to the east. The harness jingled, the horse's hooves clopped, the wagon wheels rolled over the gravel, and the wood frame groaned. I pictured in my mind a hundred times the screech of the horse after it was shot, leaving us stranded in the middle of the drive. I didn't want to die in this godforsaken island before having the chance to find true happiness. I rather liked life, and though I had considered ending it myself at one point in the distant past, I felt very differently about it now. Having finally found the woman I wanted to spend my life with, that life had suddenly become far more precious. Perhaps because it had become precious to someone else.

"Are you doing well, lad?" Barker called back.

"As well as can be expected, sir. Do you see anyone?"

"No one."

"How much farther?"

"A couple of hundred yards at most."

Eventually, we reached the edge of the cliff and the stairs to the harbor. Lord Hargrave's killer had either gone or was in hiding. That did not mean that everything would be all right.

"Damn and blast," my employer rumbled.

I sat up and looked out. The *Eugénie* was nowhere to be found, but in the gloom I could see a body floating in the water.

Both of us jumped out of the cart and took the stone steps as quickly as we dared. Once we reached the docks, Barker began pulling his jacket and boots off. He slid off his braces and pulled his shirt over his head.

"Keep an eye on those cliffs," he said. "I'll be completely defenseless in the water."

As I drew my pistol, he dived into the water, to recover the body. I had little doubt he was too late.

Once he reached the still form, he turned it over and, wrapping an arm around, stroked toward the beach. It was Delacroix. I could not mistake his bulletlike bald head. I began to follow the Guv along the dock, having scooped up his clothes.

I spied something on the dock then. It was a crumpled piece of paper. Thrusting it in my pocket, I hurried on. Barker's feet touched bottom, and he pulled the body up on shore. There was a ruddy stain about Delacroix's abdomen. Barker unceremoniously tore open the Frenchman's shirt. There were several wounds there.

"Stab wounds," Barker said.

"Why didn't he just shoot him?" I asked. "Could there be two killers?"

"It is too early to theorize," Barker said, and began to don his shirt again.

His trousers and shoes were sodden, but he would change in the house. Carefully, he lifted the Sûreté inspector onto his shoulder. The man was nearly as bulky as he and now sodden from the water. Without a word, he carried Delacroix up the steps. I could hear his chest heaving, much like the Percheron on the cliff above us, but Barker was not the kind to complain.

"Sir," I said. "I found a note crumpled on the dock."

"Did you? What does it say?"

I pulled it from my pocket. "It is in French. Let me translate. It says: *I am staying with the ambassador. Return to Le Havre until you are summoned. We shall have our sea bass another time. Delacroix.*"

"That doesn't make sense," Barker said. "Why turn the *Eugénie* away and then go there after it is gone?"

"I don't know, sir. Perhaps he changed his mind."

We reached the top, and as gently as possible, he laid the mortal remains of Delacroix in the wagon. He rebuttoned his shirt, smoothed his jacket, and even reached up and twisted his waxed mustache, which had drooped in the water.

"He will surely be missed in Paris. Not just anyone could have overpowered him and killed him in this fashion. If it is one man on this island, his skills have just increased in my estimation."

We moved the cart about slowly and rearranged the barrel to cover Barker's left flank. I walked beside the cart, keeping an eye out for any movement.

"Sir! Stop the cart!"

"Whoa! What is, lad?"

"Look!"

I pointed to the lone flagpole that overlooked the harbor. The flag had been taken down and now lay in shreds on the ground.

"We are stranded," Barker said.

"Surely someone will come by tomorrow," I argued.

"They like their privacy on Godolphin Island, Thomas. I'm afraid there will be no aid from outside. We must look to our own survival."

It occurred to me then that someone was out there somewhere perhaps watching us, gloating at the destruction he had caused.

The cart wended its way back to the house like a funeral cortege. No sooner did we arrive than the French ambassador came to the door.

"Stop him!" Barker called, pointing at him. Immediately, I leaped down and pushed Monsieur Gascoigne back into the house.

"What has happened? Who have you got there in the cart? Let me pass!" he bawled.

"Only if you wish to be the next casualty, sir. I'm afraid you must stay inside. It's the only way to guarantee your survival. I'm afraid the victim is Monsieur Delacroix."

"I've known Antoine Delacroix for twenty years. I've known Richard even longer. Two of my closest friends have died today!"

"I don't want you to be the third, sir. I'm sorry for your loss."

"How was he killed?" he asked. "Was he shot?"

"No, sir," I said. "I'm afraid he was stabbed."

"How is that possible? He taught fencing and single stick! No street apache in Paris was his match!"

"I don't know, sir, but we're going to find out."

Barker arrived from the stable a few minutes later. I could not understand what had become of Lord Hargrave's assassin. He had disappeared as suddenly as he had come.

"He's dead?" the Frenchman asked, as if he had not believed me when I told him.

"Delacroix?" Barker asked. "Oh, quite dead. Tell me, sir, if you recognize this note."

Gascoigne took the crumpled paper from his hand and read over the note several times, trying to make sense of it.

"This is not Antoine's handwriting, monsieur."

"I rather suspected that. The only interesting portion of the note is the last sentence, concerning the sea bass. It implies that whoever wrote and delivered this note was present when Delacroix mentioned returning to the boat. He has been masquerading as one of us."

CHAPTER SEVEN

In our absence, Colonel Fraser had seen to it that our host's
body was brought in. That is, he had led four male servants out
to the terrace and stood there unafraid and resolute staring into
the forest while the young men had wrapped the body in a blanket
and carried it slinglike into the hall, or so Cesar told me as soon as
we entered. The old man had some brass.

"They carried him in and were going to set him down, but the
blood, you see, was seeping all over the blanket. They set him
down in the hall, on the hardwood, rather than stain the carpet.
But what was to be done with him? Well! It turns out there is a
crypt in the basement; they carried him down the steps to lie temporarily with Lady Hargrave's forebears, until arrangements can
be made."

"Did you help?" I asked. We were loitering in the hall, but there
had been a breakdown in decorum since the master's death and
we were not questioned.

"No, I was washing my hair over and over downstairs. There
were fragments of bone and flesh still in it. It was appalling. I

couldn't get them out. I heard the gardener and three footmen carried him in."

"It's a wonder the colonel wasn't shot, standing there in the open like that."

"Gentlemen!" Barker's voice rumbled. He was in the drawing room by the fireplace. "I wonder if you would be so kind as to come in here. We have much to discuss, regarding our current situation. Ladies, if you are not informed of what is decided afterward, or you have concerns about the outcome, by all means speak to me. It is not our wish to deliberately exclude you."

The men moved at once into the drawing room as if by unspoken agreement. They didn't talk until seated, but there were several questioning looks. I should state that I was the only subordinate present. No valets or servants of any kind were there. They had closed ranks. The group consisted of the ambassador, Colonel Fraser, Dr. Anstruther, Paul and Percy Burrell, Algernon Kerry, Barker and myself. Cesar had cut along to whatever duties needed tending.

"Gentlemen, we are in a predicament. I regret to inform you that I pulled Monsieur Delacroix's body from the harbor. Someone or some group is intent upon killing us for no apparent motive. I should also state that I am not merely a guest here. I was hired as security for this event."

Kerry, Cesar's master, spoke up first. "You're not doing very well at it, in my opinion. Why should he need a bodyguard? This is just a house party, after all."

Barker turned slightly and looked at the ambassador. The latter moved forward in his chair and spoke.

"Lord Hargrave and I were in governmental negotiations of the highest order, regarding our two countries. We were using this party to also finalize our plans. I'm afraid I cannot say more on the matter."

"Who exactly are you, Barker?" Colonel Fraser demanded. "Who do you work for?"

"I am a private enquiry agent. My offices are hard by Scotland Yard. His Lordship called us to his offices and discussed the situation. I escorted Mrs. Ashleigh here, who is Lady Hargrave's closest friend. Her Ladyship will vouch for the fact that her husband hired me."

"But what are we to do?" asked the eldest son, Paul, a man in his midthirties. He was a good-looking man, who looked like an athlete. His face was ashen, however.

"I suppose we should be calling you 'Your Lordship' now," the colonel said.

"Never mind that. My father is dead, along with that poor Frenchman. What are we going to do to assure no one else will die?"

"The red flag has been torn down and shredded. If somehow we can get a makeshift one up and flying again, we might be able to attract a passing boat."

"Perhaps," the colonel said. "But it will be at their great peril. Someone would be risking life and limb to put the flag up again. Whoever killed His Lordship obviously does not want to be bothered with passing vessels."

Percy, the youngest Burrell son and one closer to my own age, spoke up. He looked completely at sea.

"May we assume that whoever killed my father had political reasons for doing so?"

Barker deferred once again to the French ambassador. The latter stroked his Imperial mustache and glared at us with his bulbous eyes.

"There is no well-organized group or organization intent upon threatening an alliance between England and France, save perhaps the Germans or the Russians who are intent upon weakening us both. His Lordship assured us the Home Office has carefully watched all political groups in England. To our knowledge, no one was aware that Richard—Lord Hargrave—and I were to meet."

"And yet our father is dead," the younger son continued.

"Oui, monsieur."

"And on your side, were there any organizations against a treaty?"

"A few," he admitted. "But none of them knew I was leaving the country, the Sûreté has assured us."

"What of Scotland Yard?" Barker asked. "Were they notified?"

"No, Monsieur Barker. It was accepted that this matter did not concern them. However, the Foreign Office has been informed."

"Dare we hope that if nobody contacts them in a few days, they will come to see how the treaty is coming along?"

"I'm afraid I have no answer for you."

"A message was delivered to the ambassador's boat to leave until she will be summoned later. Either before or after, the bodyguard, Mr. Delacroix, was murdered. I have determined that the message is a forgery. Someone wanted the boat to leave while we are stranded here. We have no idea how long that will be. I suggest we prepare ourselves. The French doors must be boarded or the house could be invaded at any time. We should inventory our food and ration our water. There are any number of things we should consider. One could say we find ourselves in a siege situation."

The first to speak up was Algernon Kerry. I was beginning to dislike him.

"How do we know the rest of us are in danger? Just because you say so? You are not our leader, Mr. Barker, and you cannot dictate to us. You claim someone out there means us harm. Rather than spending time counting jam jars, let us arm ourselves and track the blighter to wherever he is. There is a full gun cabinet by the window."

"Have you experience firing a gun, Mr. Kerry?"

"I was a captain in the Venezuelan army during the Border War with Brazil. I'm well acquainted with firearms."

"I will merely say that the man who shot Lord Hargrave with some accuracy and stabbed a seasoned Sûreté inspector to death is dangerous and should be approached cautiously."

"We shall do so. Meanwhile, will you and your man guard the house and the female guests while we are gone?"

"With my life, sir."

"Shall we go, gentlemen?"

The men looked at each other, then by consensus rose.

"Ambassador, I must ask that you stay behind," the Guv said. "His Lordship may be gone, but I signed a contract to protect you that I intend to fulfill."

Gascoigne looked annoyed at not getting to join the hunting party. He buried his fists into his hips and frowned thunderously. I suppose it worked within the French government, but I thought him a spoiled child.

Partridge came through then with a ring of keys and unlocked the gun cabinet. The key turned in the lock and the cabinet was opened, under the eager eyes and hands of Kerry and his cronies.

"Stop!" Barker called.

Everyone froze.

"Partridge, there is an empty space in the rack, right there in the middle. Was there a rifle in every slot?"

"Yes, sir, there was."

"And can you recall which one appears to be missing?"

Under close scrutiny, the butler went through the stock of hunting rifles there.

"It is His Lordship's Sharps Carbine, sir. It appears some ammunition is missing, also."

"May I assume that His Lordship did not possess expanding bullets?"

"Of course not, sir. These were for hunting parties on the mainland."

"The Sharps is a long-distance rifle, known for its accuracy. I suspect that His Lordship was shot with his own rifle. Is the key you are holding there usually well secured?"

"It is, sir. Always. I lock it up myself."

"Perhaps the lock was picked," Barker said.

"You may look for yourself after we are done, Mr. Barker," Algernon Kerry said. "Right now, we've got a man to capture."

The Guv had warned them but they would not be dissuaded. Within a minute the rack of rifles was denuded and men who probably had little experience with firearms were tossing odd rounds into any old gun. It seemed to me a recipe for disaster. The ambassador should have been glad to stay in the house, which was the only safe place on the island, but he was just as eager as the rest of them to get out and shoot something.

Perhaps I am being harsh toward them. Having lived when others had just died, they felt a need to do something. Anything.

Running about madly with guns was certainly more heroic than taking food inventories and boarding up windows. I had seen both murder victims firsthand, however, and whatever this fellow was, he was competent at killing and at staying alive. It could be a massacre.

"Stop them," I said in Barker's ear.

"How? They are grown men who will not listen to sense. I can stop myself. I can stop you. I stopped the ambassador due to a commitment I made. I have not committed to saving everyone."

Well armed and fortified with libations from the liquor tray, the men turned as one and marched out like a home battalion headed to the Sudan. And the minute they were gone, the women of the house appeared in ones and twos, looking accusingly at us as if we had planned and executed this maneuver ourselves. An old and established diplomat, Gascoigne knew when a crowd could not be dissuaded. He made a hasty retreat to his room.

"Where have they gone?" Millicent Fraser asked.

"After His Lordship's killer, madam," Barker answered.

"Ross can barely see beyond twenty feet. He's liable to shoot one of the party."

"They're in danger, aren't they?" Bella Anstruther asked.

"Aye, miss. The man in the woods is very accurate and has no qualms about killing another person."

"Why didn't you stop them, then?"

"I warned them. I have no authority to order them. They are grown men."

"A few of them," Mrs. Fraser acknowledged. "The rest are boys playing at soldiers."

Mrs. Ashleigh, who stood beside the colonel's wife, glanced at Barker. For once, he was on the side of caution. I did not imagine that would last long. She turned my way but I immersed myself in what was being said.

"Which way did they go?" Bella asked.

"Straight into the woods."

"Do you think he's there?"

"He could be anywhere. He seems to know the island well."

"What did you talk about in the library?" Lady Alicia asked.

"I tried to organize them and make preparations for being here for some time. Instead, they followed the suggestion of Mr. Kerry, who wanted to hunt the man down immediately."

"Was that so wrong?" a young woman asked. I suspected it was the daughter, Olivia, to whom Gascoigne was a godparent.

"He is better armed than they, and probably a better shot. A sharpshooter could take most of them down from a distance, then disappear."

"How would you handle it differently?" Mrs. Fraser asked.

"I would want to know what this man's plan is. Mr. Llewelyn and I just returned from the harbor unscathed. We would have been an easy target. If his plan is not to kill anyone who puts his head out the window, I would like to determine what it is."

I had to stop myself from smiling. You clever fellow. If you cannot convince the men, you shall convince the women instead.

CHAPTER EIGHT

The sun was setting quickly.

"So, what do we do until the hunting party returns?" Gascoigne asked from the top of the stairs. Having seen that Barker was not tarred and feathered, he had returned.

"When your boat is sinking, you must plug the holes, sir," Barker said.

"How do we begin?" Philippa asked.

"We must close and secure the front shutters on the windows facing the woods, barricade the doors, and look to see if there is any other way into Godolphin House. We must also secure the food and water as soon as possible."

"Should we confine ourselves to one floor or area within the house?"

"Only as a last resort, Your Excellency. I don't want to give up territory if there is no need to do so at this point."

Gascoigne stared at him as if still not certain whether or not to put his confidence in this strange Scotsman. With reluctance, he nodded. All of us stood and began to divide up the tasks the Guv had mentioned. Cautiously, I went out to secure the front shutters.

I wondered if the assassin were back in his roost somewhere in the woods, ready to shoot anyone who stepped out the front door. I even wondered if he were just obeying the orders of someone else and had little or no personal stake in what occurred here. I didn't trust him, of course, but I trusted Barker, to some degree, at least. Surely he wouldn't send me out to have my head explode like a Christmas cracker, I told myself. My head believed it, but my feet, the ones that had to cross the sill of the front door, they were another matter entirely.

One step. Two steps. At three, one might as well get on with it, or spend the rest of the day counting. There were large black shutters on the side of each window, probably to protect the house against squalls. The shutters were clipped to brackets mounted into the stone walls. I worked out that the clips attached in the middle to secure the window. As I fumbled with the latch, the window above me opened.

"Eh, Thomas," my friend called down from the first floor.

"What is it, Cesar?" I asked.

"How does one reach the clip up here without falling out the window?"

"Very carefully."

"Wonderful advice," he said.

"You are tall enough. If you hold on to the sill, you should be able to just reach the edge of the shutter with your other hand."

Cesar reached out unsteadily. Aside from everything else, he had to unlatch the window without being able to see the latch itself.

"What does it look like?" he asked.

"A hook with three prongs."

He braced his left hand on the wood of the sill and leaned out as far as he could. The hook holding the shutter was troublesome. At one point, he shook his right hand as if it were growing cramped.

"Got it!" he finally cried.

Just then the window over his head shattered and he cried out as shards of glass rained down upon him. That is, he and I, since I was just below him. I ducked back against the wall.

"Are you injured?" I called up to him.

"I wasn't shot, if that's what you mean. First brains and now glass. What does this fellow have against me?"

"He's just trying to frighten you. If he had wanted to shoot you, I expect you would already be dead."

"I'm covered in glass," he said. "Could you come up here and get it off me? I have no wish to be cut to ribbons."

"I'll be right there," I said, turning. As I reached the entrance, a bullet ricocheted off the stone wall by my head. The assassin had grown bored and was amusing himself at our expense.

I brought an ash can to Cesar and began picking pieces of glass off him. He was bleeding from a few cuts and splinters, but he would be well enough with some sticking plaster and a change of clothes. When we were done, I went in search of Cyrus Barker and found him in the kitchen consulting with the cook over the inventory.

"That madman has shot out one of the windows up on the first floor."

"Was anyone hurt?" he asked.

"Cesar was covered in glass, but relatively unharmed."

"Your friend seems hapless, in my opinion. Do you believe the assassin is specifically targeting him?"

"Not especially," I answered. "He's missed him twice."

"Did you get the shutters on the left side closed? The right ones have been secured."

"Everything on the front has been secured except Cesar's."

Barker looked at me steadily, or least I assumed he did. "They all have to be secured. You had better do it."

"Yes, sir."

I climbed the stair recalling that Cyrus Barker's previous assistant had died in the course of his duties. I had no desire to be a statistic for the next man. There were things I intended to get done now, things that didn't involve getting shot on an island of which no one had ever heard.

I walked down the hall to the now almost glassless window. Barker was right. It had to be closed if people were to sleep in that wing tonight. We did not want the assassin to whittle down the area we lived in until we were confined to a single room. There was shattered glass all over the carpet and poor Cesar's blood had stained some of the pieces red.

"All right, Mr. Whoever-you-are," I muttered. "Take your best shot, damn your eyes. I'm going to close this window!"

I reached around the side of the curtain and through the glass to the near edge of the shutter, then tried to reach as far as I could. I almost reached the far edge. The problem was, the shutter was latched behind. Putting my head out quickly, I could see behind the shutter to the latch, but my arm was far too thick to fit. Probably the shutters were latched and closed with some kind of long stick from outside, like a lamplighter's pole. What could I improvise here?

I left the hall and went downstairs where there were umbrellas and walking sticks in a stand. Most were far too thick for my purposes, particularly the umbrellas, but among them was a rattan cane as thin as a wand. They were fashionable a few years ago for about a week and a half, the kind that if one leaned on it, it would bend under your weight until it snapped in two. It was perfect for my purposes. Armed with my figurative slingshot, I went back to face Goliath.

Sliding the stick between the shutter and the wall was not difficult, but getting it to unlatch was. It wouldn't budge. There was a slot affixed to the wall into which the hook was held. If I could jiggle it out of the slot, I'd be done. I tried as hard as I could. And again. And again.

A bullet came just then. It hit the brick outside the window, shattering it into chips and powder that got all over my suit. I was a tempting target, lit up in the dark. He was playing with me, the way a cat plays with a mouse. I leaned over, jabbed the stick in behind the shutter and jiggled for all I was worth. The latch came loose and I swung the shutter closed. One down, one to go.

I squeezed the stick into the other side and it came free almost immediately. I was pressed against the closest shutter reaching across when another bullet came, striking the outside of the shutter. When it struck, it knocked the breath out of me. My body went cold and hot and clammy all at once. I felt sick to my stomach. Stepping back, I examined my shirt. There was no blood. The bullet had not passed through the shutter. I supposed I had not been worth the waste of an expanding bullet.

Crossing the hall, I threw myself into a chair, and debated whether or not to have apoplexy. I heard the cart horse neighing for his dinner in the stable. The ocean was lapping on the beach and the breeze billowed the curtains in the hall. I would save the apoplexy for another day.

The shutter was still hanging open. I came back, pulled it shut, and latched the two together. Then I got away from there as quickly as possible. I went downstairs again and found Barker in the hall.

"The shutters are closed, sir," I said.

"Good. You're bleeding, by the way."

"Am I?"

"Your cheek."

I reached up and touched my face. A sliver of glass was in it. There was no telling whether it had been at the initial breaking of the window or later.

"You should go down to the kitchen and see about your Brazilian friend. They have taken him there, I believe."

I went down to the basement. Cesar was seated and chatting with a housemaid. He smiled when he saw me.

"Thomas! I am good as new thanks to this angel of mercy. But look, you are bleeding, too! Sit down. She will tend to you."

"There is a man out there shooting at us for sport," I said. "He shot at me twice when I was closing your window."

"I'm sorry. Sit. This is Brigid. Brigid, Thomas works for Mr. Barker, the fellow with the dark glasses. Have you seen him?"

"No, I haven't," she answered.

"He's a big fellow." Cesar turned to me. "Is he as dangerous as he looks?"

"Probably more so. There's nothing he likes so much as a fight. It quenches his bloodlust."

"How can such a man attract a woman like Mrs. Ashleigh?"

"I have no idea," I admitted. "But they are devoted to each other."

"That's romantic," Brigid said, as she pulled the sliver from my cheek.

"Ow."

She smiled. "Be glad it wasn't a bullet."

"So, where does your Mr. Barker come from?" Cesar asked. "Is he from London?"

"Yes, by way of China. He has offices in Whitehall and a school for antagonistics in Soho."

"He sounds a very dangerous fellow. I'm glad he is helping us."

"No question," I replied, standing. "Thank you, miss. I should go and look for him."

I found him down in the front hall, talking with the butler.

"The hatches have all been battened down, sir," I said.

"So, we're safe within these walls, but we cannot stay here forever. This house party has been brought to an end, and everyone wants to go back home."

"How? We cannot signal for a boat, sir," I said. "The first man who tries it will be shot on sight. He took potshots at me while I was closing the shutter, but he wouldn't hesitate if I tried to run a flag up the flagpole."

"Agreed," Barker rumbled. "By the way, the men have returned."

"So, what do we do next? Shall we organize another expedition tomorrow with Colonel Fraser?"

"I think the notion of tracking him down with a large search party, culminating in the inevitable death of the assassin, is mere wishful thinking. Our adversary is too clever for that. However, if it keeps the men occupied, and gives everyone the illusion that something is being done, I have no objection."

"But, sir, what are we to do? You and I, I mean? How are we to get at this fellow?"

"What would you suggest, Thomas? If I were not on this island, and their fate were in your hands, what would you do?"

I thought for a moment. "I would break the search party into two parties and perform a pincerlike move. He is but one man, after all. He could not fight two groups at once."

"That is a capital suggestion, lad, provided he can be maneuvered into a spot from which he cannot escape. Don't forget, however, that we endanger the life of every member of the group once they step out of Godolphin House. The men here are not hired soldiers or pawns to do with as we choose. Have you any other suggestions?"

"If we could barricade ourselves in the lighthouse, we could sound the signal to passing ships."

"Another excellent idea," Barker said. "Mind you, we endanger the life of anyone who arrives to save us, but that cannot be helped. There are thirty people here whom we must try to save."

"You're saying it is up to us, then, to find this fellow, track him down, and subdue or kill him," I said.

"Aye."

"When?"

"Later tonight. There is a full moon."

"We're going out in the dark to track this fellow down ourselves," I repeated.

"He will not anticipate it and may be unprepared. It is the only logical choice."

"What will Mrs. Ashleigh say?"

"Good hunting, I hope."

CHAPTER NINE

"How did the hunting party fare?" I asked.

"There was no sign of our killer. As I said, the killer has found himself someplace to hide. The men are obviously disappointed. I believe they hoped to bag him as a trophy. Has anyone tried to get in?"

"No, sir. It was relatively quiet here."

We went downstairs and found ourselves in an impromptu war council. The woman had drawn the returned party into the empty dining room, and was questioning them.

"Perhaps our hunt has sent him scurrying back to where he came from," Percy suggested.

"I hope not. I want to kill that blackguard for shooting Papa."

"You shouldn't say such things," his sister, Olivia, said.

"I don't care. He's got to pay for what he has done. That's only fair, isn't it?"

I looked across the table at Barker and saw a slight smile on his lips beneath that great mustache of his. No doubt he could offer a sermon on forgiveness but just then it wouldn't be taken. For that matter, I have seen the Guv seek his own vengeance on at least a few occasions.

"Where could he be hiding?" Colonel Fraser asked no one in particular.

"He'd need some kind of shelter, I suppose," Kerry said.

"Perhaps among the rocks on the beach," the French ambassador replied, filling his glass with burgundy.

"You are being quiet, Barker," Fraser noted.

My employer roused himself from his reverie.

"It was a reconnaissance expedition," he said. "You men did excellent work, I'm certain. We shall try again tomorrow. If we are trapped here, so is he."

"Perhaps we can outflank him," Kerry suggested.

"Reminds me of the days I spent tiger hunting in Simla," the Colonel added. It was his way, I suppose, to suggest that he was well traveled and competent. Barker had some scars that I was certain had been made by a giant cat, but he made no reference to them.

"It's got to be some sort of foreign spy or assassin," Paul Burrell stated, changing the subject. "My father was rather high up in the diplomatic service, as the ambassador will attest."

Mrs. Ashleigh spoke up. "I can't imagine why anyone would shoot Richard. He was such a good and gentle man. It cannot be for anything he had done. He must have represented something to someone. A foreign government, perhaps."

"The Germans," Gascoigne grumbled. "Or the Russians."

Barker sat motionless and silent in the middle of the table, secure behind those smoky quartz lenses.

You sly beggar, I thought, looking across at him. You suspect one of the people at this table. You are evaluating everything they say.

"It is not fair for him to be struck down now, of all times," Philippa went on. "He was going to retire next year."

I did something stupid then. I looked over at Philippa Ashleigh. She was staring at me directly. Somehow she had gotten into her head that I was responsible for both keeping Cyrus Barker safe, which I was not, and for convincing him at some point to retire, as well. He certainly didn't need the money. Rather it was the stimulation he craved. He was a natural manhunter. Being stranded here was torture to the rest of us, but to him it must have been a treat. If it weren't for us, I had little doubt he'd been sleeping rough out on the beach somewhere, drinking rainwater from puddles and setting well-devised traps to capture his adversary, whoever he was. The truth was, I could no more control him than she could. I glanced away.

"Can we talk about anything but him?" Bella Anstruther said beside me. "You make him sound like a demon. He's only a man after all."

Colonel Fraser clapped his hands.

"Bravo, Miss Anstruther! Your father taught you well. A man this fellow is, and sooner or later men make mistakes. And when he does, we'll pounce."

There we were in one of the most unique and interesting locations in all the world. The grounds approached perfection, the house was sumptuous, the guest list of some interest, the food at least adequate, and everyone was having a terrible time. The thought of imminent and violent death will do that to one.

"Where is your mother?" I asked Olivia Burrell. She was an attractive and unwed young woman and I was courting disaster just speaking to her, but I hoped to have some news to give to Cyrus Barker.

"She has been given a heavy dose of laudanum. She should sleep until morning."

"How is the family coping?"

"Our father was everything to us."

"I'm sorry we are stranded here during your time of grief."

"Obviously, that cannot be helped."

I noticed her fingers were moving nervously on the table. She saw me look and spoke.

"Mrs. Ashleigh has organized an impromptu music night to help us. I'm trying to recall the chords to Edvard Grieg's Suite no. 1."

"We're to have an entertainment?" I asked.

"She thought it the best way to distract everyone."

Philippa caught up with me a few minutes afterward. "What can you do? Can you sing or play?"

"I can sing better than Mr. Barker, but that isn't saying very much. I can't play a note."

"Ah," she said, disappointed.

"I have won several eisteddfods, however, and have about thirty stories and poems memorized. Would Mr. Poe's 'Annabel Lee' do? It is full of melodrama."

"It would be perfect. Bless you, Thomas."

Chairs were set up in the ballroom for the performance and a playbill created on a chalkboard from the nursery. Philippa would begin with some Chopin. Lady Alicia would sing accompanied by Mrs. Fraser on pianoforte. Colonel Fraser would sing the sentimental favorite "Loch Lomond," then Mr. Kerry would attempt a romantic Spanish ballad accompanied by his valet, Cesar Rojas, on the guitar. Then I would recite from Mr. Poe.

That was the program. It went rather well, considering the circumstances. Philippa was quite accomplished. Lady Alicia's voice was rather weak, but Mrs. Fraser's playing was overloud, so few noticed. The colonel was a little off-key but he was such a charming old fellow that no one seemed to mind. By the end of his song it had become a sing-along. Mr. Kerry was also rather good, or so I supposed. It's difficult to judge a song in another language. If he was good, his accompaniment was even better. Cesar was a bit of a virtuoso on his instrument, a pear-shaped Brazilian guitar. Not being musically inclined myself, I am amazed when people I know can produce such wonderful sounds from what began as a block of wood.

As for "Annabel Lee," one cannot go wrong when reciting Poe. I've always thought the man was one part hack and three parts genius. I'm certain most in the crowd had seen the poem performed before in music halls or village fetes, but it never ceases to entertain. Even Lady Alicia, whom I would consider above drawing room entertainments, applauded.

It was not until I got up to perform that I realized we had a second audience. Out in the hall most of the staff had turned the staircase into a seating area. Entertainers on this island were no doubt few and far between. A dozen footmen, maids, scullery workers, cooks, and gardeners sat with Mrs. Albans and Mrs. Tregoweth on the bottom step. Partridge stood at the foot of the stair as if willing to defend them for the impertinence of daring to show their faces at such an event. I gave him a small nod and began.

The poem was well received and I got a smile of approval from Mrs. Ashleigh, which made it all worthwhile. I could have performed a more obscure poem and done so with greater intensity and skill, but the request I had been given was to be good enough and no better. For Mrs. Ashleigh's sake, I had attempted to fit in, not to stand out.

After the performances were done, the servants scurried away and a few minutes later a treat was brought out from the kitchen: grenadine-glazed hothouse strawberries over sponge cake, a pink perfection, served with coffee. I had two portions.

She had done it, I told myself. Philippa had distracted the entire lot of us from succumbing to thoughts of death. She had that knowledge of organizing things in such a way that it seemed natural and easy when, in fact, it was not. Then she charmed the best out of everyone while making them feel she was doing them a favor by including them.

"Do you intend to use the entire jar of cold cream, Cyrus?" Philippa asked later that evening.

Barker was scooping the contents out of a jar with a spoon. "I shall buy you an entire vat of it when we return to London, my dear."

I picked up the empty jar and began to read the ingredients. "Olive oil, lanolin, glycerin, sperm whale oil, paraffin . . ."

"You mustn't lay bare a woman's beauty regimen, Thomas," she said. "And just what do you intend to do with it?"

In answer, Barker crossed to the fireplace and reached up under the flue. He broke off a chunk of soot and began to crumble it into the bowl.

"You intend to go out in blackface, like a minstrel?"

"I intend to cover my face and hands with it, yes. I shall be moving about in the dark, and the two can be easily discerned."

"What about your shirtfront?" I asked.

"I borrowed some oilcloth from Partridge to cover it with."

Before we could protest, he tied the cloth about his throat like a scarf and began smearing the mixture all over his face.

"You look ludicrous!" Mrs. Ashleigh wailed. "Do you intend to walk through the halls looking like that?"

In response, Barker went to the window and opened it.

"Surely, you—" Philippa began, but it was too late.

Cyrus Barker had climbed out the window and was gone.

"That man!" she cried in despair.

"I'm going back to my room now," I told her.

She crossed her arms and looked vexed. So much for good hunting.

CHAPTER TEN

I awoke in the early hours to sounds of disorder in the house. There were snatches of conversation in the hall outside my door and voices raised in concern. We were not at home, however, where we could step into the hall, so Herr Schroeder, Colonel Fraser's man, and I dressed as quickly as possible to join the servants in the back hall. When we reached the kitchen, it was to find one of the male servants lying across the sill of the back door in a faint and people stepping over him to get in and out as if he weren't there.

"What has happened?" I asked to anyone who would answer. "Why is this door unlocked?"

It was the housekeeper, Mrs. Tregoweth, who answered for me as she passed by with a small bucket of water and an armful of rags.

"The male servants in the bunkhouse behind us are sick. Very sick, I'm afraid. It must have been something they ate. Could you gentlemen help? It is no place for female staff."

Without a word I took the bucket from her hand and like all the others before me stepped over the prostrate footman and hurried to the bunkhouse. Nearby another young man had collapsed in the yard near the outdoor water closet, and inside I could hear someone being violently ill. We opened the bunkhouse door and were met by an overwhelming odor of sickness. Stepping inside, we found Dr. Anstruther hard at work, while several young men moaned in agony.

"What's going on, sir?" I asked.

"It's poison, I think," the doctor said. "These men had steak and mushroom pie last night as a treat, but I suspect some toadstools were picked by mistake."

"How bad is it? Will they be all right?"

"I cannot guarantee that all will survive the night," he murmured in my ear.

"How can I help?" I asked.

"Collect all the chamber pots you can find, and make up some hot, soapy water and some mops. See if there are any more buckets. Oh, and look for any disinfectant such as bleach borax or ammonia."

"Yes, sir!" I said. Schroeder and I were glad of the charge to get out of the sour stench of the bunkhouse. In every corner the men were vomiting, their skin pale and sweaty, their eyes rolling in their heads, barely conscious of their surroundings. The butler had removed his jacket and was mopping up the mess from the floor with a determined look on his face. We went back into the house to the kitchen.

Mrs. Albans was pumping water into a pot, to be set on the stove when it was full. The tears were running down her raw face. As gently as I could, I pulled her out of the way and began working the pump myself, while Schroeder went in search of chamber pots.

"*Beth sydd o'i le?*" I asked her in Welsh, for surely with a name like Albans we were from the same country. "What's wrong?"

"I've been picking mushrooms since I was a tweeny," she said in our native tongue. "I recognize a toadstool when I see one! I don't know how this happened. I was very careful. I always am!"

"It's awfully easy to confuse the death cap with a normal mushroom," I said.

"Nae ydy!" she cried indignantly. "Not to me! Isn't my steak and mushroom pie a blue-ribbon winner at the agricultural fair? Death caps are small. I only picked big ones, to be certain!"

I wanted to state the obvious, that she was in her sixties and might need spectacles, but she was probably already feeling enough guilt from what had occurred. If one of the boys died, she might take to her bed in grief.

"The men are young and strong," I said. "I'm sure they'll be fine in a couple of days."

"I made it for them as a treat, for all the extra work required of them this week. You know young men. You're one yourself. They're always hungry, and they've always been partial to my meat pies."

"Of course," I said, letting her talk. Like the young men in the yard, she had to get everything out of her system if she were going to begin to heal.

The tears were dripping off her pudgy face into the pot. I began filling the stove with more wood, knowing this tragedy would keep us occupied for hours. I'd read a few books on poisons on the Guv's orders. Toadstool poisoning was a particularly nasty and protracted way to die.

I looked up and noticed we were being watched by the housekeeper. I nodded to her to indicate I was trying to keep Mrs. Albans calm. She smiled and nodded in return and went on with her duties. I decided to try a different tack.

"Dr. Anstruther's a good chap. I'm sure he's got this matter in hand. But won't Her Ladyship and the French ambassador be wanting their breakfast soon?"

Her hands went to her face. Her grief had made her forget her normal duties. Immediately she went to the larder and brought out a basket of eggs and a side of bacon. I reached up for the pans hanging overhead and began pulling them down.

"Sarey!" she bellowed to one of the kitchen staff. I left her to get on with her work.

I came upon Cyrus Barker in the yard tending to the fellow I had first encountered in the doorway. The Guv was dressed but without his collar and tie and the coal had been removed from his face. He held the young man by the scruff of the neck as he vomited into a bucket between his legs. There was a large blue bottle in the Guv's hand. I recognized it. It was ipecac.

"The more poison he gets rid of, the less he will ingest," he explained.

"The cook claims she can tell a death cap from an edible mushroom. She never made such a mistake."

"She would if it was already chopped up and added to the other mushrooms," Barker said.

"The killer—"

"He must have brought the mushrooms he picked himself into the house. I doubt he knew it would be fed to the stable boys and other servants. More likely, he hoped to poison the entire house party."

"Who is this blasted fellow, and what does he have against this house?" I wondered aloud.

"I wish I had an answer for you. The only thing I know for sure is that he is an excellent marksman, and knows a toadstool from less dangerous fungi."

"Someone local who knows the island, perhaps? A former employee? He knew just where to go for the toadstools."

"Perhaps. That's it, young fellow. You purge that gall from your system!"

The latter was addressed to the young man who was being sick again. If the sheer volume of matter he was expelling was any indication, he would survive the ordeal.

"If this chap had not crawled to the back door and alerted everyone, his bunkmates might have all died in the it beds," I said.

"Another work of the assassin," Barker said.

"Assassin," I said, shaking my head.

"You believe there is no such thing?"

"No, I don't. Not as an occupation. Maybe in one of Burton's Arabian Nights tales, but not on an island half an hour's ferry trip off the coast of England."

"Not everyone in England is English or lives by our values. Some people grew up in far different circumstances."

I thought of Barker, growing up as a street urchin in Foochow and traveling all over the China seas before coming to England. Then I thought of Cesar Rojas. England must be a very different place than Rio de Janeiro or wherever it was he came from.

"Perhaps," I said, which meant "you're probably right but I don't feel like surrendering the argument at the moment."

"Water," the poor lad beside Barker croaked. I immediately ran into the kitchen and fetched some. By then eggs and bacon and kidneys were sizzling in pans and toast was cooking on the fire, and there was a full staff alongside Mrs. Albans preparing the meal. One would think it was any other day.

I took the water out and he drank it, then was violently ill again because of it. He was on the mend, however, and so too were some of his comrades. There was a good deal of work to be done yet. Over the next couple of hours we mopped and disinfected the bunkhouse, doused every lad in buckets of water, washed them down, dressed them in clean nightshirts, burned the old ones, changed their bedding, opened all the bunkhouse windows, and even brought in a bouquet of fresh flowers from the garden, which the bunkhouse had never seen before.

Then and only then were the women, highborn and low, allowed in to minister to the sick men after we were certain they were out of the shooter's sights. Their patients were still feverish and perspiring freely. Lady Hargrave, still reeling from the death of her husband the day before, applied cold compresses to their foreheads. Dr. Anstruther hovered about from patient to patient with the aid of his daughters. He still had concerns over two of the servants, whose condition was very grave. Barker and I gathered and emptied the last of the buckets over the side of the cliff, then carried them down some narrow steps to be washed in the sea. There are no duties too humble for anyone when a crisis occurs. When we were done, we carried the cleansed buckets up again.

Eventually, we sat ourselves in the grass by the hut and leaned against the clapboards, exhausted.

"He is improvising," he said.

"The assassin?"

"Aye. He accurately assassinated Lord Hargrave, but this time he did not succeed. There were not enough toadstools to kill his victims, and the young men were not his intended targets. However, he is creative. He is changing his tactics. I wonder what he might try next."

We went into breakfast, which was served at nearly ten due to the crisis. There were no footmen present to serve, but I noticed that the coffee was being replaced with a new silver carafe by a maid. The butler, Partridge, had looked grim in the hut, but now his eyes looked glazed. No doubt he was trying to work out how to replace a roomful of male servants. His eyes fell on me. I turned my attention to the conversation.

"We can't just sit here all day and wait for the blighter to come kill us," Colonel Fraser was saying. "We have to go out and track him down, successfully this time."

"Gentlemen, I will put three questions to you. First of all, how did His Lordship come to be shot with his own rifle?"

"My word," the Colonel muttered. "His own gun! This is intolerable."

"My second question is, how did the killer know to bring special ammunition for a rifle he knew would already be waiting here for him?

"And lastly, how did the assassin break into a locked cabinet?"

"Where is the key kept?" the French ambassador asked.

"In my nightstand drawer, sir, unless His Lordship specifically requested it," Partridge said, looking rather deflated. "I haven't used it since His Lordship attended a hunting party last year."

"This fellow," Gascoigne said, "he comes and goes like a ghost. He poisons the staff, he shoots my old friend, he holds us all hostage. It's almost as if . . ."

"As if?" Barker repeated.

"As if everything were arranged for him."

"Aye. It is time we noted who comes and goes on this island. Thomas?"

"Yes, sir?"

"Please prepare a list of every person here, male or female, both guest and servant."

"Yes, sir."

CHAPTER ELEVEN

I noted that Barker was sitting in that way he has when he has been up all night, which occurs often enough for me to recognize. He leans forward just slightly with his chin down, staring over the top of his glasses, totally relaxed. His body uses the smallest amount of energy, enough to keep him upright. Beside him Mrs. Ashleigh was conversing with young Lady Alicia, and I could not be sure whether she noticed the change or not. There were no seats assigned for breakfast so I had filled my plate with eggs, bacon, and black pudding and sat beside him. I hoped he would tell me about his night excursion in his own good time.

"The man's got himself a hidey-hole on this island, and no mistake," he finally said to me. "I searched for him for hours late last night. He made no fire. My estimation of him has been decidedly elevated. This is not a random person with a grievance, in my opinion. It is either someone who has made a long and carefully worked out plan or an actual paid killer of some kind, someone with a unique set of skills contracted to come here and eliminate some or all of us."

"So which is it?" I asked. "All of us?"

"No, or he'd have shot you and Cesar both last night."

"Does it change matters much if he's highly trained?"

"I suppose not, but it makes our duty more difficult."

"Sir, what duty do you mean precisely? I mean which one in particular?"

"We were hired not necessarily to bodyguard Lord Hargrave, but the ambassador. His Lordship was not aware of any plot against himself, although looking in hindsight, there was one."

"Are you certain it wasn't a case of mistaken identity? This paid assassin had never clapped eyes on the two men before and mistook one for the other?"

"Perhaps. Stranger things have occurred. Chance is a factor too often discounted. But I doubt it. He is too professional. More so than I. You see, I was slapdash in our contract. Certainly, I was to guard the ambassador, but what of our client? And are we simply to let everyone else on the island perish? Would the ambassador find that morally acceptable?"

"That's just semantics," I said.

"It is? Would it hold in a court of law? Lad, we have failed. I have failed. Lord Hargrave is dead."

"Yes, but you can't be held responsible for that. You checked the island—"

"I am responsible, Thomas, and so are you. We can no longer hold up our heads among our peers and say that we never lost a client. Someone, in fact someone important, is dead because we failed. I don't imagine Mr. Gascoigne is much impressed with the cleverness of the common English detective at the moment."

"We had no reason to think anyone was on the island."

"It doesn't matter," he said.

"Sometimes people fail."

Barker thumped the table with his fist, making every utensil jump.

"Not if I have anything to say about it."

I looked up. All eyes in the room were upon us.

"We'll get him, sir," I whispered. "Professional or otherwise."

"We will," he muttered. "I will accept nothing less."

Cyrus Barker left me in charge of the house and led a second expedition around the island with most of the men. They were heavily armed. It was important to be seen doing something. Under normal circumstances he would wait out the assassin until he came in on his own or made a mistake, but now we were being watched and graded.

They returned a little the worse for wear. One of the footmen had stepped into a fox trap that was last seen leaning against the fireplace in the bunkhouse. According to Barker it had been well concealed. He'd have blundered into it himself if he had been walking in that direction. I began to be convinced that Lord Hargrave's killer was an individual with a few uncommon skills.

In the afternoon, Colonel Fraser unveiled a plan for a blind he had designed to put near the flagpole, and thereby raise a makeshift flag to attract rescuers. The Guv agreed on the principle that it couldn't hurt, at least, and might even help a little.

"It was inspired by the brave young men now recovering from that coward's attempt to slaughter them," the colonel said. "The gardener has agreed to make it for us within the hour."

The barricade built that afternoon was about six feet high by a similar width. The wood was two boards thick, stabilized by perpendicular logs. I was not sure how it would fare against an expanding bullet, but I hoped we would never find out.

There was no red cloth to be had in Godolphin House, and no extra flag, but Gwendolyn Anstruther had a claret-colored dress that she was willing to sacrifice to the rescue effort and it should do well enough. After all, no ship would sail past simply because the flag was not a proper flag or a certain shade of red. Anyway, Barker seemed to think it was a good idea, even if he didn't initiate it. We helped lift the barricade into the dogcart, and the island horse pulled it to the north end with us following afoot.

It was a brisk, windy day. The air was warm and drowsy from the sun, but suddenly a cold wind would curl around you before continuing on its way. Our neckwear was fluttering over our shoulders making a nuisance, and hats had to be pushed down hard on one's head, or they'd be blown off the cliff.

We set the barricade down on the south side of the pole. The colonel had the honors, attaching a rope through the lower cleat on the metal, and tying a knot. Then he reached for the upper cleat. There was a sudden pop, with a kind of wheeze, and Colonel Fraser cried out. I looked in his direction and saw that there was blood on his sleeve. He had been shot in the hand. Barker seized him bodily and pulled him down, and the rest of us stepped behind the barricade or fell to the ground.

A second rapport came, with an almost apologetic cough, and this time it struck the flagpole with a tang of metal on metal. It ricocheted and thudded into the wood of the barricade. I was close by it, and as I knelt, something fell at my feet. It was the top cleat. There was now no way to attach the flag at the top.

"What direction are the bullets coming from?" Barker growled, having pulled a brace of pistols from his coat.

"South!" cried one man.

"No, east!" said another.

My employer moved to the northwest corner of the wooden structure and peered around the corner for a full minute. None of us moved, save one, Cesar Rojas. He crouched beside Barker.

"Here, sir. I brought this along," he said, handing him a portable telescope.

"Thank you, Mr. Rojas," he said, and took it. He stretched out the nest of tubes as he had done thousands of times in his previous life as a ship's captain in the China Sea, and viewed the scene. Most of us sat up, growing tired of lying about on the ground, and waited. A minute went by. Two minutes.

"Nothing," he finally said, closing the telescope with a snap. "Are you all right, Colonel?"

"The bullet passed right through my hand," Fraser said. "That will not improve my rheumatism."

We were impressed. The man at seventy-three was making jokes about having just been shot. We, less than a third of his age, could only hope for as much sangfroid.

I handed him my handkerchief, which he wrapped around his hand. The hand was wrinkled and spotted and browned from days spent under a Khyber sun. The bullet had cut through the flesh and missed the tarsals, but the tendons and muscles were shredded. He would have limited use of it from now on. Fortunately it was his left hand, and he favored his right.

"We could tie the other end around the pole," Barker suggested.

"He would only shoot through the rope, and probably the man tying it. Admit it, Mr. Barker. We have been stymied."

The Guv exhaled a bushelful of air.

"We must take the flag with us, then. We'll raise it later when we've taken care of this rascal."

A far more somber and dispirited group left the flagpole than the one that had arrived. The most dissatisfied was Algernon Kerry.

"We should have done something," he muttered. "We're like a pack of dogs returning with our tails between our legs."

"What would you have us do?" I asked.

"Charge the blighter. Some of us would die, but we'd get him, finally."

"We don't know which direction he shot from, or how far away. He could shoot us all down for target practice."

"Well, we've got to do something, don't we? Not stand around all day, hiding in the house like a flock of chickens in a storm!"

"We'll get him eventually," I said.

"Thank you," he said, "but I don't need vague assurances from somebody's servant."

That closed my mouth for the rest of the journey. I suppose I understood. He was trying to appear proper husband material for Miss Olivia Burrell, but so far he had not cut a very fine figure.

"Why does your master look so ill?" I asked Cesar sotto voce.

"He had yellow fever earlier this year," he explained.

For once, I did not believe him. There was something wrong with Kerry, I thought, and it wasn't some kind of fever. I had seen him acting furtive; he was hiding something. He had not touched the wine at dinner, but perhaps he was a secret drinker. That might make him caustic and ill-tempered.

Once inside Godolphin House again we had to admit to the women and to the ambassador, who had stayed behind at Barker's request, that we were unsuccessful. As strange as it sounded, we were all being held in a house by one man with a long rifle.

The women circled around the colonel as if he were Wellington injured at Waterloo, and helped him down to the kitchen and the bandage drawer. The last I heard Fraser was claiming a sticking plaster would fix him up fine.

Most of the rest of the party had retreated to the liquor cabinet for Scotch and sodas. It wasn't Dutch courage they were searching for, it was the frustration of not being able to do anything. The fellow loose on the island, whoever he was, was thwarting us at every turn. Paul Burrell, the eldest son, was taking it particularly hard. I did not drink, of course, because Barker did not. I noticed again that Kerry didn't drink, either.

"I'm going to go lie down before dinner," he said to no one in particular, and took himself away.

Looking over to my employer, I saw he noted Kerry leaving, as well. It occurred to me that this was not a good time to have secrets.

That afternoon was spent in games, if one can believe that. All the men were bruised by the events of the day, and the women seemed to encourage them to relax. Several rounds of whist were played, with Mrs. Fraser making a big show of helping her husband with his cards. There was also a tournament of sorts at the billiards table, with every man available to play. Barker fared no better than I, but then he has little respect for games of any sort, other than strategy games such as chess and go. Kerry did not come down until dinner. For all I knew he could be bingeing on absinthe in his room, or smoking opium.

When he returned at dinner, he was immaculate. Cesar had shaved him as well as cut and brilliantined his hair. He wore a white military jacket with some sort of pin upon it. The colonel immediately questioned him about it.

"Oh, this," he said. "It was for the Battle of the Brena Movement, a campaign in the War of the Pacific near Lima."

Kerry surprised me. First of all, he told the story directly and with self-effacement as any proper soldier would. Secondly, he seemed to be making an effort in front of the ladies. It worked in his favor. His unruliness over the past two meals came off as world-weariness. He had seen and done too much off in the wild jungles of South America. He mentioned malaria and yellow fever and he was immediately forgiven for any past remarks. He was nearly as popular as the colonel.

At dinner, Paul Burrell excused himself from whatever plans there might be for the evening. With his new position came new obligations. He must go over his father's papers in the family safe. I wondered if he was playing for sympathy on the part of Lady Alicia. He could not compete with the colonel or Kerry, but he was demonstrating signs of a person who took his obligations seriously.

I inferred that Burrell had never been given access before to his father's papers. I would further infer that the party to find a wife for Paul was another sign that Lord Hargrave was not greatly impressed by his eldest son. I have not a great circle of friends but I have ears and they have often heard the lament of the son who did not meet his father's expectations. Our fathers are a stony generation, difficult to impress and sparing in their approval. I can certainly attest to being a disappointment, but let he who is without sin cast the first stone. Fathers were sons once and eventually made peace with their own fathers. Meanwhile, there is a generation of young men who feel inadequate and have none willing to offer advice or encouragement. I mention this in passing because of Burrell, but it is a common English affliction and I feel the nation has suffered because of it.

After dinner, Barker walked about the old building, making sure the doors were secure, questioning the French ambassador on matters of security, and talking to the staff. The latter did not know what to make of him, being neither fish nor fowl, but then Cyrus Barker was not particularly concerned at any time what others thought of him, or whether they talked about him, as long as he could get on with his work. This opinion had stood him in good stead, but in this case would come back to haunt him.

CHAPTER TWELVE

Apparently, Barker and Mrs. Ashleigh were both early risers. After I had performed my toilet, I stepped up to the first floor where they were already seated in a nook by the main staircase.

"Good morning," I said to both of them.

"Lad," the Guv said, and pointed toward the chair with his chin. "I want you to hear this."

I sat and turned toward Philippa, because Barker indicated she was to tell me. I had no idea what it would be, and could not imagine.

"I was here eight years ago," she said. "In fact, many times before and since. Anyway, Celia was throwing another party and Algernon Kerry was a guest. Celia had intimated to me that there had been an understanding between the two families regarding him and Olivia since childhood, but since then things were not going well for the Kerrys. His father had left for the Continent with a stage actress and there was no hope for reconciliation. Of course, these things happen from time to time, even in good families. It could have been overlooked, but the problem was Algernon himself. At dinner the first night he got drunk. Lord Hargrave overlooked it, though it was bad form. The second night Mr. Kerry grew belligerent. At dinner, he questioned being married off, comparing it to livestock cultivation. He questioned His Lordship's politics and the impracticality of the island as an estate."

"What happened then?" I asked.

She paused, as if for dramatic effect. "Lord Hargrave spoke to Paul and told him to have a word with Algie about his behavior. Paul said he would and did. It was assumed that the matter was settled. Kerry was reasonable all day, but come dinnertime, he tossed off two glasses right off and began to give his opinion on the prime minister, Her Majesty, and the Archbishop of Canterbury. None of his opinions were very flattering."

"What did His Lordship do?"

"He didn't take it lying down, and he was prepared. A ferry had been summoned and was ready and waiting, and when the guest began to hold forth, Richard and Partridge, who was a more formidable man in those days, scooped him up and hustled him out the door. He was off the island in five minutes, and banned for life."

"Well, not for life, surely," I said. "He is here again."

"I understand he apologized very nicely, recently, I mean. He's been off in South America for several years. Apparently, he made something of himself. He owns a company there, Paititi Limited. It's some sort of rubber plantation. One can make a fortune in South America on the strangest of things. Anyway, being successful, and apologizing for his behavior years ago, was enough to convince His Lordship, or perhaps Celia who could always bend him to her will. And of course, Olivia has never married, in spite of several suitors, so perhaps he had won her heart. So, he was invited. He has been rather forthright, I'll admit, but I expect this is his attempt at good manners. Not everyone can be a host's dream. In case you have not noticed, Thomas, he has drunk nothing but water since he arrived."

"Considering what is at stake here, I suppose he could go half a week without a drink, or he could drink at night. I suppose I could ask Cesar. I'm sure he would tell me," I said.

"There's no need for that," Cyrus Barker said. "I've just searched his room. It seemed the fastest way to answer many of my questions about him."

"By yourself?" I asked. "Why didn't you ask me?"

"You were getting ready. I had Philippa keep an eye out for anyone."

"Where was Kerry?"

"In Paul Burrell's room, trying to push forward his own plan, I'm sure."

"And Cesar?"

"Working in the kitchen, in exchange for a good breakfast."

"I kept an eye out in case the Brazilian servant arrived," Philippa said. "In fact, he did climb the stairs, so immediately I asked him if he would fetch a pitcher of water for us, which of course he was obliged to get from the kitchen. By the time he returned, Cyrus was seated again."

"What did you find?" I asked Barker.

"Well, first of all, his time in South America appears valid. He has a bankbook for Paititi Limited, with offices in Manaus, Brazil, and Lima, Peru. There is a letter of introduction from the king of Brazil, and others from various ministers and dignitaries. The medals he wore the other night were stamped with the seal for the War of the Pacific, which I recall reading about a few years ago. In short, his story appears genuine."

I was rather unsatisfied. By now I thought my instincts were rather good, and they told me there was something rotten about the fellow.

"Did you find anything?" I asked.

In answer, Barker reached into his waistcoat pocket and flipped a small piece of crystal onto a journal on the table in front of me. Reaching out, I picked it up. It was hard, white, and translucent.

"What is it? Quartz?"

"No, Thomas, it is cocaine. Mr. Kerry appears to have transferred his abuse of alcohol to this drug. It is produced in South

America and can be made soluble in water and injected, or crushed and inhaled. The natives mix it with lime and make a drink of it, but I saw no apparatus to make it that way. I suspect Mr. Kerry must take it several times a day."

"Is it illegal?"

"No, but it does raise some questions. For instance, someone who is a slave to a drug would have difficulty running a company the size of Paititi Limited."

"It seems obvious he relies upon Cesar for everything. He works him too hard. Let us hope he at least pays him well."

"Use of the drug results in a higher level of energy and irritability, such as when Kerry spoke aggressively at dinner. It is followed by a period of extreme lethargy."

"Kerry always retires early."

"Precisely."

"So, he is not the ideal candidate for Ms. Olivia's hand."

"No," Mrs. Ashleigh stated with some degree of authority.

"However, our purpose here is to protect the ambassador, not to engage in matchmaking," Barker said.

"And then you searched his room, which you have always claimed is the sort of activity in which our agency does not indulge, and which sets it apart from detectives. And you," I said, actually pointing at Mrs. Ashleigh, "not only encouraged him, but aided him in this illegal enterprise. What you have to say for yourself?"

"He wasn't going to admit he used cocaine," she said.

I waved my arms, imploring to the gods. "So, he uses cocaine? It doesn't mean he is tied to any murders. I mean the fellow is an absolute bounder. I'd like to horsewhip him behind the stable. That doesn't make him a killer."

"It doesn't make him innocent, either. For now, his use of cocaine is just an interesting fact. We'll have to see if it has any further bearing upon the case."

"I cannot say anything to Celia about him without admitting searching his rooms, harmless as it was," Philippa continued, eyeing me for any sign of disagreement.

"So what are we supposed to do until help arrives?" I asked.

"We cannot sit here every day or barricade ourselves in our rooms."

"Upon my soul, you're an optimistic fellow, Mr. Llewelyn. What makes you think help will arrive, or any of us shall be alive by that remote date?"

"You really think he intends to kill everyone?"

"He shall try, at least. I suspect he is following a list and will not kill us out of turn. Were it a matter of simply killing people, you and Mr. Rojas would be dead."

I tried not to dwell on what might have happened. It only made me worry more.

"I admit that so far I have not had the opportunity to hunt for our shooter," I said, "but there has to be more we can do to solve this case beyond hunting for him and reeling from his attacks."

"Agreed," Barker said. "Let us proceed with the theory that the man in the woods intends to kill some or all of us."

"Very well."

"Can we work on the assumption that he wishes to kill either all of us or a subset of all of us?"

"We can."

"Who has he killed so far?"

"His Lordship, and Delacroix."

"Let us assume that Delacroix was killed for attempting to leave the island. Who was the intended target?"

"His Lordship."

"Why?"

"I haven't the slightest idea."

"Nor have I. Don't you think we should find out?"

"Certainly," I said. "But how?"

"By rattling the family closet for skeletons. That alway seems to work."

"Very well. How should we start? You think Her Ladyship will allow you to rattle the family skeletons?" I asked. "Just like that?"

"Why not? I have her oldest and dearest friend to convince her."

Philippa frowned. She had just been finessed into doing his bidding. I was glad to see it was someone else for a change.

"What shall I do in the meantime, sir?"

"I want you to engage Mr. Cesar in conversation and squeeze him like a lime until there is nothing left but pulp."

"Without him noticing it, of course," I said.

"Of course. In a conversational tone, or he might inform his master that we are looking into his past."

"You suspect Kerry is connected to the murders somehow?"

"Allow me to ask you a question in turn. Why would a man who made such an ass of himself here eight years ago not only accept an invitation but seemingly court it? Mr. Kerry no longer needs money. His company is a success. Does he actually care for Olivia Burrell, a spinster in her late twenties? There are younger and wealthier prospects for him in London."

"You make her sound positively ancient," Philippa chided. "She's a very sweet girl."

"Whom London society had little use for."

"Well, she does live out here on this godforsaken isle, and she is third in line for the inheritance."

I thought about what he said.

"I wonder how much money Paul is now worth," I said.

"That is why I want to see Lord Hargrave's will."

I stood and offered a hand to Mrs. Ashleigh. She was in a black dress covered in jet with a full bustle, and rising was not especially easy.

"Good luck, then, to both of you. It might not be easy to convince Lady Hargrave to allow you to peep into the family's private papers. Remember, God cannot abide secrets, and none can remain hidden forever."

He held out an elbow and his companion took it, and they moved off together. As for myself, I took the back stairs to the kitchen, which is how I first arrived.

Cesar was in the silver room, polishing with his sleeves rolled up beside a mountain of flatware, coffee servers, salvers, and other kitchen utensils. It seemed perfect for what I needed.

"Can I give you a hand with that?" I asked.

"Oh, would you? I like helping, but they seem to give me the hardest and dirtiest jobs. Roll up your sleeves or you will ruin your cuffs."

"We'll make short work of this lot," I said, unlinking my cuffs. "So, how long have you been in England, and how are you finding it so far?"

"About a month now. I never knew a place could be so cold."

"This is summer," I said. "You should see it in January."

"I hope I will be out of here and back in Brazil long before then."

"Oh?" I asked, picking up a teapot and taking a rag to it. "Does Mr. Kerry intend to return to South America? I assumed he was staying here."

"If he does stay, I may return alone. I much prefer the equator to the North Pole."

"Why stay at all, for that matter? I'm sure you have your reasons for being loyal, but your master doesn't treat you very well."

"That's just his way. He is gruff with everyone. And he is out of sorts. He somehow embarrassed himself here once, and he is anxious to make up for it with the family."

"Does he favor Miss Burrell?"

"I gather they were unofficially betrothed for many years and he hopes to reconcile with her."

"He certainly made a good impression the other evening in his military jacket."

"He was a war hero. He was decorated for it. The war was hellish. Often it was one hundred and twenty degrees in the jungle. There was malaria, yellow fever, and slaughter. They fought with machetes sometimes. The king of Bolivia hired English mercenaries, hoping to train his army. Many of them died, but three survived. One of them was Mr. Kerry. They became heroes. We called them *Os Tres Tigres,* the three tigers."

CHAPTER THIRTEEN

Three tigers," I prompted.

"Si," Cesar responded. "Are you familiar with the War of the Pacific? There is no reason why a European should be. It was a border war between Bolivia and Chile. Peru became involved, which only made it a bigger mess. The area in dispute was a desert. It is ironic, no? People fighting over a desert? But there are nitrates in the desert that Chile wanted, and land, too. They fought over, well, whatever people fight over. Taxation and tariffs and tyranny. The Chilean army occupied Antofagasta in '79, and Bolivia declared war, and Bolivia asked Peru to join in because of an agreement between the two countries. Does it really matter why a war starts?"

"I suppose not."

"Anyway, we read about it in Rio rather carefully because refugees might come south, or Brazil might become involved. Chile was the best equipped of the armies, while Bolivia, in spite of their having declared war, was the worst equipped. Peru was more powerful, but soon Lima was occupied. The Peruvian ambassador put out a call for mercenaries and military experts. It attracted competent soldiers as well as ne'er-do-wells. As I heard it, three men met in a camp outside of Lima. They had been made captains by the Peruvian government based merely on the fact that they were English. They respected your military skills, you see. The men were my master, Algernon Kerry, Capitán Nigel Pelham of the Bengal Lancers, and Capitán Jack Hillary. All of them had come to South America after having felt unwanted in their own country. Hillary was a good businessman and could trade supplies and suggest ways to hamper the enemy. What is a war anyway, but a business enterprise? Pelham was an expert soldier. He was as ruthless as a soldier could be. In fact, there were rumors afoot that he had committed atrocities in the past. Then there was my master. He can drill and drive men, and turn a group of fighters into a disciplined army. Among the three of them, they could lead an army over the mountains, through jungles, and even across the desert. Unfortunately, they could not fight a larger and better equipped army forever. Having won many battles and been decorated, they lost the war. Bolivia and Peru eventually sued for peace. The Three Tigers, now wanted men, left for the interior of Brazil hoping to seek their fortunes along the Amazon.

"Soon they arrived in Manaus, the capital city of the rubber boom, the *ciclo de borracha*. There they prospered and founded Paititi Limited, one of the most successful companies in the Putumayo basin."

"How did you meet your employer?" I asked.

"I was working as a bookkeeper in Manaus, but not doing very well for myself, I'm afraid. Mr. Kerry posted a need for a manservant and I applied and was hired. People in my part of the world often change positions as our personal fortunes rise and fall. Anyway, everything went well until this year."

"What happened?"

"This year, Paititi Limited was dissolved."

"How so, if it was so profitable?" I asked.

"Up until last year the company was allowed to use slave labor. King Pedro II made it illegal. Without free native labor, the rubber could no longer be produced profitably. The three owners decided to sell the company at its best market value rather than wait for its inevitable decline. Mr. Kerry is here in England to sell the remaining rubber reserves. Captain Pelham and Mr. Hillary are in Manaus closing down the corporation and locating a buyer."

"So, these 'three tigers' will all retire rich men. What becomes of you?"

"I don't expect generosity from any of them. I'll need to find another situation. I shall leave Manaus and go back to Rio."

"Do you have any idea why someone would try to kill the ambassador?"

Cesar shook his head. "I'm sorry. We have been caught up in the company's plans, and have not read any news about Europe, but I understand there are anarchists here and unrest. I must admit that even in Brazil assassinations are not uncommon."

"You could stay here in London," I suggested, lifting a ladle.

"I'm sorry, Thomas, and I mean no disrespect to your country, but I am wasting away. The food here is inedible. I can barely keep it down. Mostly I live on chocolate bars. Even the coffee here is undrinkable. It is a tragedy to see beans I have watched grow on the hills of my homeland turned to mulch and overboiled in your restaurants."

"And you're cold," I added.

"Oh, yes, so very cold. Give me the steaming jungles of the Amazon over this frigid country, please. I vow to be gone long before September arrives. I have never seen snow before but I could not survive your autumn or winter."

I could not help but chuckle. It was perhaps sixty-five degrees Fahrenheit.

"So, is it true?" Cesar went on.

"Is what true?"

"That you gentlemen are detectives? It is the talk of the kitchen. I must admit I have made a joke at your employer's expense. I have suggested he is two men in a costume, one sitting on another's shoulders."

"I'm sure he has heard worse," I said.

"But has he seen worse—worse than His Lordship's being shot at in such a manner? Or being shot at as you and I were the other day?"

"I don't know about worse, but we've often seen men killed in as violent a method. Certainly, I am no stranger to being shot at."

"Have you always wanted a life of adventure?"

"Good heavens, no. I would prefer to work in a bookstore somewhere and scribble poetry."

"I know what you mean," Cesar said. "I miss my old work as a bookkeeper. And here we are trapped on an island and being fired upon by an insane person! I want to go home, to a simple life. I see no reason why Mr. Kerry would wish to return to this country."

"It's not always like this," I said. "Well, not for most people, anyway."

"Is Mr. Barker a capable person? Do you think you will be able to catch whoever is out there shooting at us?"

"He is like cream, Cesar. Sooner or later, he always rises to the top. I don't fancy anyone's chances who goes against him. You have to understand this is meat and drink to him, and the worse the situation becomes, the more he prefers it."

"That doesn't make sense."

"You play chess?"

"Sometimes, yes."

"Would you rather play someone who challenges you, or that you can easily beat?"

"I wouldn't know," he admitted. "I generally lose!"

We both laughed, but at the wrong time. The housekeeper chose that moment to enter the room. We immediately turned to polishing as hard as we could. She set down a few new pieces to be polished, then gave us a stern look and left.

"Do you know what I miss most of all?" he asked. "Siestas. I am not a steam engine that can be run all hours of the day. A nap in the afternoon replenishes the body."

"I have told Mr. Barker that on several occasions. I believe he assumes I am making a joke."

"I would not dare try that sort of thing with Mr. Kerry. He has a temper."

"So I've noticed. Surely there are easier masters to work for."

"I have worked for harder men, and for less money. The only

real complaint I've had with my current master is bringing me to this part of the world where it's always cold and people are shooting at me."

I nodded in sympathy. Actually, I thought it a fine day, but I suppose when one is accustomed to equatorial heat this might be bracing. I helped Cesar with the last of the silver and then returned upstairs. As far as I could tell, I had not aroused the Brazilian's suspicions. At the same time, I felt rather guilty. I was tricking a fellow who had been nothing but kind to me. Still, I was accustomed to doing that sort of thing now, and I hadn't really done him any harm.

Returning upstairs, I saw that Barker had been installed in His Lordship's rooms, and Mrs. Ashleigh in his former room next door. The door connecting them was open, which under normal circumstances might have caused some danger to her reputation.

"Ah, Thomas," he said. "As you see, we are moving."

Looking in, I saw Philippa sitting by the fire in the Guv's old room reading a book and looking contented enough, given the circumstances. To my mind, she was safer at that moment than anyone else in the house, myself included.

Pulling Barker aside, I gave him a verbatim account of what had transpired between Rojas and me. Everything save for comparing masters, anyway.

"You did not press him on the cocaine?" he asked.

"I did not see how to work it in," I admitted. "I'll try again later, if you'd like."

"Mmmph."

No "good work, lad." No "you are improving." No "thank you for your efforts."

"Lad, go retrieve your luggage. You'll share His Lordship's room with me."

"Yes, sir."

When I reached my room in the servants' quarters, it was unoccupied. Herr Schroeder was nowhere to be found. The German was a disagreeable fellow, and I had not relished sharing a room with him, but he had been innocuous enough. At least he did not snore. I could not say the same about my employer.

Out in the hall, I noticed one of the footmen, one of the fellows whom I had helped after he was poisoned with the mushrooms.

"What has become of Herr Schroeder?"

"He is being detained under guard, sir."

"Do you have any idea why?"

"Mr. Partridge has informed the staff that Herr Schroeder was discovered lurking outside the ambassador's room armed."

"Armed? I assume you mean a firearm of some sort."

"That was what I assumed as well. Mr. Partridge is not the sort of person from whom one asks for clarification."

"I understand what you mean, precisely."

Returning to the room, I told the Guv what I had heard about Herr Schroeder being detained.

"We shall say nothing about it until the colonel brings it up. Let us take a leaf from Lord Hargrave's book and try some diplomacy."

We went downstairs to dinner and endured Kerry's remarks without comment. He and Paul Burrell were becoming thick as thieves. I was concerned that the ambassador didn't see what sort of person Kerry was.

Afterward, there was no special entertainment set aside for our amusement. We spoke to various people individually, trying to gather more facts. We returned to Barker's rooms about nine o'clock. Barker went to the window and looked through the shutters at the night sky.

"We have a new development."

I felt the muscles in my back tense. It is impossible for one to think and worry for twenty-four hours. For small amounts of time one forgets until reminded of the danger again.

"What is it?"

"The lighthouse has not been lit tonight. It is nearly ten."

"Has something happened to Flannan?"

"Possibly. Let us speak to the colonel."

We went downstairs and into the library. The ambassador, Colonel Fraser, Algernon Kerry, and the Burrells were seated with whisky and sodas at their elbow. Partridge hovered nearby. The men were holding some kind of council, I assumed. Our arrival did not arouse any joy. On the contrary, in fact. They looked suspicious.

"Colonel, might I have a word?" Barker asked.

Fraser pushed himself out of his seat slowly. He was over seventy, after all, though he had that vigor some men have at that age. He came out into the hall with a guarded expression on his face, though unlike the rest of them he was unfailingly polite.

"How can I help you, Mr. Barker?"

"The lighthouse has not been lit this evening. I'm concerned about the keeper, Mr. Flannan."

"Hmmm. We should send out a search party."

"There is no need to go to the trouble. If someone will guard the house and in particular Mrs. Ashleigh's door, Mr. Llewelyn and I shall go and investigate."

Fraser frowned in thought. It was obvious that he did not fully trust us, but there was nothing dangerous in what we had proposed, nothing for anyone in the house, anyway.

"That would be helpful, I suppose," he said.

"If you need to discuss this with your colleagues, the lad and I can wait here."

That was a criticism on my employer's part, suggesting the colonel was not fully leading the group. In short, that it was a mob.

"I don't need to discuss anything with them," he replied.

"I am gratified to hear it," Barker said. He has a rough voice but when he needs to he can make it sound quite honeyed. "I shall let you get back to your discussion. If Thomas and I are not back in an hour, expect the worst."

"Very well," Fraser said, as if he expected just that.

"I think that pistols are in order, Mr. Llewelyn," he said. "Not that they will work over a hundred yards."

We went back upstairs and, ever discreet, Barker knocked on the outside door and told Mrs. Ashleigh that we would be leaving but someone would be watching outside. We then went to our own rooms and began to prepare.

Barker carries a brace of English-made Colt Peacemakers. I've seen him carry as many as four of them. I watched as he slipped the pair into the waistband of his trousers, handles forward.

"You haven't brought your coat?" I asked, referring to his heavy leather coat with built-in holsters and pockets for lead plating. He is known for it in London.

"Too cumbersome and too hot."

"Not by Cesar Rojas's standards. He claims he has been cold since he arrived."

I unpacked my own pair of pistols, Webley Mark IIIs with short-nosed barrels. True, they would be useless beyond even fifty yards, but anything within that, I could hit. I had even beaten Barker once or twice in the shooting range in our cellar. I jammed them into my pockets.

Barker retrieved a dark lantern from his luggage, and a pack of vestas. Then he locked both doors tightly. We met Percy Burrell in the hall. He was seated by the staircase. Seeing her well guarded, we went down the stair and in a few moments out through the front door.

The moon turned the entire scene before us a deep indigo blue. I looked up at it. It was full in the cloudless sky and one could make out the features of the so-called man in the moon. I know that scientists claim they are merely mountain ranges on that far-off sphere, but I liked to think of the benevolent or at least benign fellow who watches over us every night.

Barker suddenly raised an arm and pointed in the opposite direction, almost over my shoulder. The shattered window up on the first floor where Cesar had been shot at was lit by a small light, like a dark lantern. As I gazed at it in wonder, it flickered in and out.

"Someone is signaling!"

CHAPTER FOURTEEN

We ran back into the building and across the hall to the staircase. Barker took the stairs two at a time, a feat I could not attempt. When we reached the hallway, we could see a small lamp on the floor at the far end of the hall. Wordlessly, we crossed to it. It lay with an air of innocence, as if it had been set there an hour before and was valiantly fighting against the dark ever since. We knew better.

Barker looked out at the night between the shutters. The glass had not been replaced. That would require a trip to the mainland.

"No one is signaling from the other side," he said. "The rascal has scarpered."

"He must still be in the hall."

Just then the guests came up the stairs to see what the commotion was about, or came out of their rooms, mingling with the former. Our quarry, no doubt, mingled among them. I wondered if this inside accomplice might be a woman.

"What's going on?" the colonel asked when he reached us.

We explained that we had seen someone signaling at the window, but no sign of him was found, save the lamp when we arrived. Everyone looked accusingly at the little oil lamp, but it refused to give up its secrets.

"Colonel, Thomas and I shall go on with the business we discussed earlier. I suggest you question the whereabouts of everyone in the house during the last ten minutes, verifying as many as you can."

"Right."

"The Lord willing, we shall return shortly."

We pushed through the crowd, which was discussing this new development among themselves. Soon we stepped back out into the night.

"Have you ever noticed—" I began, but I never had the chance to finish. Our assassin shot at us, hitting the brick wall. Quickly, I followed Barker around the side of Godolphin House and among the safety of the outbuildings.

"I believe we have moved up on the assassin's list," Barker stated, as if the question were academic, which it most certainly was not.

"Sir, I am getting heartily tired of being shot at."

"Then let us do our level best to confound him. Come along."

Barker began to run, bent low, toward the lighthouse, and I followed in his broad wake. At that moment, "lighthouse" was a misnomer. The tower was black against the sky. The moon was bright that evening and I suspected that a shooter would have no trouble finding us in the dark. How Barker managed to see in near blackness with his dark spectacles remained a mystery to me, but then many things about my employer evoked my curiosity.

We reached the lighthouse without incident, and threw open the door. Inside, the gas was lit, but we heard no sound. I stepped to the staircase and looked upward.

"Mr. Flannan!"

Cyrus Barker brushed by me and began to climb the stair. At the first level, there was a landing with a door. He opened it and we stepped inside. It was the living quarters, with two beds, a table with chairs, and a small kitchen. There were cards on the table and a cup of tea. I put a finger into the cup and found the tea stone-cold.

"He could have been missing since last night."

"Aye."

I looked about. There were tins of food.

"What do you suppose our shooter is living on?" I asked. "There are no fauna here."

"Gulls," Barker replied.

"Really?"

"Fulmer, cormorants. He might even eat fish. He's very resourceful."

"You sound as though you almost admire him."

The Guv shook his head. "Not admire. Respect. I wish I could have had a glimpse of him. I like to see the faces of people who are trying to kill me."

There was nothing to see in the room. We climbed up to the gallery.

"It's a crocus burner," Barker said. "One of John Wigham's designs. Perhaps I can get it started."

He lit the oil lamp. I carried it and raised the glass housing. Inside the mechanism had been smashed as if with a hammer, or the butt of a rifle. There would be no illumination coming anytime soon, no people from the mainland or nearby islands wondering why the lamp was not lit.

I stepped outside onto the gallery and circled the tower. No one was there.

"There is not a sign of Flannan, sir. I even looked over the side to see if he had fallen or been pushed."

"He could not leave the island, and if he were thrown into the sea, his body would drift to shore."

"In any case, this is not a promising sign for his safety."

"Agreed. There is nothing we can do here. Let us return to the house."

We picked our way to the ground floor and set out. So far our luck had held out, but no more. The clouds parted, the moon shone down upon us, and there was that popping sound. Barker staggered.

"Sir!"

We had reached the shelter of the labyrinth. Without stopping, my employer entered. I followed behind. Once inside the relative safety of the tall bushes, Barker sat down.

"How badly are you hurt?"

He looked up at me. Blood was trickling down his face.

"A flesh wound, lad," he said. "He grazed me."

"Do you think he did it intentionally?"

"No, the Sharps is not that accurate. He had hoped for a kill, but he'll have to try harder. I'm not going to hand him my life."

He pulled a handkerchief from his pocket and used it to stanch the blood. I gave him mine as well.

"This is good," he said.

"That you've been shot?"

"Now that we have been forced in here, it occurs to me that this is the only part of the island we have not explored. Perhaps he has his camp here. We will examine it. But keep to the shadows. I presume he is in the woods to the north."

"Is it wise to go crawling about a maze in the middle of the night?"

"No, Thomas. It's utter folly, but one must play the hand one is dealt."

I looked about. "Speaking of folly."

Barker actually chuckled, then groaned.

"Don't make me laugh when I'm bleeding," he said.

The Guv stood again and raised the Colt pistol in his hand. It was possible, I supposed, that while we had entered from the front, the killer might have entered from the back. It is better to be prepared. I drew my pistol and crept along beside the wall of box hedge.

It would have been a diversion during the day, but at night, with someone shooting at you, the maze seemed nightmarish. The narrow walls on each side were menacing, as if closing in on me. They were perhaps seven feet tall and spiny, grasping at my clothes as I hurried along.

"Left! Always take the first left. Stop!"

I nearly ran into him.

"Yes?"

"Give me a piece of paper from your notebook."

I complied, pulling out my notebook and giving him one sheet. He spiked it on to a thorny bush at my eye level, not his, and we moved on. Barker opened the trap on his lantern, shining a small beam of light onto the ground before us. Within a few minutes he stopped.

"There," he said, pointing down to an area of the grass that had been dug into.

Barker reached into his cuff and retrieved his dagger, which he generally kept there in a sheath. He dug into the shallow earth with the blade. Within five minutes he had unearthed a bit of ash and a skull the size of a golf ball. An avian skull.

"It looks like a cormorant," he said. "He made an exceedingly small fire and left almost no trace. Do you understand how clever this fellow is? He might be some kind of native. Or he was trained by one. Trained very well."

"Who said the English cannot learn?" I countered.

"It was probably a Welshman."

He continued to dig. The next thing he unearthed was a bit of wood about five inches long, charred, and covered with a pattern of thin slats.

"Some sort of wicker, perhaps," he said.

"I recognize this," I said. "It's part of a coracle! I had one as a youth."

"What is a coracle?" he asked.

"It's a tiny boat. Not much more than a hoop stretched with rattan weave or canvas, propelled by a single oar. Do you suppose that's how he came to the island?"

"It would explain why he came without food or arms. He probably had no room on the vessel."

"It's a rolling sea out there. Only a madman would take a coracle out into open ocean."

"Or a very determined one."

We continued moving forward, guns drawn. I held my Webley up near my shoulder, while Barker held his pointing at the ground in front of him. Every shootist has his own methods. Barker was crouched low, so as not to be a target due to his height. I had no such problem.

The two of us were creeping along, gazing at the ground revealed by the bull's-eye lantern. I glanced over at Barker to make some comment when I saw the gleam of two eyes in the darkness, almost directly over his shoulder.

"Sir!" I shouted, straightening out my arms so that my revolver passed over my employer's shoulder. He wheeled and raised both his Colt and the lantern. The light swung in an arc, illuminating the tall hedge across from us. Vertically wedged into it was the body of Noah Flannan, the lighthouse keeper.

"I hazard that we are near the front entrance," Barker said. "Our killer would not go to the trouble of carrying the body deeper into the labyrinth."

I have no great experience with labyrinths. In fact I'm not sure anyone has, outside of Theseus, but I understand that there are two kinds, the true, which is difficult to get through but is quite rare, and the ornamental. The latter is easier to get through, but looks beautiful from the upper floors of the house, which was their intended purpose. There was no need to bring a ball of string in fear of being stranded here for hours. At most one might take a wrong turn or two, though in the dark it was naturally more difficult. I suppose also the chance that one might be shot at or discover a corpse didn't make it any easier.

Having met Noah Flannan only once, I could not say what kind of man he was. I suspected those content to run lighthouses were naturally solitary and distrustful of people. We did not know nor would we ever know the circumstances of his death, or for that matter of his life. Had he been a bachelor all his life? Did he have anyone to mourn him? Either way he had abruptly stepped into the void as all of us must someday do, and in the same manner, alone.

"Help me, lad," Barker said, taking Flannan by his cold, waxen hand and pulling him slowly from the grasp of the hedge. Rigor mortis had set in, which I knew meant he had been dead for several hours. The branches put up a fight, and when they finally let go of the prize he was festooned with leaves and twigs.

Flannan was a scrawny little fellow, tanned by the wind and sun, and now that he was dead, he reminded me of a desiccated mummy, or one of these people they find preserved in bogs. A crop of small white hairs stuck out of his tanned chin.

"How did he die?" I asked.

Barker indicated a wound on Flannan's neck. "He was stabbed."

"That wound looks too wide for a knife."

"I suspect it is a spear wound."

"A spear wound? Are you sure?"

"I grew up in China, lad. I know a spear when I see one."

"But he's got a rifle! Why would he need a spear? Perhaps the rifle came with the bayonet."

"I tell you, it is a spear. The wound is practically round."

I actually sat down in the damp grass and pondered this. "But surely he didn't lose the rifle. You don't suppose there is a second person running around the island, do you?"

Barker shrugged his heavy shoulders.

Such an eloquent man, and such a turn of phrase. Perhaps when the case was done, if I were alive to hear them, he would tell me all his thoughts.

The exit was half a dozen feet beyond. The corpse had been brought here and jammed into the hedges in order to dispose of it. Unless it was to have the opposite effect, to shock and disturb whoever found it.

"This fellow seems determined to break the morale of everyone on the island."

"That is the wisest thing you've said all day, Thomas."

I wasn't sure whether that was a compliment or not.

"Let us return to Godolphin House," Barker continued. "Philippa will start to worry."

We came out of the labyrinth, skirted the wood slowly, and then ran across the lawn to the safety of the jumble of outbuildings. No one shot at us, nor did anyone throw a spear. We entered the back door, climbed to the ground floor to tell the colonel what we had encountered, and then continued upstairs. We nodded to Percy Burrell and went into our room.

Philippa Ashleigh was seated on an ottoman facing the door. She wore a choker of pearls and an evening gown of crushed blue velvet. Her fiery hair was pulled back loosely. As we entered the room she lowered the barrel of Barker's .45-caliber Colt revolver, which had been pointed at the door. She looked faintly disappointed.

CHAPTER FIFTEEN

The meals were starting to be a trial. Literally, I mean. Conversation would start, generally about something trivial such as who was related to whom among the local families, then Mr. Algernon Kerry would think it necessary to state an opinion. He was one of those horribly overopinionated guests that were the bane of any host's existence. It wasn't he alone, or even the Burrell boys, who were calling Kerry a prophet.

It was M. Gascoigne, who would not let off preaching how wonderful the late Mr. Delacroix of the Sûreté was and how deficient Mr. Barker was in comparison. It was more subtle than that, but not by much. Any suggestion the Guv made was either questioned or unwillingly accepted. One would have to go to the House of Lords to see such lukewarm acquiescence. It went right up my nose. If there had been any way off the island, I'd have told Kerry and Gascoigne that I wouldn't give tuppence for both of them together, and gone back to London.

Paul Burrell seemed to agree with everything his old school friend said, and when he offered an opinion, Percy Burrell tended to side with his brother. Of the group of male guests only Colonel

Fraser and Dr. Anstruther refused to say anything critical of my employer.

"This is not getting us anywhere, gentlemen," the colonel said at breakfast the next morning. I was sure he was accustomed to playing mediator between warring factions. "We need to work together if we are going to get off this island."

"I noticed Mr. Barker and his 'lad' have moved into His Lordship's former room. I'm sure that must be very convenient. It's a wonder he stopped there."

There was an intake of breath around the table.

"What are you inferring, sir?" Barker asked.

"His Lordship is barely cold in the grave, yet you are acquiring what is his."

"I asked Her Ladyship to borrow the room, since it was at the foot of the steps. It seemed the most convenient spot to defend everyone."

"Myself included?" Kerry asked.

"Everyone."

"I don't need your protection, Barker. I don't even think you provide any. You were brought here, I understand, because Her Ladyship wanted to meet you, not out of any respect for your abilities. You are fortunate that your lady friend was close to the family. Now you're in a spot and over your head. There should have been a proper squad of soldiers here. Instead, we get you and Little Tich here."

I had sat there in the Royal United Service Institution and heard Barker suggest the same thing, but His Lordship had turned him down. He's not the type to argue, however. He says nothing until he decides to dismantle your head. Now he reached for his tumbler of water and drank from it with no sign of irritation. He felt it, I knew, but he showed no sign. I could only do likewise. Little Tich notwithstanding.

"You know, Your Excellency, you don't need a Scotsman to protect you. We can do that collectively, and not by cowering in the house with the women, if you ladies will forgive the phrase."

"Some of us feel safer with Mr. Barker in the house," someone said. I looked over. It was Philippa Ashleigh. Now we're in for it, I thought.

"Well, you would, considering you've been installed in the room beside him."

"Installed? Mr. Kerry, you make me sound like a drain or a water closet."

There was a nervous chuckle at the remark.

"That's awfully convenient for you, Mrs. Ashleigh. I hope the other women feel as safe as you do."

"Why wouldn't they, Mr. Kerry?"

"I'm not sure they are willing to pay the price of admission," he drawled.

"Admission to what, exactly, Mr. Kerry?" Philippa asked.

"I believe we are all wondering that ourselves, ma'am."

"Too far, too far," I heard the colonel mutter. His wife seemed ready to faint. People all began talking at once, but the loudest sound was Barker's chair scraping as he rose from it, all fifteen stone of him.

"Come, Philippa," Barker said, raising an elbow to her. He came around and she took it. They proceeded from the room.

I couldn't tell what was going on in his head. Once they were gone, Kerry pounced.

"Are you still here? Go back to the servants' hall, boy."

I felt my face flush, but I wouldn't go down without a fight.

"I don't believe I'm your guest, sir. In fact, I hear the last time you were here you were escorted from the island for drunkenness."

"You little guttersnipe. Paul!"

"Cut along, Mr. Llewelyn," Paul Burrell murmured.

I stood and bowed. "My pleasure, sir. Ladies."

My leave-taking would be neither too quick nor too slow. My employer had taught me how to leave a room with one's head held high.

We had been beaten but for a time only. We had lost the battle, but not the war. My own condition was unimportant. I worked for Cyrus Barker and was paid well, no matter what the case. But I worried about him. He was a true Scotsman and could brood with the best of them. He'll speak of patience and Asian philosophy, but deep down he held strong feelings. Now we were on this infernal island, facing Hell Bay, and his friends were few and far between. I had to keep the black dogs from tearing him down.

Neither of them had even had a chance to eat. Kerry had started haranguing them early. I ran to the kitchen to request a couple of private breakfasts to be delivered to the first floor. They took pity on me and fed me too, right there in the kitchen.

I did not want to intrude on Barker and Mrs. Ashleigh's privacy, and I didn't feel like anyone else's company. I took myself to the library, to a quiet and secluded corner, and looked for a book. Spenser's *Faerie Queene* came to hand. I had read it at university, but one rarely has a chance to enjoy a book there. One is busy trying to ingest it for the next essay. This was my chance to read it for pleasure, if there was a thing on the planet called pleasure anymore. I had my doubts.

The chair was soft, the light was bright, the book awaited me. It was difficult to begin, but some books are worth the effort. I persevered. It was close to forty-five minutes of hard work before I actually fell asleep in the chair, and anyway, I didn't sleep more than half an hour.

Rubbing my face awake, I took the book with me up to the first floor, reasoning that their breakfast must be over by now.

Failure, I thought. Oh, I was well acquainted with it myself, but not as an employee of Cyrus Barker, private enquiry agent. Don't think he never failed, because of course he did. He was only a man, after all. But it didn't happen often, and we rarely had our faces rubbed in it. I didn't much care for it, Algernon Kerry with his ill temper and his sneering ways. I'm just a bloke, I know. A collier's brat from Gwent, literally no one. He was the Honorable. Shouldn't he act like it? I was a human being after all, and I wanted nothing from him.

What was the bee in his bonnet? Was he naturally ill-tempered? Had we done something to him we didn't understand? Had I frowned when he spoke unkindly to Cesar, or was he angry that I had carried the bags one minute and sat at the same table by him the next?

I suppose it was not me at all. It was Barker he had issue with, and his assumption that he was in charge. Some people just have to hold the reins in order to feel secure, and Kerry was one of those people. Barker isn't one of those people per se, unless he is trying to accomplish something important. As long as people are safe and everyone is being treated fairly, people can do or say or think whatever they like.

One can think about someone's motivations for a time, but one eventually runs out of material. Kerry was true to himself. Gascoigne could not get over the death of his friend, and now he had put himself in danger.

Eventually I went upstairs again, and found Barker reading also. We were not supposed to have easy days here. The man in the woods was seeing to that.

He was making a good show of it, but I knew the morning conversation had cut. He was brooding over it. Mrs. Ashleigh was, as well. She had been grossly insulted, and as if to prove her point, she did not enter our room. Barker and I spent the day reading, our meals brought to us on a tray.

It was nearly nine o'clock that evening when there was a sudden rap upon our door. I got up from my chair and answered it.

"Cesar, what is it?" I asked.

"I must speak to Mr. Barker," he said, looking agitated.

"What is it?" Barker asked over my shoulder.

"Sir, I brought a drink to Mr. Burrell in the study, but the doors are locked and I cannot rouse him by calling. I thought I would consult you before trying to break one down. They are very heavy doors."

Barker slipped on his evening jacket and stretched out a palm. "Lead the way, sir."

We hurried down the hall to the staircase.

At the bottom of the stair a party of concerned guests had already formed. The colonel was calling out Burrell's name, hoping to get some kind of response. Meanwhile, Kerry was jiggling the handle roughly and beating on the door.

"Where is the key?" the Guv asked.

"The butler is bringing it," Fraser said.

Barker pushed his way through and knelt down to look in the keyhole. There was no key on the other side obstructing the lock. The Guv pulled the skeleton key he habitually kept in his waistcoat pocket and began to work it in the lock. By the time the butler arrived with the house keys Barker had the door open. In a rush we all stepped inside.

A fire was going in the grate and Burrell was seated at a large desk covered over with important papers. I noticed right off the knife thrust down through his dress shirt into his chest. Paul Burrell had not survived forty-eight hours as the heir of Godolphin House.

CHAPTER SIXTEEN

A few hours before we had been talking with Paul Burrell across the table, and now his eyes were staring vaguely into the beyond. No matter how many crimes we investigate, and how many bodies I am forced to view, I can never fathom the calm glare corpses have, as if stopped in the middle of a thought. Paul's head was leaning back against the high-backed chair, and his eyes were focused or focusless toward the right, as if he'd watched the blade enter his breast, which he probably had.

The Guv and I had discussed the rumor that a corpse's eyes would capture the last image they saw. We both agreed the idea was ridiculous, and yet, there is so little on this earth one can be certain of. As Paul Burrell lay collapsed in his chair, I searched his irises for some kind of image. I found nothing save the light fixture reflected in his eyes.

"How did the killer get out of the room?" Kerry asked. Normally there would be police constables underfoot, making sure that no one inappropriate came in. Kerry seemed the very definition of the word.

"Obviously he had the key," Gascoigne stated.

"Or one like it."

"Just what are you implying, Mr. Kerry?"

"You tell me, Mr. Barker. You were hired to protect us and so far four of us are dead. Six more were nearly poisoned to death."

"Oh, come now!" I said. "The first bullet came out of nowhere and without warning."

"I hardly think your testimony counts, considering you work for him, old boy. I'm sure you are being well paid."

"I—" I began, but Barker cut me off.

"Mr. Kerry is welcome to his opinion, Mr. Llewelyn. After all, his life is at stake just as much as anyone's. Mr. Burrell, are you of the same opinion?"

The latter was directed at Percy Burrell, the youngest son and presumably the heir.

"I don't know," he said. "You were hired as a bodyguard and now my father and my brother are dead."

"Colonel?"

"It's deuced bad luck is all, but it is your watch, old man."

"Thank you. Ambassador, what is your opinion?"

The Frenchman stared at the floor with his heavy-lidded round eyes, weighing the matter seriously.

"I cannot help but think that Delacroix would have at least saved the heir from dying."

Barker gave a cold smile. As for me, I was angry as a wet cat. Damn and blast every one of them for the ungrateful wretches they were. I suspect they would have all been dead by now without my employer.

"I suggest we go through the family papers carefully, Mr. Burrell. They may have some bearing upon the case. If that is all, I hope you will excuse me, gentlemen."

"I'm not done, Barker!" Kerry said. "There is still the matter of that passkey you possess. You could have come in here and killed Paul when he was going through his papers. He was a friend of mine, who stood by me when others wouldn't."

"You accuse me of murder?" Barker asked.

"I do. Nobody else had a key, except on the housekeeper's ring."

"And what reason would I have?"

"How in hell should I know? What reason would that madman outside have who has been shooting at us for days? You might be in league with him. I don't know you from Adam."

I reached across to a table where a three-day-old copy of the *Times* lay. I turned to Barker's advertisement, which I suspected His Lordship had seen a week ago.

"Here," I said. "Here's our advertisement, which appears daily. What more proof do you need? Obviously the *Times* finds us reliable."

"How do we know you are this fellow; that you are who you claim to be?" Kerry asked.

"The question is moot," Barker said. "Most of us have never met and we don't carry complete proof of our identity. Now that I have resigned, who will oversee everyone's protection?"

"We'll get along fine without you, sir," Kerry replied.

"Every man for himself?" Barker asked, setting the passkey down on the table.

"No." Kerry looked about at the group of men. "The colonel could do it. We will take orders from a military man."

"I've been in two wars," Barker stated.

"Which ones?" the colonel asked.

I noticed he had not accepted Kerry's offer. He was merely considering the matter. I thought he had been wondering about Barker's past.

"The Taiping Rebellion and the Boshin War."

"Went native, did you?" Fraser asked, with a hint of disapproval in his voice.

"Sometimes it was necessary in order to live."

"Wait," I said, suddenly remembering. I pulled a pocket watch from my pocket. "This is from the Prince of Wales. We worked with the palace on several occasions."

Kerry looked it over. The watch was engraved.

Presented to Cyrus Barker for services rendered.
The Prince of Wales

"Anyone can engrave a watch for a few shillings. The more unscrupulous ones will put on whatever you like."

The problem with taking as many antagonistics classes as I have is that one's mind starts picturing how to grass a fellow that one knows is completely unfeasible. In this case, I fantasized about raising my right limb, pivoting on my left, and wiping that smirk off Kerry's face with the heel of my boot.

"Mrs. Ashleigh has known me for decades, and has been telling Her Ladyship about me for nearly as long."

"Hearsay," Kerry said.

"You should stand for the House of Commons, sir," Barker said. "You debate well."

I almost pointed out that Barker was a thirty-third-degree Mason, but he had sworn me to secrecy about the matter, and anyway, some trust them, while others do not.

"There are too many questions about you, Barker," the aristocrat continued. "Who are your parents? Why do you hide behind the spectacles? I've heard you have a lot of money, but no one seems to know how you earned it. Two nights ago I saw you climb out of a window and down an almost sheer wall with just your fingers. Where were you going?"

"To track this fellow at night when he was at his most vulnerable," Barker answered.

"Or perhaps to rendezvous with him."

"Raising suspicions, sir, is not the same as providing proof, no matter how good at it you might be."

"If we have suspicions about you, Barker, we cannot fully trust you. The colonel I trust implicitly."

"Is that the general consensus, gentlemen?" the Guv asked, looking about.

No one would fully answer his gaze.

"Very well," Barker said. "You have my resignation. We will accept a payment at a later date for what duties we have done to this point."

"Hear, hear," Kerry said, with a chuckle.

"Come along, Thomas. Good evening, gentlemen."

I have seen Cyrus Barker when his blood was up. He punches

things, generally things that could withstand the abuse such as brick walls or marble. This time he did nothing, causing me to wonder if one can ever really know a person well enough to anticipate him.

The house suddenly seemed as large as a castle again. Every step seemed to scorch dignity. We had never been treated to such abuse. Even the Guv's enemies respect him. As angry as I was with Kerry, I was equally furious with the ambassador and young Percy. Not as good as Delacroix! I should have reminded Gascoigne that his vaunted detective was now a corpse, while Barker was very much alive. When we reached Barker's room I threw myself into a chair. Seizing a Staffordshire statuette from a table, I'm afraid I snapped his neck.

"Mr. Llewelyn," Barker chided. "We are guests here. Besides, that is a pitiful way to treat Old Tom Morris, a credit to my race."

"Sorry, sir. Kerry just made me so furious!"

He picked up the two pieces. "Perhaps we can get it repaired in the morning."

"Why not," I said bitterly. "We have plenty of time now. Sacked! I cannot believe it."

The inner door opened and Mrs. Ashleigh swept in.

"Sacked?" she asked.

"Aye."

"Thought as much. I have not fared much better with Celia. Whenever I ask a probing question she says she really can't bear to discuss the matter, then goes on for half an hour about how she feels, physically and emotionally."

Barker scratched under his chin and thought. "Let someone else worry about the French ambassador."

"And what shall we do in the meantime?" I asked.

Barker turned to Philippa. "My dear, do you have a penny in your reticule?"

Mrs. Ashleigh reached for her reticule, a crocheted bag of pale pink, and began rummaging around in it as if it were three times its size. Finally, she pulled out a change purse, and having dug around in that for a minute, finally put a penny into my employer's outsized palm.

"Thank you. Thomas, note please that we have a new client, and that she has paid us a retainer."

I chuckled. Barker can be unintentionally funny sometimes. "I see. And what does she want us to do?"

"To investigate what is really going on here on Godolphin Isle, and to get to the bottom of this, so we can leave. Oh, and to protect her, of course."

"What about everyone else?" I asked.

"We can make no guarantees, Thomas. A very competent killer is out there somewhere on the grounds, intent upon murdering whom he will, and he's carrying what I might consider the deadliest weapon on the planet. Meanwhile, we are trapped like sheep in a pen. To promise that everyone will emerge unscathed is madness and folly. What I can promise is to investigate as quickly as possible and to do my best to close with my adversary. I do not envy the colonel. Saving everyone will be a near impossible task."

Barker sat on the bed and began removing his shoes.

"We were not sacked. We resigned. Under pressure, it is true, but the choice was ours."

He pulled his limbs up onto the bed and crossed them, lotus fashion. He settled a hand loosely on each knee, doing one of his meditation exercises to calm himself. It was more than I could stand. I jumped out of the chair.

"I'm going for a walk," I said.

"Don't get yourself shot," he replied as an afterthought. He was already going into wherever his mind went at such times.

"This is why they don't want you, you know," I couldn't help saying.

He made no response. His mind was no longer in the brain, perhaps not even on the island.

I left. I needed that walk. Mrs. Ashleigh followed me into the hall, looking very grave.

"You heard?" I asked.

"Of course," she said. "We are disgraced. All of us."

"I'm sorry, ma'am."

"Detection is not like laying bricks or knitting a scarf. There are a thousand possible outcomes."

"Yes."

"I could have done without the looks of pity," she said.

"No doubt. He's meditating like a Buddhist holy man! At least one of us is taking it lightly."

"Oh, no, Thomas, believe me. He is taking it very seriously. You should know him well enough by now to understand he always feels things keenly. He will still triumph."

"Not today, ma'am."

"If not today, then tomorrow."

"I'm going for a walk," I said.

"Be—"

"Yes, ma'am. I'll be careful."

I seized my hat and stick and stepped outside. Then I kicked the step. Godolphin House felt nothing, and I succeeded only in stubbing my toe. Then I began to walk across the lawn.

As I walked I began to ask questions. That is what I do best. Why did he assess and not shoot me? Oh, he shot at me, but he could have killed me if he wanted to. He shot Lord Hargrave. He stabbed Paul Burrell, Delacroix, and Flannan. He poisoned the male servants, although they ultimately lived. He shot at Cesar. Come to think of it, he shot at him twice. Surely he didn't come here just to terrorize a Brazilian servant. There appeared to be no rhyme or reason. He was killing indiscriminately but not, as Barker said, opportunistically, or Cesar and I would be dead. What was his plan? Did he have one? Was he merely passing time?

I reached the short wall by the cliff and wasted close to half an hour simply throwing rocks over it into the ocean. No matter how hard I threw the splash was nothing compared to the crashing waves beating against the boulders below. It seemed somehow symbolic of what we had accomplished so far.

My anger eventually evaporated to be replaced by fatigue and listlessness. What was I accomplishing? If I threw in enough rocks perhaps we could walk to Land's End.

I put my head on again and headed back toward the house. It was another ironically beautiful evening. Nature is beautiful, I told myself, but nothing but evil dwelt continuously in the hearts of men.

CHAPTER SEVENTEEN

The next morning before breakfast I found myself still seething from our exile. I left by the back door, took the narrow stone staircase to the beach, and walked until I could no longer see that accursed house. Then I stripped down and dove into the ocean. The water was bracing and salty, lashing my skin like an astringent, but it felt wonderful after everything I had gone through. At first I had thought this island a paradise, but now I contemplated just swimming away and never coming back, no matter how dangerous it was. It was just a feeling, though, and it quickly dissipated after a swim in the briny ocean.

Invigorated, I swam back to the beach and donned my clothes again. When I was fully dressed I shook out my curly hair like a dog after a bath. Then I threw my jacket over my shoulder and began to head back. The beach was little more than rock and in places was no more than half a dozen feet from the side of the cliff. As I walked, something small, like a pebble, struck me on the top of the head. I yelped and looked up.

Not more than twenty feet above me, the killer was seated on a rock ledge. He was the man I had spoken to in the hall on the first day, when the guests and serving staff were getting acquainted with the inhabitants of the island. He was tanned and wore a singlet with braces, the shirt damp from his wet hair. No doubt he had had the same idea as I did a little earlier. He had a rifle cradled in his arm negligently, and was smoking a cigarette that looked hand-rolled. It occurred to me I was facing the ocean and there was nothing I could hide behind. I was a perfect target. But then, I live by my wits.

"Morning!" I called, waving to him.

"Good morning," he replied.

"Enjoying your stay?"

"Immensely," he replied. "The best holiday in years."

"Is there anything you need?"

"Nothing you can provide me with, Mr. Llewelyn."

"You have the advantage of me, sir," I said.

"And I intend to keep it that way. Good day."

I walked away quickly, my mind taking impressions. A British accent, well educated. He was tanned, but not around the edges of his shirt. He wore long pants, dark brown, stuffed into black boots, heavily scuffed. He carried the gun as if he were well acquainted with it. His beard and hair were slightly longer than the last time I saw him, and both looked a shade or two lighter from being out of doors in the sun all day.

When I reached the stone staircase leading up to the cannon and the outbuildings, I stopped because my heart was hammering in my chest. I'd cheated the Reaper again through my sheer foolishness. This work would be the death of me yet.

I hurried inside and up the mahogany staircase to Barker's room, interrupting his thoughts. I told him the man himself was outside, and that I had seen him a second time. He jumped from the bed and retraced my footsteps outside, even faster than I had made them. Fast as he was, he was not fast enough. The stranger was gone.

The Guv crossed to stand right beneath where the assassin had sat, and then without a word began to climb. My route to the top of the cliff was more circuitous but far less strenuous.

"Here, I think," I said, pointing to a spot where the grass and dirt had been disturbed. From just overhead I found a novel view of the spot where I had bowed to the fellow. It would have been a clean shot to kill me. The only thing I might have had to recommend myself was that I was unimportant and not a major target, though he had poisoned half a dozen servants, as well.

My employer bent and picked something from the grass—the fag end of the cigarette, which was still hot. He sniffed the burned end, then broke up the cylinder to get at the unburned tobacco inside.

"Shag," he said, "with a bit of latakia for flavor."

"I hardly call roasting tobacco over a fire made from camel dung 'flavor.' The stuff smells dreadful."

"I did not invent it, lad. I am merely reporting it."

"Shag with latakia. That's a popular blend in London, isn't it?"

"It is, but how did you know that? You only rarely smoke."

"Sir, I've been fetching your tobacco for five years now. It would be foolish if I didn't learn something about it."

"True," he said. "In other parts of the world, it is known as 'British blend' because we tend to favor it. Did the assassin look English to you?"

"I'd say so, yes."

"Describe him for me."

"Thirty to thirty-five. Light brown hair, short beard. He wore a brown jacket and trousers, with no tie or waistcoat."

"Plus fours or long trousers?"

"Trousers, as I recall. Tucked into boots."

"He still carried a rifle? A Sharps?"

"I'm afraid I couldn't tell one rifle from another, sir."

"You must remind me when we get back to give you a cramming course in rifles."

"You seem rather certain we shall both return safely, sir. I suspect the fellow intends otherwise."

"You can count upon both, Thomas. Be sure to put it in your daybook when we get back to the room."

"Yes, sir."

We looked across the expanse of the island from the harbor to the lighthouse on the other side. Barker climbed still higher to the top of the ledge and looked across open sea toward Land's End and the coast.

"Nowhere to be found," I said, merely to have something to say.

"I don't suppose he attracted your attention to parlay."

"No, but you know, if he hadn't dropped the pebble on my head, I might not have seen him."

"It's as if he were trying to hide within his environment," Barker said. "As if he were trained to do so."

"Yes, I suppose so. Do you mean military training? Where are we fighting now? We're out of Afghanistan, mostly out of India. There is the Sudan, but that's mostly desert warfare. This is a far cry from the desert. Unless they are training at Sandringham or someplace, I don't see where he could have picked up the experience."

"There are a number of officers and ex-officers that hire out."

"Perhaps," I said, "but not generally against their own country."

"I think the longer one is away from England, the more complicated one's allegiances become."

"Maybe he's against the French."

"Maybe he is in favor of money and not scrupulous about where it comes from."

"I like money," I said. "But I wouldn't kill for it. It is repugnant."

"Aye, to you. You have a certain moral rectitude which others lack. Having this lack could be most beneficial, financially speaking."

"You mean killing for money? I couldn't do it."

"The more training one undergoes, the more one kills, the less difficult the next killing will become."

"Precisely."

"So is this fellow, Mr. X, if you prefer, is he here to settle his own score or someone else's?"

"That's not the most important question."

I thought a moment, and it came to me.

"Is the person who hired him also on this island?"

"Ah," Barker said. "Enlightenment."

We climbed down again and began to walk toward the house. Naturally, my eye was scanning everywhere for the slightest movement. This fella had me as nervous as a fox. It occurred to me that in my excitement I had flushed Barker from safety into the open. If he were shot now, any hope of getting off the island alive would plummet.

"So how are we to find his client, if I may use the word for so horrible a concept?"

"By questioning everyone," he said, pulling out his pouch.

Barker stopped to light his pipe. It occurred to me that he didn't often do things subtly.

There was a pop and a whine and suddenly Barker's head jerked and he pulled the pipe from his teeth. The bowl had shattered into pieces. It was his old traveling pipe, a meerschaum carved in his image. He smoked it on the first day of my employ.

Barker held the stem in his hand.

"That was my favorite pipe!" he thundered.

"Those he doesn't kill outright, sir, he likes to use for target practice. I'm sure you can have another one made."

"But I'd broken it in!"

"Let us step inside before he decides to do you real harm."

As we trotted out of danger, the Guv turned and threw the pipe stem toward the woods in anger. I'm sure the assassin quaked in fear.

We stepped inside and climbed the staircase. There was a seating area near the head of the stairs with a couple of sofas and some chairs. Mrs. Ashleigh was seated in one of the latter.

"I thought we might risk dining together in my room. We are already disgraced, and I do not wish to eat alone."

"As you wish. Thomas shall eat in the dining room."

"I shall?" I asked. "Why?"

"To gather whatever facts and opinions you might find relevant and to use your presence to cast question upon their decision."

"I see. It shall be a working dinner, then."

"If you would be so good."

"Very well, sir."

I changed into my evening kit and went downstairs, passing the cart with Barker and Philippa Ashleigh's dinner upon it. It was a tête-à-tête, so my presence was not necessary. I took my seat and greeted the sisters Anstruther, who seemed glad enough to see me. A few minutes later Kerry took his seat. He was shaking out his serviette when our eyes met.

"What is he doing here?" he asked.

I answered for myself. "I am a guest here, same as yourself."

"Since your boss at least had the manners not to appear where he is not wanted, I assumed you would take your proper place at the servants' table. You are hardly a guest and most certainly not the same as me."

"Thank you, sir," I said, adopting my best Old Etonian accent. "I am most relieved to hear it."

"You are rather a fish out of water, Mr. Llewelyn. You should be eating with your master at least. Where is your sense?"

I smiled at him, as if we were passing pleasantries.

"Unused and packed away, I'm afraid. Like your manners."

"See here, you little . . ."

"Mr. Kerry, you mustn't confuse convincing others of your opinion with convincing me. If you said it was sunny I would reach for an umbrella."

Kerry's face turned red and he glared at me like the devil himself. I picked up a roll and began to butter it. Gwendolyn looked shocked, but Bella snickered into her serviette. Her eyes went large when he muttered an oath.

"Please, sir, not in front of the ladies." I added, "I'm sure we can discuss our differences another time."

"Hear, hear," the French ambassador concurred. "By all means, let us discuss this matter later, *non*?"

"Of course," Fraser murmured.

"Colonel," I said, "have you located some new evidence regarding the case? Do you have any suspects in the murder?"

"I will be questioning someone after dinner, actually. Someone from inside the house."

It was on the tip of my tongue to ask him, but after coming so close to insulting one guest, I would not press another.

"Oh, good. I'm so glad to hear it."

I turned and started a conversation with Bella as our soup was taken away and the turbot brought in. It appeared I would learn nothing new to take back to Barker.

"But Colonel." Olivia Burrell, of all people, spoke up. "Who is it, what have you found out? I want to know who it is who has murdered my brother!"

"I really could not say at this point. We haven't asked the man any questions."

"Is it Mr. Barker? All the other men seem to be accounted for."

"No, Miss Olivia, it is not Mr. Barker. It is not a guest at all. It is, in fact, a servant."

At that point, he murmured something under his breath in that way that elderly gentlemen have. I wanted to ask him to repeat himself, but dared not. At that point, another young woman came to my rescue. It was Miss Bella Anstruther.

"I'm sorry. I didn't hear that. What did you say, Colonel?"

"I said, young lady, that the person we will be questioning is my own valet."

"I don't understand," Bella said. "How could it be your valet? What reason would a valet have to kill anyone?"

"Mr. Schroeder—Heinrich Schroeder—who has been with me for several years, is Alsatian."

"Is that important?"

The ambassador spoke up. "I am responsible for trying to force Germany to return Alsace-Lorraine to France. Naturally, many people in that region despise me for trying to take their citizenship from them, but they are the aggressors in the conflict. And there have to be concessions."

"Do you have any proof that he killed my brother?" Olivia pursued.

"None," the colonel admitted, "but we were concerned for the safety of the ambassador, whom you will recall Mr. Barker was hired to protect. Mr. Schroeder had a gun. To be more precise, an assassin's pistol, which can be hidden in the palm and shoots just one bullet."

The women all spoke at once. "Oh, how terrible." "Oh," said both Anstruther girls, Miss Olivia, and Lady Alicia. Had she been there, Mrs. Ashleigh might have said the same thing. It was as if every woman when she was sixteen were taught if something frightening were mentioned at the table, one was to utter that word.

"Here now." Kerry finally spoke up. "Little pitchers."

It was another attack upon me but belated and ineffectual. I had won the table through being the first to show good manners. Sometimes one uses what one can. I pretended not to hear the remark.

The turbot gave way to pheasant, complete with tail feathers. I don't generally care for animals that still look alive on my plate. I wondered if anything here were not imported from elsewhere. The wine was from France, the butter and cheese from Jersey, the beef and lobster from Scotland. I began to suspect that Godolphin Island was some sort of consolation prize. Someone had been banished as far away from court as possible, only they never realized the slight.

I wanted to press the colonel a little as to how his own valet was now a suspect, and carrying a gun right under his nose, so to speak, but I could not do so without making him look bad and me uncouth for asking.

What was it about the colonel that engendered everyone's good opinion, so that even when he took over Barker's position, so to speak, we still wanted his approval? Perhaps it was we felt sorry for him. His wife glowered beside him, stuffing herself full of pheasant, as if it were her last meal.

We finished with coffee and Bakewell tart. Mrs. Albans was not a very good cook, but her desserts were excellent, and I think well of any woman who makes good pies and tarts. Even the coffee was tolerable, as if, having literally left England, Land of Bad Coffee, the beverage had improved automatically. No more of import was said. Kerry tried to ignore me as we rose after dinner to separate from the ladies. Then something happened. It was small, and not very important yet, but it would be. As I moved to pass down the row of chairs, one of the women turned and regarded me. She had ignored me all three days, but I had somehow come to her attention as if I had dropped out of the sky. She smiled at me. Not to be ungallant, I smiled back. It was Olivia Burrell. If Mrs. Ashleigh had seen us, she would have thrown a fit.

CHAPTER EIGHTEEN

It had been a long and eventful evening after an equally long afternoon. In fact, the entire day was full of tragedy, danger, and death, with little respite. My nerves were shot, and I'm sure I wasn't the only one on the island that felt that way. All I wanted was a good night's sleep. It wouldn't come. I tossed and turned for half an hour. The thought occurred to me that perhaps there was information about the killings in Heinriche's luggage. Nothing obvious of course, which could be found by flipping through his philosophy books. The Germans were clever. Perhaps a code. Pin-pricks in a book. A note inserted in the spine. Something. Since the whole house was abed, and I was awake, I decided to return to my old room for a look-around.

I made my way down the back stair to my room and began to let myself in. The door was unlocked. I was certain I had locked it myself. I debated going back and telling Barker that someone might be in my room, but it seemed like a lot of effort. After debating for a moment, I walked into the room.

We all know the nursery tale of the three bears: a family of bears arrives home and finds the rooms disturbed and a girl named

Goldilocks in their beds. As it happens, someone had been sleeping in my bed, and she was still there. She even had a head full of golden curls, from what I could see.

"Excuse me?" I asked.

My visitor sat up immediately. Her blond hair without pins or bands cascaded over her shoulders. Her large eyes were blue, her skin pale, and her lips red as ripe strawberries. She was wearing a frothy nightgown held up by the thinnest of straps. They seemed too fragile to hold the gown, which might fall to the floor at the slightest movement.

"Miss Burrell," I murmured.

She clutched the blanket, my blanket, to her bosom.

"Mr. Llewelyn, I'm sure you must think me the most forward of women."

"I would think no such thing," I assured her. "But what brings you here?"

She drew up her limbs, encircling them with her arms. I would pinch myself if I were not otherwise occupied, to make sure I wasn't dreaming. Young men have notions of finding a beautiful woman in their beds, but that is what they are, mere dreams.

"To see you. I'll be frank with you. It seems the only way. I need safety, Thomas. I may call you Thomas, may I not?"

"Of course. You say you need safety?"

"I believe I am to be the next victim. First my father was killed. And my older brother. I'm next in line."

"That isn't necessarily true, Miss—"

"Olivia. My name is Olivia."

"Olivia, then. Your father was involved in international politics. There is little to suggest someone is coming after the family."

She suddenly burst into tears. She was clearly overwrought. "I don't want to die. I'm still young. I haven't done anything yet! I haven't been to Paris, for example. Last year I had the chance but I postponed it. What an idiot I was!"

"You'll get to go, yet," I said. "I'm sure of it. We'll get this fellow, and everything will return to the way it was."

"Do you promise? Can you promise?"

I came forward and dared sit on the corner of the bed. "Mr.

Barker and I are doing our best to protect everyone. You understand he cannot protect one person above everyone else."

She pushed herself a little closer to me on the bed. "I would not expect him to. But I thought you might. You look like the sort of fellow who could protect a girl very well."

"Thank you, but you must forgive me. You haven't spoken to me this entire time. Now suddenly you are here. There was no need to take this drastic step. You could have spoken to me in the hall. In fact, why did you not ask Mr. Kerry to protect you? He has access to your father's guns, and I'm sure he would be only too glad to protect you. He is a war hero, after all."

"I'm willing to marry Algernon to please my mother. I don't have much choice. I'm a spinster, you see, at the advanced age of twenty-seven. My prospects are few. I suppose I should have accepted one of the proposals I received several years ago when it appeared that I had so many choices. But this is different. I need protection now, desperately, and I don't think Algernon can give it to me. But I think you can."

"Are you offering yourself to me in exchange for protection?"

She wiped her eyes with my sheet.

"Forgive me," I went on, "but is that not a high price to pay? As I said before, why did you not simply ask me in the hallway? I would do my best to protect you."

"If you came to care for me, you might try harder."

I smiled at the turn of phrase. "You wanted me to care for you, but only temporarily?"

She shrugged her bare shoulders, and I watched with at least some degree of interest as one of the straps of her nightgown slid off.

"I'm sorry, I can't think beyond the next few days. I'm not trying to trick you."

"You genuinely believe your life is in danger."

"I do. I am convinced of it."

"No, there has got to be more to it than that. Why me?"

She gave me a puzzled, even frustrated look. She gathered my blankets around her and moved to the other edge of the bed. My resolve began to wane. "Whatever do you mean?" she said.

"You could have gone to your brothers, or the colonel, or Mr. Barker. There is no need for you to trade favors."

"I didn't speak to you, but that doesn't mean I hadn't noticed you. You're a good-looking fellow. You seem nice, kind, even trustworthy."

"Thank you for the compliments, Olivia, but I'd like the truth."

"The truth," she echoed, as if in thought. "Sometimes it is difficult to tell the truth. Very well, I shall risk it. Just this once. You see, I'm not known for being brave. The truth is, I didn't want to die a virgin. I wanted to experience intimacy just once, with someone who might be gentle, who might act as if I matter to him. I would like to matter to someone. I fear I'm not worth much to my mother, except what I can make on the open market. I've become a problem to her. 'What shall we do about Olivia?' she has asked when she thought I was out of earshot."

"I'm sorry," I said, and I genuinely meant it.

"In books, perhaps not the kind you read, authors hint at what might occur on one's wedding night, as if it were the most wonderful experience of one's life, the union of two people, flesh to flesh, so to speak. I would like to have that experience before I die. I assumed I had all the time in the world."

"Of course you won't die," I insisted. "You're not doomed. It is the fear speaking through you."

"It is as if a cloud is hanging over my head. Something told me this was the only option. You see, I am being frankly honest with you, am I not? I have never been so honest with anyone before in my life. Certainly not with someone of your sex."

"I understand."

"So, do we strike a deal, Mr. Llewelyn? Thomas? Will you protect me with your life in exchange for what I can give you?"

I thought about it. This half-naked girl was in my bed. Barker need not know. I could even be a cad and not hold up my end of the bargain. Or I could be her protector, when in fact she was in little danger, and reap the benefits.

She shrugged again, slipping out of the final strap, and the nightgown began to slide. I reached out, hoping my hands would encounter silk and not silken flesh. I stopped it just in time.

"I cannot," I said. "I'm sorry. I've given my heart to another. In fact, she has owned it for a while now."

"I feared as much," she said. "You seem too nice of a fellow. Are you married?"

"Not yet, but I hope to be soon."

"She is not on the island, I assume."

"No."

"Then what is the problem? She need never know."

I slid the straps back onto her incredibly soft shoulders. "I would know."

She sat back, leaning against my pillow. "You see? Scruples. You don't know how rare they are these days. Algernon has never worried about scruples. Neither have any of my other suitors. I rather thought they had gone the way of Camelot and Knight Errantry. You're making a mistake, you know, but I admire you for it."

"Thank you."

"I would have done my best to make it worth your while. I desperately want to live. As I said, I haven't done anything yet."

"I accept your boon, Olivia. I shall do my best to protect you. I'll speak to Barker, without mentioning this, of course, and see if I can keep a close eye upon you because of a premonition you had that you in particular are in danger."

"For what price?" she asked, struggling into a dressing gown by the side of the bed.

"None. Because you asked for it."

"What about the other part?"

"I can do nothing about that, I'm afraid," I answered. "Tempting as it is."

"I think you're not tempted at all. Your heart is full of that other girl. Is she a blonde, like me?"

"No. She is dark. A Jewess. I knew I wanted her the minute I saw her."

"I thought men liked blondes."

"I'm sorry. If I turn you down in my own bed it is not out of any flaw I see."

"Perhaps I could show you more," she said, beginning to tug on the strap again.

"Stop! Believe me, this is hard enough as it is. I could not live with myself if I were unfaithful, even if she never found out. I should know, and that is bad enough."

"Very well, if that is your final offer. I accept. Can you help me leave without being seen?

"Of course."

"You'll really protect me?" she asked, turning back.

"I said I would. My word is my bond, as Mr. Barker says."

"And you won't tell anyone about this?"

"Not a word, upon my honor."

"Would you do me another favor?"

"Another one?" I asked. "The first was difficult enough! Very well, what is it?"

She looked at me steadily. "Don't be in a hurry to throw away your life."

"I'm afraid that contradicts the first request."

"I'm a woman. I'm allowed to contradict myself. I would be so incredibly upset if you gave your life just to save mine. For that Jewess's sake, as well as my own. Don't do anything foolhardy."

"I'm sorry, I cannot promise that. It is my duty, Miss Burrell. I have sworn to protect the party. This is my occupation, danger-ous as it is."

She leaned forward then and kissed me on the cheek. I'd have avoided it if I could. It was innocent, but not that innocent. Then I took her hand and led her silently down the hall to the kitchen, which I found empty for the first time since we had arrived.

We looked about, and it seemed safe for her to return upstairs. I watched her go, gliding as lightly up the stair as a fairy from a storybook.

When she was gone, I went into the kitchen, put a bucket in the sink, and pumped water until it was full. I lifted it onto the counter and then, with no more preamble, plunged my face into it. The water was ice-cold and bracing. It killed any auxiliary ardor in my veins.

Then a heavy hand seized me by the back of the neck and thrust my head deeper into the water. I flailed about, trying to find pur-chase. I hadn't properly caught a breath before putting my face in the bucket. Someone was trying to drown me. I kicked back at the legs of my assailant, and my fingers ripped at his shoulders. Finally, I got hold of the lip of the bucket and pushed with all my might to get my face out of the water.

The hand suddenly released me and I sputtered and coughed water into the sink.

My hair and my face were dripping water and I couldn't see who it was. A towel was pressed into my hand and I quickly wiped my eyes. It was the last person I expected to see. It was Partridge, the butler.

"What in hell?"

The old fellow grimaced angrily. I'd say he was approaching sixty, but had not yet reached it. He was large and in his livery with its expansive white shirt bib, he looked intimidating.

"Mr. Llewelyn, is there anything I need to know regarding Miss Burrell?"

I make no claim to Barker's genius, but I can add two and two. The butler must have given her his keys. Perhaps she had not told him anything, but he looked capable of addition as well.

"I promised her," I said, between coughing and wiping water from my face, "to do what I could to protect her, without requiring anything in return."

"Miss Burrell is concerned that she shall become the next victim," Partridge said.

"So she told me."

"She is overwrought. She demanded I unlock her room. I did so, knowing that you had moved to another!"

"Does that mean you do not believe her fears are valid?" I asked him. Butlers do not get to where they are without acquiring some sense.

He tapped his jowly chin in thought. He was not the kind to give an opinion lightly. "It is too early to tell," he said. "Mr. Flannan has just been killed, and he is not in line for the inheritance. So far the lord and his heir have died. His Lordship could have been shot randomly or he could have been the intended target. There is no way to tell."

"Mr. Partridge," I said. "I swear to you by all that is holy that I have not asked anything from Miss Burrell in exchange for offering to protect her. I ask you for something instead."

Partridge frowned with a pair of bushy brows.

"You may ask," he said.

"Would you be willing to be questioned by Mr. Barker regarding the events that have occurred this week?"

"Only if I may refuse to answer any question which I feel may compromise the family. You must understand that I hold many secrets regarding Godolphin House."

"Understand? Sir, I am counting on it! You must realize that we are doing our best to lay hands upon this killer, and that anything you say, even the most chance fact, may open the case to us, and reveal the killer's methods and motive."

"But I assumed Mr. Barker had given up on the case, having been asked to retire from it."

"You don't know Mr. Barker then. He does not give up or give in, and the more pressure that is brought to bear merely makes him more keen."

"I understand now why Her Ladyship has wanted to meet him for some years. He seems a unique individual."

"Unique, indeed. I'm not sure the world could hold two of him, without cracking open."

"Then by all means, let us go speak to your employer. I suspect there is a great danger to this family at present, and in spite of the current situation in which he finds himself, Mr. Barker might be the very man who can resolve it."

Partridge led me up the back staircase. He must have gone up and down those stairs a hundred times a day, but his tread was steady and strong. He would serve this family for years to come.

I opened the door to the master's old suite. Barker was seated in one of the old armchairs, and wearing an Asian-style dressing gown over his waistcoat with little gold medallions on a black background. He was reading a book from the library. It was a biography of Oliver Cromwell. He looked up as we entered.

"Mr. Barker, sir," I said, "Partridge is concerned about the safety of the Burrell family, and has offered to answer some questions you might put to him."

The look he gave us was the kind a cat gives when offered a fresh kipper.

CHAPTER NINETEEN

Won't you have a seat, Mr. Partridge?" Barker asked, offering a chair in front of him.

"It is just 'Partridge,' sir, and I prefer to stand."

"I prefer conversation at eye level, if you don't mind, please."

It was a request but there was iron behind it. Reluctantly, the head servant sat down in the chair, but at the very edge. Servants sitting in chairs set a very bad precedent.

"Thank you," Barker continued. "Now tell me, how long have you worked here?"

"Forty-two years this June, sir. I was hired when I was fourteen to mix mortar for the masons building the outer walls."

"That is an admirable record. I assume you were hired by Her Ladyship's father. When did he die?"

"Let me see," Partridge said, stroking his chin. Though the household was in chaos, he was still freshly shaven. He was the force of order below stairs, and perhaps in many ways above.

"That was in sixty-eight, if my memory serves."

"Was the new master well received?" Barker asked, leaning forward with his forearms resting on his knees.

"There were those who thought a natural son was preferable, but there was none to be had and His Lordship was always kind and thoughtful and deferred so much to his wife in most matters, but then few felt the need to hold a grudge against him, even if he wasn't a natural Scillonian."

"What kind of master was he?" the Guv asked.

"He was a good one. Strict, but fair. He wouldn't be disobeyed or cheated in any way, but he indulged his wife, always coming up with ways to please her. That folly, the labyrinth. It was a gift for her fiftieth birthday. It was a lot of trouble getting all of the box hedge bushes here by ferry and planted. Some might have given up, but not he. He must please Milady."

"To your recollection, did His Lordship have any enemies?"

Partridge frowned, his shaggy eyebrows meeting over his hawk nose, giving him a raptorlike appearance. "Naturally I was not privy to His Lordship's professional secrets. However, I know his policies were not popular among the eastern Europeans. He was an outspoken man, particularly over matters he was passionate about."

"Do you know if he had any argument with any individuals?"

"Not to my knowledge, sir. He was a most amiable man."

And so the deification begins, I thought. All the man's accomplishments are magnified, while all his sins are swept under the rug. It merely makes it more difficult for an enquiry agent to go about his duties. I heard the Guv give an audible sigh. He would try another tack.

"How old is this house?" Barker asked.

"It was built in 1733."

"To your knowledge, are there any secret passageways or entrances?"

"No, sir."

"Are you aware of any attempt to blackmail the family?"

"No, sir."

"Have you ever heard the name Harold Throgmorton?"

"No, sir."

"Yolanda Tisher?"

"No, sir."

"Have you ever heard the Bromley Boarding School mentioned?"

"No, sir."

"Is everything you are telling me the truth?"

"No, sir."

"Are you protecting the family?"

"Yes, sir."

"I thought as much."

"I am a sagacious man, sir. I'm not in the habit of giving glib answers, nor would I give away any family secrets without consulting the family."

"Partridge, I was hired by His Lordship for a purpose. You would not stop a glazier from filling the window in the north wing."

"According to the new lord, sir, you have been sacked."

That was like a slap in the face. Momentarily, Cyrus Barker's brows rose above the twin discs of his spectacles, then sank again.

"I would expect no less from a man like you to keep his silence, but in doing so, you may be doing the family you work for irreparable harm."

The Guv stood and crossed to the window, peering out between the shutters and looking out at the copse of trees, as if daring a bullet to come out of them.

"I like this place, and what the family has done to it. They took a barren rock and made an oasis of it. I have tried to do the same kind of thing at my residence in South London. I fully understand the amount of time, money, resources, and backbreaking work involved in making and maintaining this little paradise. Obviously, His Lordship loved his wife very much in order to lavish so much attention here. Someday, when this is over, I hope to be invited to return and see this place under more normal circumstances. What I would not like to do is to come here and find Godolphin House boarded up and decayed, the woods gone wild, and the island deserted because the family was wiped out one by one by a man with a personal vendetta."

I'll say this about the old retainer. He knew how to keep his mouth closed.

"There is a secret here, Partridge, perhaps several, and you know what it is. For the good of the family, give me something to work with! A clue, an old legend, a chance remark. Help me get to the bottom of this, so these guests may go home and the Burrell family can begin to heal."

"That will take a while, sir."

"Aye, it will."

The butler still sat as silent as the tomb. Barker left the window and began to pace in front of the butler.

"Partridge, so far we have both been on the same side, so to speak, but at some point I'm going to have to remove my gloves and attack this family, the way a carpenter does a worm-eaten old table, with a hand plane and glass paper, in order to expose the rotten wood. You cannot put me off the island the way Mr. Kerry was put off a decade ago. I can do this the gentlemanly way, or I can be as rough as necessary to accomplish my objective. Butlers are not known for their imaginations but I do not believe you require a demonstration of how rough I can be. You are a repository of family secrets. Perhaps the only repository. Give me something, for the good of Godolphin House."

There was nothing. Not even the slightest movement. Partridge might as well have been carved in stone.

"We're wasting our time, Thomas. Let us see what information we can wrest from Her Ladyship."

As he passed behind the chair, Barker leaned over, so that his mouth was close to the butler's ear.

"The only woman I care about is in mortal danger, because she was doing a favor for your mistress. Forgive me if I do not feel especially generous."

My employer left the room. I followed in his wake. We were on the stairway before we finally heard Partridge call from the room.

"Very well!"

Barker turned immediately around.

"Very well for you," he rumbled.

We strode back into His Lordship's former chambers.

"This had better be worth my while," the Guv stated.

"There is a secret passage."

Partridge crossed to the bookcases, as if deep in thought. He reached forward for the final book on one of the middle shelves. The spine gave way revealing a handle inside the book. By lifting the handle the entire row of middle shelves opened on hinges, revealing a corridor.

"It is the family mausoleum," the head servant corrected.

Of course! We had heard mention of it after returning from our first reconnaissance when His Lordship had been recovered by Colonel Fraser and the manservants. The area provided by the opened shelves was wide enough for men to carry a coffin through. We stepped forward into the darkness. Partridge scraped a vesta on the wall and it flared in the dark. He took down a lantern from a shelf and lit it. In the gloom I saw stairs going both up and down. Barker shook his head in disapproval.

"The mortuary is this way, sir," Partridge said, raising the lantern and heading east, down the narrow corridor.

"Is the mortuary as old as the house?"

"I believe so, sir. This is the only way to inter family members on the island. Otherwise, they would need to be exported to the mainland."

He came to a gated room, filled with stone tombs. Barker stopped him before he unlocked the gate, and taking the lantern, examined the lock.

"There are fresh scratches on this lock," he said, "but they could have been made when His Lordship was interred."

"Speaking of which, sir, His Lordship and Master Paul have not been given a proper service. For the good of the family, it would be best if it happened soon."

"Is the family Church of England, Partridge?"

"No, sir, they are Catholic."

Obviously, there would be no way to have an open casket. Lord Hargrave was essentially headless. If the killer was not caught soon, the body would molder and the coffin would have to be sealed. There was so much to consider.

The butler opened the lock and swung open the gate, which protested with a loud squeak. Barker immediately pushed his way among the graves. Some were ornate, but most were made of plain slabs of marble. Barker appeared to be looking for something.

"Ah," he finally said, reaching between the wall and one of the graves. He lifted a disreputable-looking blanket.

"What have you got there?" I asked.

"Our assassin's nest. I believe he has been sleeping here for most of a week."

"In a mausoleum?" I demanded.

"By the grave of the very man he killed?" Partridge asked, at just about the same time.

Barker folded the blanket and laid it on one of the graves. "I believe this fellow is not bound by superstition and would not fear sleeping among the graves. I have no doubt he has done it before. Here he is out of the elements, dry, and until now, private. He can even sneak into the kitchen for a crust of bread and other food.

"As for sleeping atop your late master's crypt, I doubt the assassin has any interest in a body once it's dead. He came here to hide and to rest, locked safely in here and probably sleeping there on the floor."

"How do you possibly know that, sir?" I asked.

"By imagining how I would survive on an island such as this. It seems the best way."

"But you don't know him. How can you guess how he will act?"

"I came here looking for a place where he might sleep and discovered a blanket, did I not?"

I stamped the floor, which was lain with flagstones.

"It makes a rather hard bed," I said.

"I have slept in worse conditions, and it is only temporary. Partridge, did I spy a door leading away from Godolphin House?"

"Yes, sir," the butler admitted.

"Lead on, then."

Partridge led us out, and locked the gate again, then we continued down the corridor, lit by the lantern. There were dusty crates at the sides, and cobwebby barrels that may have once held ale. At the end of the passage there was a door in the stone wall. When the butler opened it I could feel a change in the atmosphere and hear the ocean crashing on the rocks, as if at a distance.

I glanced at Barker, and saw that he had pulled his Colt. I cursed myself for leaving my revolver in my room. This fellow was dangerous, and I had no business going about unarmed. It was possible, even likely, that the assassin was still nearby.

It was a long, narrow tunnel, sometimes giving way to steps. At one point the tunnel zigzagged and as we turned I heard the roar of the ocean closer. Then Partridge lowered his lantern. We came to the entrance and found ourselves at the mouth of a natural cave some thirty feet or more off the ground, with no obvious way to get down. I leaned forward and craned my neck to look up. It was perhaps another twenty feet to the wall, which as a boy, the butler had helped build. I looked down again. It was almost a sheer drop.

"Not an easy climb," I said.

"No, but a determined man can do it," Barker stated. "I assume he has a rope."

"Why shouldn't he?" I said. "He seems to have had the run of the house since he arrived. It's a wonder he hasn't killed us all in our beds!"

I kicked a small rock in anger, and watched it fall to the rocks below. I may have noticed this little cave during our first day and discounted that it led anywhere.

"Partridge, are you aware of any arrangement between a member of the household or staff and this fellow, whoever he is?"

"No, sir."

"And are you telling me the truth this time?"

Partridge came very near to smiling. "Yes, sir, I am. That's not to say that there isn't one, but I have seen no sign of it. I suppose it is possible that he has moved about at night without alerting anyone."

"Would Mrs. Albans have noticed if food were missing?"

"She might. I shall broach the subject with her, if you wish."

"Aye, do. And the gardener. See if some of the tools are missing.

Suggest he take an inventory if possible. I think that's enough for now."

We retreated down the zigzag corridor again, until we passed through the door. Once there, Barker closed it and pointed toward the lock.

"May I see the key?"

Partridge pulled a large ring of keys from his pocket and eventually found an old and rusty key which turned in the lock.

"Is yours the only key ring?"

"There used to be another, sir, but it was misplaced years ago," the butler said.

"We must assume that they are now in this man's possession. Help me, lad."

He seized one of the barrels and rolled it over against the door. We followed with two more, and lifted a crate on top of all three of them.

"He'll be sleeping outside tonight, I'll reckon," the Guv said, with a grim smile on his lips.

As we reached the back of the library bookcases he turned to regard the staircases going up and down.

"Where does this come out?" he asked, pointing to one.

"To the inglenook in the kitchen fireplace."

"I see. And the one going up?"

"There's a panel up on the first floor, by the standing clock."

"Do the young people in the family know about those secret passageways?"

"Oh, yes, sir. They played upon them as children. One could not keep such a secret from them for long."

"And the servants? Do they use the passage from time to time? It seems convenient."

"Occasionally. I have ordered them not to. It is dangerous, and they could break things, including limbs. Most of them are young, however, and they don't always listen."

"So, even before our arrival, the killer has had full access to the house, from cellar to attic. That stops now."

CHAPTER TWENTY

Thomas," Barker said as we climbed the stairs again. It was perhaps ten o'clock in the evening. "Have I demonstrated patience to you?"

"In what way, sir?" I asked.

"When I learned Colonel Fraser was holding Herr Schroeder, did I immediately run to ask the circumstances or question the man himself?"

"No, sir. Far from it. You didn't even mention him when you last spoke with the colonel."

"Then I may feel justified in asking for the particulars now. They've held him for days. Would you like to accompany me?"

"I would, sir, but I have something to report."

Barker stopped on the top step and regarded me intently, trying to fathom what I would say before I said it. He indicated one of the chairs on the landing. We were getting full use of the furniture on the first floor. We sat.

"What has happened?" he asked.

I told him about Miss Burrell. I had no way of knowing what

was important and what was not. Barker listened intently, as he always does, rubbing his nails under his chin as he thought.

"And you in no way encouraged this?" he finally asked.

"No, sir! Of course not."

"I meant before. Could anything you said or did be miscon-strued?"

"I didn't speak to her, and as far as I recall, didn't even look at her."

"You have an effect upon women, I have noticed. Either they want to mother you or else pull your hair out. There is generally no stage between the two."

"I've noticed that."

"Do you intend to help her?"

"Not without your permission, sir."

His hand moved and began to stroke his mustache. "I'm watching a woman of my own."

"True," I said.

"And I wonder how well I am doing. Our opinion that we are protecting these women may just be that, mere opinion. Speaking of which, let me look in on Philippa a moment."

We knocked, and upon being summoned, stepped inside.

"I'm getting bored, Cyrus," she warned as we entered. "Miss Austen and the beauty of *Sanditon* can only capture my interest so long."

"What is it you wish to do?" the Guv asked.

"Take a walk. Talk to somebody who possesses a brain."

"I'm afraid it is dangerous."

"I know it is dangerous. Yet you walk about. Must I give the speech about how fortunate you are to be a man and not a woman?"

"I don't think that will be necessary," he said.

"Do not treat me like a child."

"I would not presume."

"Miss Burrell is feeling nervous and neglected," I suggested. "Perhaps she'd like a little company."

"What do you mean by 'nervous and neglected,' Thomas? Have you been flirting again?"

"Quite the opposite, ma'am. I have been the proverbial bucket of cold water."

"It might be good," Barker said, adjusting his pearl tie pin in the mirror, "to draw her out about the other guests. What opinions has she formed about the party, if any? Her father has just died, as well as her brother."

"The death of a father makes a great change in a girl's life," Philippa said. "Her chief defender is gone, and now she must either become an adult or marry someone who shall treat her like a child for the rest of her life."

"That is simplistic," I said. "Or cynical."

Barker's eyebrows rose above his lenses. I had dared challenge something Philippa said.

The corner of Mrs. Ashleigh's mouth went up on one side. I hazarded a guess that she was rarely treated in such a fashion.

"It was," she admitted. "Simplistic, at least. Some fathers don't bother to defend their daughters at all. And some daughters rarely need it."

"I must accept your word for it," I said, hoping to smooth the feathers I had just ruffled.

"Please do," she said, still looking ready to pounce. "Are you asking me to spy for you, Cyrus?"

"Miss Burrell might be inclined to withdraw if I question her, but you can tease information from her without being obvious. That is, if you are willing."

"I suppose I could try," she said, as if it were a lot of trouble.

"You don't have to."

"I said I would try, did I not?"

She looked at me, as if to confirm what she said.

"Yes! Yes, you did."

"That's settled, then."

"Thank you, my dear. If you need a breath of fresh air later, take the lad with you."

"I've rather gone off the idea," she said. "But I'll go speak to Olivia."

"We were going to speak to the colonel about his valet, Schroeder."

"You will let me know what happens, won't you?"

"Of course," Barker replied.

The atmosphere in the room was too charged for my liking. Barker looked at me as if I were going to laugh at his answer to Mrs. Ashleigh. I took the opportunity to step into the hall, where it was safer. Barker joined me almost immediately.

True to form, he did not discuss Philippa in public. He was not the kind of man who complained behind a woman's back, thereby making her an object of ridicule and he someone to be pitied. I would do my best to never be that kind of man myself.

It was getting on ten thirty and I was concerned that the colonel had gone to bed early, as septuagenarians are prone to do. When we knocked, however, he answered the door immediately, and then without a word stepped into the hall.

"You came about Heinrich Schroeder," Fraser said.

"We have. Has he confessed to anything?"

"No. He was found armed by the ambassador's door, but he claims he had kept the weapon in his pocket since we became stranded, out of necessity."

"What kind of weapon was it?" my employer asked.

"A Turbiaux palm pistol," Fraser said. "Why don't we talk somewhere more private? Perhaps His Lordship's old room? I'll go speak to my wife."

"Very well, Colonel," Barker said. "I'm sure we have much to discuss."

Fifteen minutes later we were in our new room with a bottle of port and three glasses. The latter was the colonel's idea. Barker's hand looked outsized holding the small glass.

"Colonel Fraser," Barker said. "I understand the need for secrecy in this mission, but please do not take me for a simpleton. Lord Hargrave was once your aide-de-camp. I suspect you are not simply a guest. Are you by chance the director of the Royal United Services Institution?"

"Why would you say that?" Fraser asked.

"You are too old for military service, but not necessarily to run an agency that specializes in monitoring espionage. You also appear to be in excellent shape for your age."

"Thank you. This was supposed to be my last act as director. Richard was poised to take over the organization. Alas, such things were not to be."

"What will you do now?" I asked. "Will you stay on as director?"

"Perhaps temporarily, until a suitable replacement can be chosen and vetted. I promised my wife we would take a holiday to Lisbon. It is long overdue."

"Do you know if anyone objected to Lord Hargrave's taking over the agency? Did he step on any toes by doing so?"

"Not that I'm aware, but I'll begin an investigation as soon as we get back to London."

"Whom do you suppose is out there shooting at us?"

"Some sort of hireling, I think," the colonel stated. "He would have made short work of us by now if he had a vendetta of his own. He's an excellent shootist. I know that much."

"He shot a pipe out of my mouth yesterday."

"Did he, by Jove? Well, it goes to show he's just toying with us."

"He killed the lighthouse keeper with a spear. One he had fashioned himself, I believe."

"Whoever the blighter is, he has seen action in jungles before. Africa, perhaps, or Borneo."

"Most likely. We've learned how he got in to kill Paul Burrell. There is a passage coming up behind the library bookcase. We have blocked it."

"Good! We can sleep better at night, knowing he is locked out. Although I'm wondering what he should try next."

"I imagine we shall not have long to wait. Now, about your valet."

"Schroeder."

"Aye. Is there a chance he is a spy for the German government?"

"A chance? It is a certainty. He's a spy, but not a very good one. I have kept him on and used him to relay faulty information to the German military for years."

"Why was he hanging about the ambassador's door?"

"As said, he was born an Alsatian and Gascoigne was responsible for annexing his homeland to France. I'm certain he was aware the ambassador would be on the island. I could not say whether he had orders to kill him, or if he tried on his own volition out of national pride. Not that it matters either way."

"Has he confessed to being a spy?"

"Not yet, but we haven't been lighting any fires under his feet. We've been polite so far. That may end if Kerry has his wish."

"Do you suppose he and the man outside are working together?"

"I think our assassin is working with someone, but I doubt it is Schroeder. I don't believe he has the brains."

"What if it is the other way around?" I suggested. "Schroeder finds out information and sends it outside by candlelight signal."

"It's possible, I suppose, but the two men are an odd combination," the colonel said.

"Agreed. Where are you keeping Mr. Schroeder?" Barker asked.

"In the cellar, in the linen room."

"Colonel, you are in charge. May we speak to the prisoner?"

"About that . . ." Fraser said, looking at the floor. "It was not my wish that you be taken off the investigation. That was Kerry's doing, along with the Burrells, who seem to fall in with whatever he says. Do not think that I agree with their assessment. In fact, Richard and I decided together to hire you. I'd have spoken, but my position is a secret."

"I am glad to hear it."

"In fact, as director of the RUSI, I would like to renegotiate your contract. I would like you to track down this fellow, not only for the sake of the ambassador, but for everyone's safety."

"Thank you, Colonel, but I already have a new client."

Fraser leaned forward in his chair, a bundle of dry sticks in a tweed coat, yet still very much alive and alert.

"Do you, by Jove? Imagine that."

"However, my duties are very similar to what you proposed. I have been on the case since last night."

"Good! I didn't know you and I was rather concerned you might sulk over your treatment."

"I have spent my entire career ignoring what men such as Kerry or the Burrells think. I see no reason to begin now. Shall we go see Schroeder?"

The director of the Royal United Services rubbed his dry hands together.

"By all means, let's," he said.

CHAPTER TWENTY-ONE

We woke Heinrich Schroeder by unlocking the door. He sat up in the cot he was sleeping on and put a hand to his eyes when the colonel turned up the gas. He wore neither a tie, nor braces, in case he tried to do himself a mischief. I would judge him to be approaching forty.

Schroeder was an angular-looking fellow. He possessed a long jaw, high cheekbones, and a tall forehead. All his bones seemed outsized, with a thin layer of skin to hold them together. He had blond, almost colorless hair that didn't extend down below the tip of his ears. It made him look older than he was. He had blue eyes that looked almost silver in a certain light.

"Schroeder, sit up!" Fraser said to his former valet. "Mr. Barker here wants to ask you some questions."

"Anything I can do to help," the man said solemnly. All his features seemed regular, but when they went together, they produced a stern-looking man.

"I understand that you were outside the ambassador's door," Barker began, "and that there was a weapon in your pocket. What were you doing there?"

"I wanted to catch a glimpse of him."

"The man was trying to steal your homeland? Forgive me. I've been told a little of your past."

"*Ja.* I wanted to look in the face of the man who destroyed my family and my people."

"And you just happened to be carrying a gun on your person?"

Fraser put the weapon on the table. It was some sort of miniature gun. It was a disc with a very short barrel on one side and a plungerlike trigger on the other. Such a device could contain no more than one bullet and that one of a small caliber. Its purpose was to shoot someone up close, preferably in the soft spots where it could do the most damage. It was an assassin's pistol.

"I have carried it about since we arrived. I have had it for years. I forgot I carried it."

"You had no plans, then, to shoot the ambassador?"

"Of course not. If I shot him, there would be no way to escape."

"You are under no orders from your former government to kill him?"

"I would not. I live in London now. Besides, I am a pacifist."

Barker smiled. "A pacifist with a pistol?"

"I saw an advertisement for it in a service magazine. 'Carry it to protect the family you work for,' it said. A pistol is not only designed to harm. It can protect, as well. The situation we were in warranted that I carry it. I had no intent to harm the French ambassador, I swear it."

"What do you know of the person shooting at us from the woods?"

"Nothing, sir. I'm as much in the dark as you."

"Were you familiar with this house before this visit?"

"I have been here before as the colonel's valet, yes."

"Have you been helping as a footman?"

"Yes, sir. I have done the work before. Mr. Partridge assigned me to the duties. He said Dr. Anstruther still has some of the poisoned footmen resting in bed."

"Did you have specific duties assigned to you?"

"No, sir. When the bell was rung by one of the guests, Mr. Rojas and I would see to it. Whichever was the fastest got the work."

Barker gave a wintry smile. "Which one of you got most of the work?"

Schroeder sat up straighter. "He may be younger, but he is only a Brazilian. He has no concept of tradition and pride in one's work. He's a mere pup. He shall only learn by studying a more advanced and better trained servant such as myself."

"It is fortunate you came along when you did," my employer said.

"Yes, sir, it is."

"How came you to work for Colonel Fraser?"

"The usual way. I applied to an agency for servants. Many people in Britain have a prejudice against Germans, but we make excellent servants. We are precise and efficient and we have a fine memory. The colonel was impressed with my background. I don't know what standards they have in South America, but they must be low. The Brazilian is always lurking about, and speaking to whomever he chooses. He gets by on his charm and youth. If the situation were not so dire, Mr. Rojas would soon find himself packing."

"He means well," I said, feeling the need to defend him, since he was not here to defend himself.

"*Ja,*" Schroeder said. "He does. But he is imprecise. He throws Mr. Kerry's cases around as if they were a bunch of bananas. A case should be handled gently and efficiently so it lasts for generations."

"This is all very enlightening, Mr. Schroeder," Barker said, "but it doesn't explain why you were going about armed."

"Of course I am armed, sir. I noticed you are armed. There is an insane person outside firing upon us. All of us are carrying such weapons as we may. None of us want to die and we must protect the women."

"But you were near the ambassador's door."

Schroeder actually jumped from his cot in anger.

"I have been near his door a dozen times every day! So was every other footman. The reason I was stopped was because I am German. No Englishman trusts a German, or a Frenchman or a Russian, for that matter. It is difficult being Alsatian and living in London. Waiters are rude to you. People make jokes about how you pronounce your words. One would never treat an Englishman that way in Berlin or Hamburg. We know how to treat a guest!"

"Where were you when His Lordship was shot?"

"I'm not sure. I was downstairs, either in the kitchen or in my room." He suddenly stood, very agitated. "I don't know anything about whoever is shooting at us. I didn't kill Mr. Burrell. He seemed a fine fellow and did not deserve to die so young."

"What were you doing in the hall by the ambassador's room?"

"I was hoping to see the ambassador. I said that!"

"To see him, or to speak to him?"

"Just to see him. I was curious! I wouldn't have anything to say to such a person."

"You wouldn't wish to avenge yourself on the man who signed the treaty giving away your country?"

"It doesn't matter so much anymore. I have lived in England for many years now. Most of my family is dead."

He sat down as abruptly as he had stood. He put down his head and ran a hand through his cropped hair.

"Is that the only reason you were in the hall?" Barker continued.

"I wasn't waving a candle about, if that is what you're suggesting."

"I was wondering if you were alone."

Schroeder rolled his eyes in exasperation. "Sir, I am not a spy. I was not conspiring with anyone!"

"No, but you might have simply been talking to someone."

"Who?" the colonel asked.

"As Heinrich has admitted, he has been here before. Romances sometimes spring up at house parties, and not merely among the guests."

"There was no such girl," he said quickly.

"Ah, but if you were to admit it, you might get her sacked," I said.

"There was no such girl!"

"Is your valet known to be a lady-killer, Colonel Fraser?"

"I'm blowed. Didn't know the blighter had it in him."

"I tell you, there is no such girl!" the valet said, flushing scarlet.

Barker turned to me. Somehow he has gotten into his head that I am an expert in matters of the heart.

"If you had an assignation to meet a girl, why would you bring a pistol?"

I shrugged my shoulders. "Several reasons. If she were frightened, I might show her I could protect her. If I barely knew her, I might wish to appear dangerous, which is romantic. Or I might feign an interest in killing the ambassador for the same reason, an anarchist disguised as a valet. There are all sorts of ploys to impress a young girl."

"And I suppose you know them all, you rascal," Barker said.

"Well, you asked. You're not going to tell Mrs. Ashleigh, are you?"

Barker leaned his head to the side, as if considering the matter.

"Ha!" The colonel chuckled. "My valet is something of a dog. A below-stairs Lothario. Who would have thought?"

"I'm nothing of the kind, sir. I don't flit from girl to girl, and I don't romance anyone from our own household. But sooner or later I should like to marry. Before it's too late, if you take my meaning, sir."

"Mr. Schroeder," Barker said. "You must understand that we are trying to catch this killer. Has anything occurred to you or seemed suspicious regarding anyone here that suggests he or she might be colluding with the killer, or has some other motive we need to know about?"

"No, sir."

That was it. There would be no getting anything out of this one.

"Mr. Schroeder, I hope you understand the penalty for spying in Britain. It is the firing squad. If you are very fortunate, after several years in jail, you might be traded back to Germany for an English spy."

"I'm not a spy, sir!" Schroeder insisted.

"I am glad to hear it. Of course, you understand we cannot simply take your word for it. I'm afraid you'll have to remain locked up until the matter is resolved."

"But there are not enough valets, sir. Who will look after the colonel properly? Certainly not the Brazilian!"

"If you recall anything, please speak to the colonel."

"Yes, sir."

We rose, and left the room. Fraser carefully locked the door.

"Did you believe him?" he asked.

"Not a word," Barker said.

"Nor I."

It occurred to me that a single but well-armed man was exactly what Miss Olivia Burrell was looking for. I didn't mind him being locked away.

By then it was after eleven and I was tired. Now, when working for Cyrus Barker, it is never good to be the one to suggest we stop for the night. It's judged as a sort of moral weakness on my part. On the other hand, he will go on as long as he feels that there is work to be done, which may include working until dawn. He himself would never admit to tiredness, of course. The best course, I've found, is to show a willingness to go on while looking as knackered as possible. Yawning is too obvious. Rubbing the forehead every fifteen minutes is always a good bet, as is standing for a few seconds with one's eyes closed.

"You look tired, lad. Let us stop for the night."

"Is there something else we could do, sir? Has anything been left undone?"

"Probably, but everything I can think of requires talking to others, and most everyone is abed for the night. We'll get a good start in the morning."

"If you say so, sir."

I crawled into my bed right around midnight and lay watching Barker smoking a final pipe in bed in the dark. I suppose this is a rather hazardous endeavor, but it might lead to a solution in the case, so I did not object, nor did I fall asleep until he had smoked it down to ash. The room was only lit by his tiny brazier of burning tobacco. It occurred to me he had brought a spare.

As I lay I ruminated on the irony of Olivia Burrell's offer. Diffident as I was, I had tried whenever possible to speak to any eligible woman my age. None had ever offered herself to me, a peach ripe for plucking, so to speak, and now I had turned her down, having recently pledged myself to another. I suppose there were those who would have kept their mouth shut about the courtship to one and the offer to the other. The question I was debating to myself was whether I would have had such scruples before I met Cyrus Barker, or had he influenced me for the better? I rather hoped the first was true, but I could not fully convince myself. One wants to be the best version of oneself. The spirit is willing but, ah, the flesh.

CHAPTER TWENTY-TWO

B ring me Mr. Rojas," Barker said, just like that. No "Good morning" or anything. Once awake, Barker is always working at something. I generally need coffee and a crumpet before the old coconut begins to function.

I got out of bed, rubbing my eyes.

"Yes, sir."

I threw on a change of clothes and tied my shoes. On the one hand the Guv wanted Rojas now. On the other, I represented the agency and must be well groomed. I seized a brush and attacked my hair.

"Back in a moment," I said, and was off.

I tracked Cesar down in the kitchen. I had no idea how long he had been awake. He always seemed full of energy.

"Thomas, have you come for breakfast? I could bring a tray to your room."

"No, that won't be necessary. But Mr. Barker has a few questions for you regarding Mr. Kerry. Could you come up?"

"*Si, si.* I have a tray to deliver, but I will be there in about five minutes, no?"

"I'll tell him you are coming."

In the kitchen they were frying eggs, bacon, and potatoes. Coffee was brewing, and a large pot of tea was on the stove. I debated hanging about for a moment, but Barker seemed a trifle impatient. I went upstairs and said Cesar was coming.

A few minutes later, there was a knock at the door and I opened it.

"How may I help you, Mr. Barker?" Cesar asked, stepping into the room. "Is there something I can bring you?"

"Just information, Mr. Rojas. Have a seat."

"Aside from helping as a footman, I have been making myself useful to Colonel Fraser, since his valet is detained. Sir, do you know if Mr. Schroeder will be returned to his duties soon?"

"I think it unlikely, sir," Barker admitted. "Why do you ask?"

"I did not wish to see him get himself into trouble."

"Did the two of you become friendly during your time here?"

"No, sir. Not particularly. He kept to himself. A very private and formal man he is."

"He didn't, for example, show you his pistol?"

"Pistol? No, sir. I had no idea he carried such an engine."

"Did he leave the room at any time in the evenings?"

"Yes, sir. About ten o'clock for ten minutes. I assumed it was to perform his ablutions."

"I see. How did he spend his free time? Did he, for example, engage in ciphers or work with puzzles?"

"No, sir. He read when he wasn't working. He was a student of philosophy: Schopenhauer, Goethe, and Nietzsche."

"It is not the customary reading list for a valet."

"Decidedly not, Mr. Barker," Cesar said. "Philosophy is not of much use for helping a man dress or looking after his suits."

"How did you come to be a valet yourself?"

"Originally, I was a bookkeeper in Rio de Janeiro, but I was lured to Manaus during the rubber boom. My mother warned me not to go. It is a wild frontier city and wicked. The natives were being exploited and worked to death. The businesses came and went quickly. My last business failed, and I was without a situation, with little money to get home. I answered an advertisement for a manservant, though I had no experience in that line. Mr. Kerry hired me."

"And what sort of employer is he?" Barker asked.

"A demanding one, if I must be perfectly honest. But he pays well, and he said he might take me to Europe. I had always wanted to see Europe, Mr. Barker."

"Mr. Kerry was business partners with Mr. Pelham and Mr. Hillary, I understand. Did you ever come in contact with these two gentlemen?"

"Yes, sir. Mr. Hillary ran the daily operations of the Paititi Rubber Company, Mr. Kerry oversaw the labor camp, and Mr. Pelham gathered investors and buyers for the raw rubber. Each to his own strengths was how Mr. Kerry described it."

"Would you say that Mr. Kerry has exaggerated his duties here? He implied that the entire company was his."

Cesar shrugged his shoulders, and restraightened his spectacles. "I suppose it is an exaggeration. I had the impression the company was owned equally among the three partners."

"You are a former bookkeeper. In your impression, was the company doing well?"

"Very well, sir. South America has a monopoly on rubber, and there are new uses for it every day. Bicycle tires, for example. But the company was being sold. Slave labor was made illegal last year."

"What sort of fellow is Mr. Hillary?"

"Very capable, I understand. He has a good head for business."

"You and Mr. Kerry came here alone. The other owners stayed behind?"

"Yes, Mr. Kerry said he had earned a holiday. He had not seen his family in years."

"What does Mr. Hillary look like?"

"Really, senhor," Cesar said. "I'm not very good with descriptions."

"Did he have, for example, one eye and a hump?"

Cesar laughed. "No, sir, he did not. A very pleasant fellow. Of medium height, clean shaven."

"Very interesting. And Mr. Pelham?"

"I have heard him called the very devil himself, if you will pardon the expression. He is very driven and some would say quite ruthless. I shudder to think how many natives have died under his exploitation."

"What is his appearance?"

"He is tall. His hair is light brown. He has a short beard."

Barker turned to me. That was exactly like the man I had seen in the kitchen the first morning.

"Did you happen to see the gentleman I was speaking with in the kitchen on the first day, Cesar?" I asked.

"When?"

"Right after we arrived."

"I suppose not. There was so much going on. I was anxious to get settled as quickly as possible. Mr. Kerry was waiting, you understand."

"Certainly," Barker said. "Did you ever hear Mr. Kerry say anything about the Burrell family? Was he anxious to come here?"

"Yes, he told me he was coming to right a wrong. Apparently, His Lordship had said something unkind to him at some time in the past. He said he would make him eat his words."

"Did he mention Miss Olivia?"

"No, sir."

"He doesn't strike you, then, as a man in love?"

"I'm sorry, sir, but I cannot picture Mr. Kerry as a lovesick swain."

"He was more interested in humiliating His Lordship and his family, perhaps."

"He was going to 'get his due.' Whatever was said between them angered Mr. Kerry very much."

"How long have Mr. Kerry and the other owners been acquainted? Since England?"

"No, sir. As I understand it, they met in the war in Bolivia."

Cesar gave Barker a brief history of the Pacific war, encompassing what he had told me, and a little more.

"Border disputes are always lively entertainment," Barker said. "Were you yourself involved in the war?"

"I? No, sir. I'm no soldier. If they needed anyone with an accountant's skills, they did not advertise it in Rio."

"I have heard some parts of the city are quite sophisticated."

"Indeed, sir! We have many fine buildings and an opera house. Entertainment arrives from Europe almost weekly. We are not some backwater."

"But Manaus is primitive in comparison."

"It is," Cesar said. "It has been freshly cut out of the jungle, which still encroaches upon it. However, new buildings are springing up every week, and new people arrive every day. Mr. Hillary says we will be the São Paulo of the north."

"You have spoken with him, then."

"Only once or twice, sir. He has no time to speak to the lowly valet of a partner. He is a busy man. I'm sure he has a company to run."

"What are Mr. Kerry's plans, Mr. Rojas, after his holiday?"

"To return to Brazil with money from the sale, and to help dissolve the Patiti Limited."

"What will become of you and your employment?"

"I have a mother that needs looking after. I shall return to the sunny beach of Copacabana. Someone is bound to need a bookkeeper."

"Not a valet?"

"Numbers are a good deal more reliable than a capricious master, or so I have found."

"How did you find London? Besides cold, I mean."

"It was very grand. Such magnificent buildings!"

"I assumed Mr. Kerry stayed at the Savoy. I've heard it is even better than Claridge's."

"Yes, indeed, sir. Nothing in South America compares to it."

"You saw the statue of Lord Nelson at Trafalgar Square? Our offices are hard by there. Right next to Scotland Yard."

"You must be a famous detective, senhor, to be in its shadow."

"It is in Whitehall, the seat of England's government."

"I am glad to hear it. I hope you catch this fellow, whoever he is."

"Oh, I know who he is, and what he's doing here. It's merely a matter of trapping him. I don't believe that will be so difficult. Were I you, Mr. Rojas, I would consider packing. Before you know it, you shall be home with your mother." Barker stood and gave one of his formal bows. "Thank you, sir. It has been a pleasure speaking with you."

Cesar gave me a questioning look, but I didn't have time to answer it. I showed him to the door.

"You've worked out who he is?" I asked. "When were you going to tell me?"

"I haven't decided yet, but it won't be today. There is still a good deal yet to do."

How much, I wondered, did my not knowing help him discover what was going on, and how much was his simply enjoying watching me flounder about? I didn't much care for either, myself. I'd find out sooner or later. Maybe I would figure out the solution myself.

"To whom shall we speak next?" I asked.

"The youngest son, or rather, I should say, the only son, has not had much to say. I'm sure he has opinions concerning what has happened these last few days."

"Has he spoken to you?" I asked.

"No, he hasn't. And you?"

"Not a word. It is odd. I mean, I have heard these theater types are generally loud and gregarious."

"They would also be able to change their appearance."

"You're implying, then, that he killed his own brother?"

"I'm merely throwing out possibilities, lad. I'm not saying I like him for the murder."

"We don't know anything about him."

"Precisely. Can you say the same of everyone else? I know more of Colonel Fraser's wife than I do of the new heir to the Godolphin estate. It is a situation I feel we should rectify."

"I wonder where he is at the moment," I said.

"I'm sure Partridge knows. I suspect he knows enough to solve this case, were he so inclined. But Partridge is an old retainer and he will say nothing. One would sooner get blood from a stone."

We went downstairs and within a few moments the butler appeared out of nowhere. Barker buttonholed him.

"Partridge," the Guv asked. "Do you know where I can find Percy Burrell?"

"Master Percy has gone to his room. He has asked not to be disturbed. I believe he said something about having a sick headache."

Barker nodded. "Thank you, Partridge."

"Very good, sir."

The butler faded again into the woodwork. When he was gone, I blew out a lungful of air in frustration.

"That's it, then."

"What is, lad?"

"He's asked not to be disturbed."

"That message was meant for the servants. I am not one of the servants."

"Of course," I said. "But we don't know where his room is, and we can't ask Partridge."

"By process of elimination, it is on the first floor. I have kept an eye on the rooms here to see who has gone in and out of each one. I assume you have done the same."

"Of course," I said.

"Then let us step into the corridor. Someone is bound to direct us to the room we seek."

It was such a logical suggestion, I don't know why I hadn't thought of it. We went upstairs and Barker leaned upon his stick until someone came out of a room. It was a maid of some sort. She was going to pass by, but Barker stopped her, most politely. Had he been wearing his bowler he would have raised it. As it was, he bowed.

"Pardon me, miss, could you direct me to Master Percy's room?"

" 'Tis there, sir," she said, indicating a door very close at hand. She had an Irish lilt to her voice. "But he isn't to be disturbed."

"Ah!" Barker said, looking crestfallen. "Some other time, then."

He turned and began to go down the stair again. What was he playing at?

The maid went down the hall and into a room. Meanwhile, the Guv had stopped halfway down the steps. He immediately reversed course and went back up and across, stopping at the door. He raised his cane and knocked loudly. I would merely have tapped. But then no one could accuse Barker of having a faint heart.

"Go away!" called a voice from within.

Barker opened the door and strode in. As was my duty, I followed.

CHAPTER TWENTY-THREE

Percy Burrell's room, like its occupant, was still making the transition to adulthood. A small army of lead Highlanders marched on the windowsill and a toy sailboat was propped in a corner. There was a stack of books on theater design on a table near the bed alongside a decanter of Scotch. Percy himself sat in a chair beside the decanter, doing his best to empty it expediently.

"What do you want?" he asked.

"To get better acquainted," Barker stated.

"I'll assume that's a joke," Burrell said, and downed half a tumbler.

Burrell was thinner than his late brother, and his hair was lighter, a color that in the sun looked auburn and in the shade looked brown. He had freckled cheeks, pale blue eyes, and a weak chin. I could not picture him as a leading man in a production of any import, especially not with his tie undone and his collar sprung.

"We have been going about asking questions of the guests and family," Barker explained. "I thought someone might have noticed something important without realizing it."

"Still haven't a clue as to who is killing my family, then?" he asked.

"Oh, I have a good idea who he is, I just don't know who is helping him or where he is hiding."

Percy frowned, as if trying to make sense of the words. The bottle was not yet half empty, but I suspected it had recently been full.

"You must forgive my manners. Have a seat, gentlemen."

Barker sat in an old leather chair, rubbed raw in the middle. I rested an elbow on the wing behind his head.

"I wish he'd get a move on."

"Whom?" I asked.

Burrell snorted, and revealed a set of horselike teeth. "Whom? Whom do you think? The killer. He's certainly taking his time about killing us. Olivia is petrified, but I wish he'd just burst in and get it all over with."

"I would think you'd be grateful that you had suddenly become the heir."

"You'd think that, wouldn't you, if you didn't know. I'd rather dig ditches than be the heir of Godolphin House. It was Paul that wanted it so much. He'd have been good at it."

"Nevertheless," my employer said coolly, "the duty has fallen in your lap. What do you intend to do about it?"

He poured himself another drink. "Isn't it obvious? I'm doing it."

"Mr. Burrell, do you know a man by the name of Jack Hillary?"

"Not that I'm aware of, but I've got a number of cousins on both sides of the family."

"Have you ever heard the name Henry Pelham?"

"Not that I can recall. Can I offer you a drink?"

He held out the bottle, though we had not a glass to pour the Scotch into if we wanted any.

"No, thank you," Barker said.

"Where was I?"

"Mr. Pelham and Mr. Hillary."

"Don't know either one," he said.

It was obvious that Burrell was getting drunk. Something about the way he drank told me he hadn't been drunk before.

"Breakfast will be served soon," my employer pointed out.

"That's why I'm drinking," Percy said. "I'll have to go downstairs and pretend to be something I'm not. You'd think that wouldn't be so hard for an actor, wouldn't you? Well, it is. That was Paul's role. I'm just the bloody understudy."

Barker frowned. He's not one who enjoys self-pity.

"It's like I'm in one of those damned dreams actors have. Nightmares, I suppose. You walk through a door in your house, a door you use every day, and suddenly you walk out on stage. The audience is there waiting for you to begin your opening line but you don't know what play you're in or what to say. So you just stand there with panic in your eyes, looking like a fool. Like the fool you actually are."

That was all it took. Barker burst from his seat, seized Percy Burrell by his spindly shoulders, and shook him like a rag doll.

"Your mother's life is in danger!" he thundered. "She and your sister need your protection. The staff, your guests, are waiting for you to step up and do your duty!"

He finally ignited a fire in Burrell's watery eyes.

"I'm no good at running an estate!" he cried.

"It doesn't matter! The responsibility is yours. Your family needs your guidance."

"I don't know how to keep them safe from a crazed lunatic!"

"Then you'll die trying, won't you?"

Burrell leaned forward and pinched the bridge of his nose. "No one has ever shown me how, you know. Paul kept it as if it were some great secret."

"Then how do you know you'll fail?"

"I'm not much good at anything except acting."

"Can you read a book?"

"Of course I can read a book. I went to Harrow and Oxford!"

"Then buy a book on running an estate. It cannot be difficult for someone with your education."

"I believe there is a book on it in the library. Paul used to dip into it for tax tables and such."

"There you are, then."

"But I'm bound to be a disappointment."

"Partridge seems like a pretty smart old fellow," I said. "I'll bet he could give you advice from time to time."

He sat for a moment, deep in thought. "Do you think so?"

"Think of it as a role. You would study how to play a role, wouldn't you?"

"Of course. When I played Bassanio in *The Merchant of Venice*, I learned the part in Italian, just to get it right."

"There you are, then. Apply the principles of being an actor to being the heir, until it starts to feel natural to you."

Percy said nothing, but sat there either deep in thought, or feeling the effects of alcohol wash over him. I could not tell which. The thing is, he didn't realize that to my employer, not actually answering back was a sign of assent.

"What are you here for again?" Percy Burrell asked.

"I was wondering if you saw anyone acting strangely under the circumstances, or someone made a comment you considered suspicious."

"Alive or dead?"

Barker gave one of his ruthless smiles. "I would prefer alive, but if it opens another line of enquiry, I won't be finicky. You've heard something, then."

"Well, a chance remark, while we were out hunting for the killer that first night."

"Who made it?"

"Algernon Kerry."

"I see. And what did he say?"

"Something about people getting what they deserve, only he wasn't talking about the killer, you see."

"Could you be a little bit more precise, Mr. Burrell? I know you've had a lot to drink, but on the other hand, you are an actor, accustomed to memorizing long passages. Where were you, to begin with?"

"By the copse of trees, on the way back home. We were facing the house, all lit up in the night. Kerry had stopped and offered me a smoke. It was some sort of South American cheroot, scented with licorice. I smoked part of it just to be polite."

"Good. Excellent, sir," the Guv said. "So, the two of you were smoking and staring at the house. Were you alone?"

"Yes. We'd been separated from the party."

"And you had your guns with you."

"Yes, Mr. Barker."

"And what did he say precisely?"

Burrell closed his eyes. "I'd mentioned that I couldn't understand why someone would go around shooting innocent people like my father, unless they were barking mad. And he said, 'Perhaps the killer feels perfectly justified in what he is doing, and believes he is righting a wrong. He may think your father was not as innocent as you believe and he got what he deserved.'"

"You must have found that unsettling."

"I did. I mean, yes, it's often a good thing to put oneself in the other man's shoes or to question someone's motives, but to accuse my father and suggest he deserved to have his brains blown out, and him lying fresh in his coffin like that . . ."

"What did you say to him?" I asked.

"Nothing. I couldn't bring myself to speak, save in anger. In fact, it was the last conversation we had. I was too young when he was first ordered to leave the island, years ago, but it appeared to me that he was a caustic sort of fellow, sharp-tongued and mean-spirited. My father had been too generous in accepting Kerry's apology and request to attend the party. But then, he was Paul's friend, not mine."

Barker crossed his arms and frowned. I suspected he was willing himself to be calm. "Your mother did not originally plan to invite Mr. Kerry to the festivities?"

"No. Apparently he sent an overture to my father, apologizing for his behavior years before, and describing his success in South

America. My parents nearly had a row over it. I recall my mother saying how polished the letter was, and Father saying he didn't think him capable of such tact."

"Do you recall the dinner party?"

"It was many years ago and I wasn't invited. Too young at the time to attend. My sister wasn't. She is two years older than I, and I thought it unfair that she and Paul got to attend and I had to stay in the nursery."

"How old was she then?"

"Fourteen, I think. Rather in the awkward stage. Pigtails and gangly legs."

The young woman I found in my bed the night before had definitely grown out of the awkward stage. In fact, I came very close to being seduced.

"When you last spoke to him," Barker asked, "did you feel Mr. Kerry knew more than he was saying, or that he was merely being—"

"An ass? Yes, I told him he was being one after the hunting party. He didn't care for my assessment. We parted company and each came back to the house on our own."

"I see. Did he come back immediately?"

"I don't know. I believe I arrived first. But then I went to play billiards. He didn't appear for an hour at best."

"So it was possible that Mr. Kerry was outside and alone for half an hour or even in the north hall signaling to a compatriot."

Burrell shrugged again. "It's possible, I suppose, but unlikely. I didn't feel he was being malicious or evil, just rude, if you know what I mean."

"We'll leave it at that," Barker said, and began to fasten Percy's collar buttons with his stubby fingers.

Percy's eyes bulged for a moment. Barker is none too gentle, and he was probably choking him in his enthusiasm to help him get ready. He pulled him to his feet, then reached behind them and put the stopper on the bottle, as if daring him to try unstopping it now.

"I suppose I'll toddle down to breakfast, then," Percy Burrell said.

"We shall see you there in twenty minutes or so."

Barker looked uncertain as to whether or not to take the decanter with him.

"You can leave it, Mr. Barker," the heir said. "It was a moment of weakness, but it has passed."

We left the room and went downstairs to our room.

"Let me play devil's advocate," I said.

"A role you were born to play."

"Now, now, there is no need for that!"

"Continue," Barker said.

"It was a stupid remark to make in front of a son who has just seen his father shot to death, but Kerry, aside from being an ass, is also a human being. A thought occurred to him and he spoke it without thinking. That doesn't mean he had an ulterior motive."

"What of the letter, then? Is it suspicious that he invited himself to this house party?"

There was a knock from the inner door. Barker stopped and unlocked it. A moment later, Mrs. Ashleigh entered from her room. She didn't want to miss anything.

"Perhaps he genuinely wanted to make amends, if for no other reason than that Olivia will receive several hundred pounds annually at least. I know it is harsh to discuss it in such terms—"

"No," Philippa broke in. "It is practical. Whom are you discussing, precisely?"

I looked to Barker, who nodded. I explained the conversation we had with the heir to the Godolphin estate, leaving out nothing but the term he had used to describe Algernon Kerry, apt as it was.

"If, as you say, Mr. Kerry insulted the family with his odious suggestion, which angered Mr. Burrell so much, perhaps it was to free himself from his company, in order to confer with whoever he intended to meet, presumably the killer."

"It's possible," I conceded, "but unlikely. Kerry is an abrasive fellow, more at home in a frontier like Brazil than a dinner party at a country house. To think he has the skill to say just the right words to free himself of Burrell's company is to give him too much credit, I think."

"You forget what he did for a living. He controlled the slaves at Paititi Limited. That requires a certain amount of coercion. It's possible what we are seeing is a performance on Mr. Kerry's part."

"A chilling thought." I replied.

"Not chilling," Philippa said. "Practical, in a diabolical way."

CHAPTER TWENTY-FOUR

A s we arrived at the dining room, Kerry was nowhere to be found. Barker asked Mrs. Ashleigh if she would be willing to ask Lady Alicia to speak to us. Not only did she agree, but the lady herself had come down to breakfast. Apparently, breakfast was the quickest way to learn if anything important had happened overnight. Mrs. Ashleigh asked if Barker could have a few words with her.

I know a Thoroughbred when I see one. Lady Alicia was near unapproachable. If I tried to speak to a woman like that, I would either babble or become tongue-tied, so I don't even try. Barker is far more egalitarian.

When Cyrus Barker invited Lady Alicia into the library, I rather thought he had his work cut out for him. I hadn't heard her say more than two words since we had arrived. I don't know whether she was naturally diffident or merely tight-lipped. Even Mrs. Ashleigh had trouble getting anything from her in the way of information. In her defense, she was reasonably attractive and if she survived the present ordeal might make some fellow a pretty if rather silent wife someday.

"Lady Alicia," the Guv said. "We are sorry for your loss and regret having to intrude upon your privacy, but I am asking questions of everyone in the hope that they might shed some light upon anything which might help us get off this island. You probably believe you don't, and in fact you may very well be right, but I would be remiss not to ask you questions. You were Paul Burrell's intended, after all. Does that seem reasonable to you?"

She nodded and adjusted her seat on the edge of her chair. She had curling chestnut-colored hair and a carefully sculpted nose that turned up nicely at the end. It was her best feature.

"Very well. Did you know Paul Burrell long?"

"We met as children at gymkhanas and county fairs," she answered in a high and cultured voice. "As I recall, he used to pull my hair. Our fathers knew each other, being the two closest landowners."

"Were there any hopes among your family of an early betrothal?"

"No, Mr. Barker. My mother would have put a stop to that, I'm afraid. She hoped for me to marry better than a Hargrave."

"Then may I ask why you haven't? You are obviously an intelligent and cultured young woman. What has brought you to a level your mother would find disappointing?"

It was not a question I would have asked. I thought he might be told to mind his own business. In fact, any other aristocrat I'd met probably would have. But then, being a private enquiry agent allows one leeway to have as much or as little tact as is required for the work.

"The family's resources have dwindled, I'm afraid. My father has debts. I had a few early offers of marriage, which I refused, but I'm running out of chances, or so my mother says. This was to be my last chance in England, you see. The next step is to try the Americans. One of the millionaire sons from Boston or Chicago might be interested in supporting a lady. It really makes me sound like a racehorse, does it not?"

I almost blushed for her. I hadn't expected her to reveal family financial problems to a pair of complete strangers. Barker seemed to take it at face value.

"Were you invited by Lady Celia?"

"I believe it was Mrs. Ashleigh who suggested my name. I gather Lady Celia just wanted to see her son married and settled."

"Were you amenable to that?"

"I have already been called a spinster publicly. It would be a relief to be married and settled. I had my heart set on it, I'm afraid. Sometimes I feel cursed."

"I do not believe in curses," Barker told her. "One makes one's own luck. Keep trying, Lady Alicia. It's a funny thing about husbands. It only takes one and you are done."

She gave a wan smile.

"I'm sure you haven't called me here to discuss my marriage woes. How may I help you?"

"Let me begin by asking if there is anything beyond the fact that people are being killed that you have found unusual here. Is anyone's behavior puzzling to you or does it seem in any way suspicious?"

"Mr. Kerry puzzles me."

"Does he? How so?"

"I've known him for ages. He was worse than Paul when he was young. A nasty little boy. I wasn't at the dinner where he disgraced himself years ago, but I saw him no more than a week later at another event. He was drunk but not belligerent.

"'I have disgraced myself, Alicia,'" he said to me. "'Papa is sending me away. You probably won't see me again, so I apologize for the mud pie I threw at your party dress on your sixth birthday.'"

"So what did you find curious?" Barker asked.

"I was surprised he came back a success. He just didn't have the knack. He tended to say what he thought and he never thought highly of anyone. I used to say his mother must have put pepper in his bottle as a child. He was a bully with a bad temper. Making money, even in South America, requires certain skills which he clearly lacks. Seeing him here with a foreign servant and a medal, it all seems impossible. He hasn't changed, you see. Still as rude as ever. So how did he succeed? Whom did he impress and how? I don't understand."

"There, you see? I had no idea you knew Mr. Kerry before this party. You have offered a fresh perspective. Does anything else puzzle you?"

"Let me think . . . I find it unusual that a doctor and his daughters were invited here. There are a few girls I know among the aristocracy that would have liked to have been asked. But then the Hargraves have always done as they liked. When one is off the mainland, one feels more pressure to conform to social standards. My mother would never wear last year's fashions, for example, while Lady Celia dresses only to please her husband. If any menu or style of decorating or activity is in fashion here this week, I am certain it is due to Mrs. Ashleigh's influence. That woman has breeding. In fact, if I know Celia, she wrote to her and asked her to take things over."

Barker turned his face my way, as if to say, "You see? I told you a woman's opinion would be helpful." Not that I disagreed, but if he were such a champion for women's opinions, why did he live in a bachelor household?

"What think you of Mrs. Fraser?"

"Smarter than she looks. Took every rubber at whist. She runs her husband around, and my papa says he is intelligent enough to be an MP."

"The French ambassador?"

"He is a bottom pincher. Oh, not mine. I saw him pinch one of the maids."

"Percy Burrell?"

"Younger brother. I saw him in a play once. A farce. I think he had more energy than talent. He always looked up to Paul. I don't know what he's going to do now."

"Lord Hargrave?"

"We knew he was in the government. He tended to drift from one department to another until he joined this new one, the Something Institute. Haven't the foggiest notion what they do, but I doubt the ambassador is here merely to pinch the maids."

"Colonel Fraser?"

"A sweet old man. Not the pinching type. Rather doddering, of course, but he must be a centenarian by now."

"Have you noticed any of the servants acting differently?"

"The dark one has been jumping about and trying to help everyone, but I suspect it was to avoid his master. I feel sorry for anyone who has to work under him. Algie is the type who pulled wings from flies, you know, and burned ants with a lens to pass the time."

"Are those impressions from years ago, or have you seen more recent evidence that he is still difficult?"

"He isn't drinking, which I suppose is a good thing. To tell the truth, I avoid him as much as possible. He doesn't look particularly well. I heard he had contracted one of those jungle diseases."

She seemed at an end, and clapped her jaw shut, as if she had said too much. I pondered whether she would be silent for days after such an outburst.

"Thank you, Lady Alicia. You have been most candid and helpful."

"Mr. Barker, if getting us off this island rests in anyone's hands, it is yours. Please track this fellow down and do whatever needs to be done. I want to go home."

Barker bowed to her. "I shall do the best I can, Your Ladyship."

She rose and gave him a look which in someone else might be considered haughty. She was an aristocrat, however, and no doubt felt that the Guv and I were no more than common peelers. I'm sure in her world that was precisely what we were.

CHAPTER TWENTY-FIVE

Breakfast was sparsely attended. The thought that someone outside the house was intent upon killing us all one by one rather put a damper on social convention. Conversation was strained, and those that tried to put on a brave face were obvious even to themselves. The colonel was telling us a long story about his time in India which, frankly, I wasn't paying strict attention to, being bracketed by the sisters Anstruther. Some of us will still obey the social conventions.

"Do you need butter, Miss Anstruther?" I asked Bella.

"Please," she said.

I reached for the dish and I was actually passing it into her hand when the house was suddenly shaken by an explosion. It was not especially loud, but it was profound. It made the cutlery on the table jump and the water in the glasses slosh. Every woman at the table shrieked at once. Barker turned in his chair and looked at me, his hand gripping Philippa's, as if to protect her.

"What devilry has that menace come up with to confound us today?" the colonel asked wearily.

Barker stood and released Philippa with a reassuring pat.

"I'm sure it's nothing," I said to my breakfast companions as I stood. It was the sort of reassuring nonsense one says at such a time. In no conceivable way was I sure that it was nothing.

Four of us—Colonel Fraser, Percy Burrell, Barker, and I—exited out the front door. Smoke rose from the back of the house. We hurried around the side, walking into a wall of dense dust and debris, and passed the bunkhouse where the young men had been recuperating. They were all standing about, covered in dirt and soot. There was something missing and it took me a moment to work it out. The outdoor privy was now little more than a gaping hole in the ground.

"Could it have ignited accidentally?" I asked. "I have heard of that happening before."

"No, Thomas," Barker said. "More likely, it was deliberately blown up. I suggest you retrieve your list of guests and servants and begin taking roll."

"You believe it was occupied?" I asked.

"I do. Blowing up an empty privy would be only a minor inconvenience and not worth the effort."

"But where do you suppose he got the dynamite?"

"He probably made it from scratch, using base materials."

I recall the characters in Jules Verne's *Mysterious Island* digging saltpeter and sulfur from the earth and making charcoal, but I had found it far-fetched at the time.

"How would someone know how to build a bomb?"

"Lad, you have built several bombs yourself."

"Yes, but that was with commercial-grade dynamite. I wouldn't know where to start if I had to do it this way."

"Aye, well, someone had the ingredients and the process locked away in his brain. Now go. See if anyone is missing."

"Yes, sir."

I pushed my way through the crowd at the kitchen door and ran upstairs to find the list I had made on my bedside table. Passing a tall dressing mirror, I noticed that I was caked in a layer of fine black powder. There were dark circles under my eyes which had begun to sting. I seized a pencil from my notebook and began checking off names. I ran downstairs again and gave the women at breakfast a fright, but only stayed long enough to count heads. I went down to the kitchen and counted everyone there before going outside to check on the male servants.

"Colonel," I called. "Is Schroeder still locked in his room?"

"He is. I checked before coming down to breakfast."

I went over to Barker, who was still standing over the malodorous hole in the ground.

"Sir, Algernon Kerry is missing."

"I suspected as much," he replied.

"That is a hellish way to go," I said.

"Agreed. I wonder if the killer felt some special antipathy toward Mr. Kerry."

I walked to the edge of the pit and looked down into the hole.

"I don't wish to speak ill of the dead, sir, but I suspect we all did. He wasn't a very pleasant fellow."

Barker nodded.

"Do you suppose this is a ruse? Kerry might not have been in there at all. He could have joined the man in the woods!"

"That's good thinking, Thomas, but I'm certain he was blown to bits. There is blood on the rocks at the base of the hole, and no one else is missing."

"Poor blighter. Do you suppose Kerry was the intended target or merely the next person unlucky enough to use the privy?"

"I suspect the assassin has been going by a list of people to kill. You may not be aware, but the gardener has been carrying on as if we weren't here. Flannan is dead, while he has been left unmolested to compost his roses."

"So, is the killer civilian or military?"

"Can a civilian shoot the pipe from a man's mouth at a hundred yards?"

"I see your point. But what I can't understand is how he does it. He seems to take a gleeful pleasure in killing us. It's like—"

"It's like he's having the time of his life," Barker growled.

"What do we do now? There is nobody to bury."

"And no priest to give him last rites."

We stopped for a moment and prayed for Kerry's soul. Though

I had no idea what his religion was, if any, we did the best we could for him. I doubt he would have done the same for us. Smoke still billowed from the pit. Eventually it would need to be covered or repaired. The gardener came forward and looked down into the hole.

Barker turned to the male servants.

"Do you gentlemen suppose you could construct a makeshift privy using scrap lumber? It will be necessary."

"We'll get to it, sir," the gardener said, pulling on his cap.

I looked at him. Like his comrades, he had prepared for our arrival, only to be met with poisonings, hardship, and fear. One man, one anonymous man, was holding all of us in his grip.

"I should have shot him when I had the chance," I said to Barker. "I should have been carrying my revolver."

"It would be best if you carried it from now on. At least until we leave the island."

Going upstairs again, I pulled my Webley out of my suitcase and made certain it was properly loaded. It wasn't merely that this man was killing people, it was that they were dying in the most ignoble of ways. Granted, one man couldn't just walk in the hall door and face everyone armed with just a pistol. But this, blowing up a fellow in his most unguarded moment or poisoning him in a way that leaves him vomiting on his knees . . . This man must hate people, I thought.

I tucked the pistol in my waistband, against my right kidney. It made me feel at least marginally safer. Then I went downstairs and out the back door again. There was activity all around. Maids were scrubbing the back windows to the kitchen. Footmen were bringing buckets of water up from the beach to throw over the paths. Men were scrubbing with brooms and brushes. A man had been killed a quarter hour before and now people were making it appear as if it had never happened.

"You're giving them all something to do," I said to Barker.

"They seem to need it."

"Have you found any evidence?"

"Blown up or blown away in the wind," my employer said.

"Mr. Kerry had family, did he not?"

"He did. You had better find Cesar and tell him to pack Mr. Kerry's belongings."

"Are you giving me something to do?" I asked.

"You look like you need it, too. You should change and wash your face while you're at it. You look like a bandicoot."

That's Barker for you. Cleanliness first. Everything reflects upon the agency, you see.

I washed and changed and went looking for Cesar. He was difficult to find. I thought perhaps he was dead as well until I found him in the chair by the window that had fallen on him. The hall was now deserted.

"Cesar?" I asked.

"I am unemployed," he said. He looked crushed.

"I know."

"It was a mistake to come here."

"Perhaps."

"He was a tyrant sometimes, but you know, I got used to it. He had his faults but he was a human being. In a way, I will miss him."

"What will you do now?" I asked, sitting down in a nearby chair I had drawn closer.

"My first thought was that I would return to Brazil, but you know, Thomas, that is thousands of miles away. I don't believe I shall ever leave this rock. I'm going to end up dead just like Mr. Kerry."

"Don't say that, Cesar. We'll get you home."

He held up a finger. "He is one man, senhor. One! Why can't we catch him? We are over a dozen. We live in fear of him? Let us organize a search party and track him down."

"We've done that half a dozen times now."

"But we're stuck here with little to do but wait. We should stay out, sleep rough, until we catch him."

"And go native, as he has?"

"*Sí!*"

"I'll suggest it to Barker."

"Forgive me, Thomas. Is your Mr. Barker all you claim he is?

Would the Frenchman who died have caught the killer by now? Could anyone catch this fellow?"

"Let Mr. Barker do his work, Cesar. He'll track down the killer in his own time. He doesn't give up. He'll go without food or sleep if necessary."

"But will that be enough? Forgive me, but I do not want to die. I like this life. Oh, not this part of it, of course, but the rest of it. There are *senhoritas* in Rio, my friend, that would break my heart. I think I would let them."

"You do that," I told him.

My mind returned to the case. What questions would the Guv ask?

"Did Mr. Kerry go down for breakfast at his usual time?"

"No, his stomach was bothering him. He suffered from ulcers, you know."

"Yes, that is an unfortunate effect of cocaine usage."

Cesar's face went blank. Somehow his pince-nez spectacles stayed perched on his nose.

"You knew, Thomas?"

"Mr. Barker knew."

"He must be very intelligent."

"He has his methods. So, Mr. Kerry took cocaine this morning and it affected his ulcers?"

"I'm not sure," Cesar said. "He was nervous. I helped him put on his best suit. You see, he was going to ask Miss Burrell to marry him today."

"What?" I asked, shocked.

"I know. Incredible, isn't it? He said it was time. His family was pressuring him to marry her, as well. If he proposed and was accepted, he told me he would split a bottle of that fine champagne with me."

"No champagne now," I said.

"No, senhor. No champagne."

I went downstairs and told Barker all that Cesar had related to me.

"So, Mr. Kerry was to propose tonight. Interesting."

"This is so messy. Kerry, who happened to be a cocaine fiend, was going to propose to Olivia Burrell to please his parents. Lord Hargrave would have let them marry, in spite of the embarrassing incident several years ago, because he wanted to see his daughter settled, but he got his head blown off."

"Life is complex," Barker said. "It only makes our work here more difficult."

"It does! You know, at home in Newington, Mac works all day to keep the house spotlessly clean. The gardeners work outside to bring the entire garden to near perfection. But it's all an illusion. It's artificial. All life is disorganized."

"Our work, Thomas, is to bring order out of chaos, no less than Mac or the Hong family who tend our gardens. People try to cover things up. They are capricious. Everybody lies to some extent. Our work is to find that thin thread, that tiny steel wire of truth, and follow it to its inevitable solution."

"Sometimes the solution doesn't make sense or it's too fantastic that someone should act in such a way."

"Our duty is to discern the truth. To understand it, to discern it, to learn from it, that may come afterward. Of course, by then we have probably started another case, which has its own problems."

CHAPTER TWENTY-SIX

I supposed when this party was planned, the concept would have been that everyone would enjoy themselves and spend much of the time talking with one another. With the host and several guests murdered, however, activities such as charades and the Minister's Cat seemed frivolous and the general spirits of the crowd were low. Catastrophes such as a death in the family might cause a normal party to break up prematurely, but we did not have that luxury. The guests played bridge or whist or billiards, or they read or sewed or talked in order to pass the time and to try not to think that they might be next to die.

Barker and I were passing through the drawing room when the Guv leaned over the sofa and spoke to Dr. Anstruther.

"Would you care for a game of billiards?" he asked.

"I'm afraid I'm not very good," the doctor said.

"Then we shall be evenly matched."

Anstruther followed us into the library, where the table stood. I set up the balls in the break box, aware that this was my employer's way of questioning him. He placed the ball on the baise-covered table and shot it with the tip of his stick.

"Had you known Lord Hargrave long, Doctor?"

"A dozen years at least. My offices are in Land's End. He came into my surgery to have a wart lanced and then he began seeing me for other things. As it turned out, we were both golfers. He put me up for his club and we have played together ever since."

"Was the invitation an attempt to bring your families closer together?"

Here Barker aimed the ivory ball in line with a red one and missed.

"As you can see, Mr. Barker, I have two unmarried daughters and he had two eligible sons, but I know my place. I understood the eldest son had to marry well. If Percy should find himself in need of a bride, however, I hoped he might look no farther than Gwendolyn or Bella. He won't find two better girls in Cornwall."

"You have every reason to be proud, sir. Mrs. Ashleigh says they are beautiful and accomplished and she is a good judge. I regret that they are in such circumstances, and shall do my best to protect them."

Anstruther tapped a ball into the pocket, and looked slightly astonished that he had done so.

"I thank you," he said.

"Is there anything you can tell me about the wounds on the bodies that might help my investigation?"

"Richard's death—Lord Hargrave, rather—was instantaneous, as was the death of the French bodyguard. He died from a stab wound under the breastbone. That is two very competent murders by the same person. This fellow is no piker."

"I see."

"I understand the killer came into the house, but the entrance has been locked. Yet someone was signaling outside, so we must assume there is an accomplice in the house. How would you suggest I keep my girls safe?"

"I would suggest all three of you move into whichever room is the largest and barricade the door at night. It is close quarters, but the safest course."

"Thank you. Of course. It sounds logical, the way you describe it. I'll do it tonight, whether the girls object to it or not."

"I've been questioning everyone, looking for something they might have seen or heard of use to me. Information that might help me learn his plan before he springs it on us. Can you think of anything that appears out of the ordinary, or some fact that might be useful?"

"I don't know if this is useful, but there is something unusual. I would not normally reveal this, but His Lordship is dead and you are the closest thing to an official on this island. You've scratched."

"What?"

"You've scratched the cue ball. That's a foul."

"So I have. What do you have to tell me?"

"His Lordship was ill. I performed an operation on him several months ago, removing a tumor from the back of his mouth, the soft palate. I suspect it had spread to his throat. I don't believe he had a year to live."

"That would certainly give him the impetus to see his sons married," Barker said.

"Indeed."

"Did His Lordship ever discuss his work?"

"With me, sir? Not a word. I gathered all his work was secret, so I didn't press him. He was very tight-lipped about what he did. Sometimes he had to break a reservation for a round of golf, but we never discussed what he did. I took it as a matter of course."

"It sounds to me, Doctor, as if you were his closest friend."

"Oh, I don't know about that. He and the colonel were very close, almost like father and son. I will admit that I owe a great deal to him. His patronage helped me to become a successful surgeon."

He stopped for a second and picked up one of the balls. Now, I understand that was against the rules. However, I saw that he was trying to stop himself from becoming emotional. His Lordship had indeed been a friend to him and he would feel that loss for some time to come. His eyes a little moist, he sniffed and set the ball down in its place again.

"Um, we were saying?"

"Would you say that His Lordship was well liked in the area?"

"I should say so. He helped several local charities and in spite of his international work always had time to judge the local flower show. I don't think you'll find anyone who suffered at his hand."

There is a look which professional men in London prefer and Dr. Anstruther seemed to personify it, even if he didn't visit London from one season to the next. He was of medium height and trim, and seemed to go in for double-breasted suits. He had wavy light-colored hair and a very trim mustache. Like most doctors I had met he had no sense of humor. Either he was born without one and hence went into medicine, or else he had had it surgically removed. He had nothing frivolous to say and I was content to let Barker do all the talking.

"You had to inform His Lordship that his illness had returned?"

"Yes, I did. He took it stoically. Beyond remarking that he had hoped for his threescore and ten, and that it was unfair to not even reach sixty, he was more concerned about his wife and family."

"Was he in pain?"

"Oh, yes, but he was a man with a strong drive to accomplish things. I suggested laudanum, but he claimed it made his head feel as if it were full of cotton, and he couldn't make good decisions."

Barker glanced my way and I knew what he was thinking: had Lord Hargrave taken laudanum when he asked us to take this case? But then I was sure he had no idea that the man in the woods would be coming to Godolphin Island.

"Did he speak to you of any personal concerns?"

"He joked about putting his affairs in order, and said he would have liked to walk Olivia down the aisle. I believe he was most concerned about Lady Celia, that she would not have someone to lean upon or to help her make decisions."

The Guv lined up another shot at the foot of the table and then stopped. "Did he imply that she was emotionally or mentally weak?"

"Both, I think. He said that when she made decisions they were often the wrong ones, so he had been making them for her for years. He loved her, but she was not a strong woman."

"I see," my employer said, and made the shot. He missed again.

Anstruther came around the table and aimed at the next ball. He sunk it in the side pocket.

"Is there anything you can say about all the murders? Was there any verisimilitude which comes to mind?"

"There was a professionalism about them all. From what I can tell, the shot to Lord Hargrave's head was dead center. The knife wound to his son was instantly fatal. The explosion that killed Algernon Kerry was at sufficient volume to kill him."

"And yet the dose of poisonous mushrooms was not sufficient to kill anyone."

"I assume that there were not enough available, or that they were not of sufficient strength to kill anyone. Difficult to gauge."

"Precisely."

"I understand there is a secret entrance that not only approaches the house, but goes all the way through it," I said. "Either the killer has been here before or he's being helped by someone."

"The person sending messages from the window," Barker stated.

"Person?" I asked. "I assume you are referring to a man."

"It doesn't take a man to send a message or to let someone into the house."

"Could he have seduced a housemaid or something?"

"Do you suppose housemaids to be of lesser virtue than other women?"

"Here now," Anstruther said. "I resent the implication. I have been watching over my daughters carefully since the first night. If they had stepped from the rooms, I would have known about it."

"I am glad to hear it, sir, but there are over a dozen women on this island, and there are all types of relationships. The killer could be someone's brother, someone's father or son. We don't know his purpose here."

"I see your problem, Mr. Barker. Your work is similar to my own. I know something is wrong with the patient, but it could have a number of causes, and I must choose the right one or it will be ineffective. It might even endanger the patient."

"Thank you, sir. You have captured my dilemma perfectly."

The doctor sunk two more balls. He was clearing the table. Cyrus Barker was obviously no billiards player. I suppose no man is expected to be good at everything. He could care less if someone thought he had no ability with the cue stick, but I found it rather embarrassing. The doctor, an admittedly mediocre player, was sweeping the table.

"Doctor, are you also Lady Hargrave's physician?"

"I am."

Two more balls went into the pocket.

"Is her health good?"

"She is well enough."

"I understand she has been sedated. Did you bring that with you, or has she used laudanum of her own?"

"That is private information, Mr. Barker. I cannot discuss it with you."

"I see. Forgive me, Doctor. Patient privacy and all that."

"Yes, sir."

Anstruther sunk the final ball. He had a preoccupied look on his face. Turning, he put his stick back in the rack.

"I need to check on my daughters," he said. "Thank you for the game."

"Well played, sir."

The doctor left. Barker picked up a piece of chalk and began chalking the tip of his stick, as if deep in thought.

Barker reached into the pocket and pulled out a red ball. He tossed it onto the table and lined up a cue ball, about halfway between two pockets. He shot. The white ball struck the red one, which hit the felt bumper at one end and jumped up into the air a few inches. It went over Barker's arm and the cue he held, then made an arc across the long table until finally it went into the right-hand pocket. The Guv grunted, put the stick in the stand on the wall, and left the room.

"Did you mean to do that?" I called after him.

He didn't answer.

CHAPTER TWENTY-SEVEN

Another day of exile had begun. Mrs. Ashleigh had been brought her breakfast, but we were expected to eat in the dining room, as always, being mere men. We were not inclined to do so early, and since we were not strictly employed, Barker and I were having a very rare morning off.

Mrs. Ashleigh was playing a hand of cards. Solitaire. It was not strictly ladylike, I supposed, but we were trapped there, and if this did not end soon, there would be further breaches of etiquette.

Seated beside her, Barker did not say a word, but pointed to where a ten could be placed alongside a knave of hearts. She moved there, and patted the stack as if it were a live thing.

"How is Lady Hargrave?" I asked.

"Difficult," she said, laying the next card. "Pass me my tea there, would you?"

He nodded and set it down near her. "How so?"

"Losing her husband and son and being trapped here. She wishes we would all go away so she can grieve for the rest of her life."

"We are here, and we cannot go anywhere until she is more forthcoming."

Philippa waved a card at him. "It is all black-and-white with you. There is no gray."

"Sometimes people expect a gray answer," he countered, "when a black-and-white one will serve."

"She is grieving!"

"While people are dying."

She played her hand and went through the stack beside her. Finding nothing to put down, she gathered up the cards.

"True," she said.

"You got nothing from her, then?"

"Do I look like the kind that would come away empty-handed? Richard was a good husband, loyal and kind, but he rather spoiled her. He anticipated her needs and now she has trouble making decisions of her own. The situation has paralyzed her, in a manner of speaking."

"I see."

"Paul was like his father, another rock to moor to. Now she is drifting. She's lost her taste for food and guests. She wants to sleep and think."

"What about Percy?"

"Percy was different. Nothing was ever expected of him. He showed no interest in law, the army, or the church. He's been acting in an amateur theater company at Land's End. He is generally far from home most of the time."

"Some men take a longer time to become what they were meant to be," Barker said. I wondered if he were speaking of himself. "Sometimes they are the better for it."

"I hope you are correct for Celia's sake. And for Percy's, for that matter."

There was a moment of silence. I assumed the discussion was over. Then I saw Barker's mustache bow into a smile.

"Yer having me on, woman," he said. Sometimes I forget he is a Scotsman. "Ye have something."

"Something," she agreed. "I don't know how helpful it is. You were looking for skeletons from the closet, were you not?"

"I was," he said. "A whole graveyard if you can manage it."

"It's ancient history, I'm afraid. Not long after coming out, she met a young man from one of the other islands. He was from a good family, and local. She didn't say it but I'm sure they were in love. They were engaged."

"When was this?"

"It must have been '55 or '56."

"And what became of him?"

"He was captain of the local lifeboat society. He was known for being fearless. He disappeared during a rescue attempt. Caught in some rigging, apparently. He washed up on the beach a few days later. The beach below us, to be precise."

"How did she react?"

"She claims she went mad for a time. She was in seclusion for over a year. A doctor came over from the mainland regularly to check on her. It was two years until she was able to enter society again. Not long after, she met Richard at a garden party. She said she was attracted to his striped jacket."

"How did you get this information from her?" the Guv asked.

"She volunteered it. She said she'd had two great loves, but that both had been taken from her. She had been with Richard thirty years, and it was not nearly enough. They were meant to be together into their old age."

"And die together in each other's arms?" he asked, a trifle harshly.

"That's the dream, isn't it? A long life and a swift death with no parting."

"Aye," he answered.

They stared at each other, sharing unspoken thoughts. I was distinctly uncomfortable.

"Did she say what his name was?"

"No. She avoided it when I asked."

"Did she say anything else?"

"Nothing. I couldn't ask any more questions without appearing to be obviously inquisitive."

"Do you think I should question her now?"

"Not yet. Let me work on her. You know, she's rather afraid of you."

"This woman, who manipulated her husband into hiring me in order to finally meet me? What is she afraid of?"

"I wish I knew. Give me two days. I shall have her ready for questioning. You will be gentle, won't you?"

"I can make no promises. Tell her that I only have a few questions for her. One in particular, in fact."

Mrs. Ashleigh frowned. "If there's just one, I can ask it for you."

"Nae," he said. "I want to be looking in her eyes when she answers me."

Mrs. Ashleigh looked troubled for a moment. She set down the cards at the end of the table. "Celia is one of my closest friends. She has been there when I needed her. I hope you do not suspect her of some crime."

"I suspect everyone and no one. I suspect myself of being especially dense at the moment."

"You shall solve this matter, Cyrus. You always do."

"I regret," Barker said, "that I have embarrassed you in any way, my dear. It was not my intent."

"You haven't. Besides, I'm not a house of cards, to be blown over by the slightest breeze."

"What shall we do now?" I asked.

"You see?" the Guv said, addressing Philippa. "The hound bays at the door, demanding sport."

"I'd like to get back to London, too," I said in my own defense.

"I have no doubt," Barker said. "Lady Hargrave is being maneuvered by Philippa, so let us move on. Why don't you speak with the kitchen staff and see if there is any missing food or suspicious activity?"

"Right," I said. "I'll push off, then."

In my defense, let me reiterate that I was young. Young people, young men especially, take chances. They delight in their own physicality. They are overflowing with vim and vigor, and so they take chances. They do stupid things. In my case, I reasoned that since I was up on the first floor and Cesar's room was in the basement, I would take the secret passage there. It would save me at least a few steps, and would provide a diversion. I had been itching to go down there again, but my time is rarely my own. Barker need not know, I told myself, which is generally how these things start, I've found.

I found the panel in the hallway, and spent several minutes looking for the latch that would unlock it before finally finding it on the frame. There was no sound, but the panel would suddenly open if pushed. I did and stepped inside. I was in a narrow passage. I stopped and lit one of the lanterns.

My way illuminated, I descended the steps. Going to the barricaded door, I tugged on the handle to see if it was still locked. It was, as was the crypt where Barker said the assassin had slept. Was he sleeping now? I wondered. Perhaps in the cave, or even at the lighthouse, on the other side of the island.

Everything seemed in order. Actually, that wasn't strictly true. It looked in order, but something told me to be on my guard. A sixth sense, perhaps. I couldn't say precisely. I thought I felt someone's presence. Had I heard a sound? I swung the lantern about, but there was nothing to be seen.

"Hello?" I said, in the palpable darkness. Yes, I know. Ridiculous. If there were someone there they were up to no earthly good, and therefore wouldn't answer.

I stood for a moment by the back panel of the bookshelves and listened. Perhaps it was someone in the library moving about a few feet away. I considered opening the secret entrance, but didn't want to give some innocent person on the other side just coming in to get a book a fit of apoplexy. I turned about to head down the stair to the basement.

Suddenly, something seized the handle of my lantern. I was in the act of turning around on the narrow staircase. I saw a blur of movement peripherally. Then something struck the back of my neck hard. My heel lost its purchase on the stair and I fell.

As I said, I was young. But I was not indestructible. This body was not built for tumbling down stairs. I hit the stone floor below. Everything hurt. Had I been knocked out by the blow, I would have fallen easily and naturally. Instead I had been tense and taut, and so had managed to hurt myself even worse. I lay spread-eagled in the darkness, waiting to see if I had broken anything. The worst thing was, the blighter had taken my lamp.

My head was banging like Big Ben itself, and there were fairy pinwheels swirling in front of my eyes. The thought occurred to me that, blast the lot, I was going to live. I'm sure the assassin was going to be disappointed.

I didn't know what he'd hit me with. It was surprisingly soft, soft compared to a cricket bat, for example. A cosh, perhaps: a leather bag filled with sand. I raised my arm, ignoring the pain in my elbow, and felt the back of my neck. There was a lump. Everything else in my body hurt, why should that part feel privileged?

One can only lie about on a cold hard floor so long. We are a race of doers. While the sun is up, we work. Slowly, I tried to stand. I hazarded this is what it was like to be ninety. Some muscles were willing to work, others weren't. Finally, I stood. Now what to do? I asked myself.

I'd been attacked. I should tell Barker. He had given me an order, however, and he expected me to complete it. Anyway, I wasn't about to climb two flights of stairs in my current condition. I fumbled with the latch and stepped into the lower hall. While I was shambling along the passage, I began to hear music. It was guitar music, coming from somewhere. Spanish music, unless I was imagining things. It grew louder as I reached Cesar's door. I knocked.

"Entra!"

Turning the knob, I stepped inside. Cesar Rojas was perched on the bed in his shirtsleeves, legs crossed in front of him, with the round guitar in his lap. It had twelve strings. I was no judge but his playing sounded quite accomplished, reminding me of classical Spanish music, both courtly and fiery at once. He was smoking a cigarette as he played.

"Eh, Thomas! What has happened to you? You look unwell."

"I fell down the stairs. H-hit from behind."

Cesar's eyebrows went up, causing his pince-nez to fall and dangle from their chain. He set aside the guitar immediately and led me to the edge of the bed to sit. Then he ran into the hall. A few minutes later, he returned with most of the staff, each of them armed with something. The housekeeper had a roll of gauze, the cook a bowl of warm water. The maid had a stack of washcloths and bottles of various patent medicines.

The next I knew, my shirt was removed, down to my singlet. My braces hung from my trousers. I was inspected all over. My knuckles were barked and bleeding; both my elbows were bruised; one shoulder was turning a yellowish purple. There was a cut across my nose. Then, of course, there was the knot on the back of my neck.

Every woman in the room managed to tsk at least once, as if I were a child who had fallen. Cotton was produced, and a half-dozen hands applied medicines, wrapped gauze, or tended bruises, while I sat, stinging from either the wound or the treatment. I would have enjoyed the cosseting of six women at once if I didn't feel so bad.

In the middle of this, Barker strolled in. Of course. He raised an eyebrow at the scene before him. He had given me a simple task, and now here I was with an imbroglio. Partridge was looking over Barker's shoulder disapprovingly. I was beguiling his staff and keeping them from their duties. Half naked, no less.

"What happened?" Barker asked flatly.

"I was struck from behind," I said.

"Where?"

"In the passage."

Hastily, I pulled up my shirt. One by one, my Florence Nightingales returned to their duties. Eventually, it was just Barker, myself, and Cesar.

The latter donned his jacket and put away his strange guitar in a case. He adjusted his pince-nez on his nose.

"I forgot to ask the staff your question, sir," I said.

My employer gave me a withering look.

CHAPTER TWENTY-EIGHT

That evening, he and Philippa dined upstairs while I sat below, among the regular guests collecting any tidbits of information I could find. The latter were few and far between because the atmosphere at these events was solemn both because of the danger and the fact that Mrs. Ashleigh had chosen to leave, while Lady Hargrave was sedated. The guests were left to fend for themselves.

When dinner was over, I went upstairs. In our room, Barker rose from his chair.

"It's time for another attempt to make an ally of Henri Gascoigne."

We found the French ambassador sitting with Colonel Fraser in his room with a brandy at their elbows. When we knocked and entered, Gascoigne frowned. Barker chose to ignore it, sitting down beside him. I sat at the far end.

"Good evening, Colonel. Your Excellency."

"Evening, Barker."

"I hope you gentlemen are coming to terms."

"That isn't your business, sir," Gascoigne said.

He glared at us with those bulbous, unfriendly eyes of his. His forehead was large but his chin was delicate. He was very sallow. I wondered how much his countenance was altered by the fact that almost an entire country despised him and conspired to kill him.

"My business is to keep you alive, sir."

"You've been sacked."

"I'm afraid you haven't the right to sack me, monsieur. You didn't initiate the contract between Lord Hargrave and myself. As far as I'm concerned, I shall protect you until I decide not to."

"You're mad!" Gascoigne said.

"I have been called worse. Now as I recall, an alliance is in the offing between Germany and England down in Zanzibar. Bismarck has gunboats down there, but if we bring in our navy, it will prove embarrassing, since our royal family is also German. I suspect the RUSI will suggest a trade, such as the island of Helgoland for Zanzibar, which I believe leaves France out in the cold."

"Hang it!" Fraser cried. "I was going to get to that eventually!"

"Meanwhile, the French explorer Colonel Montiel has been signing treaties with native kings all along the west coast and just about has the area sewn up."

"How do you know all this?" Gascoigne demanded.

"I am in the intelligence business. Though my firm is small, I have excellent information sources within the British government. As soon as Lord Hargrave told me a treaty was afoot, I began gathering information from several quarters. I now owe a number of favors, but I believe I have sufficiently educated myself on the subject of Anglo-French relations. You, monsieur, have made yourself powerful enemies in Germany by championing Alsace-Lorraine's cause for freedom."

"I am from Lorraine. It was not fair that Germany should capture my homeland by force simply because a portion of the population speaks a dialect of German."

Barker sat in that near immobile way he had, as if he were carved of wax.

"Le Figaro claims you have been attacked twice recently," he said.

"Three times, Mr. Barker. This week someone tried to throw a bomb under my carriage. It is why Delacroix came along. All these attempts on my life have been by German students, all of them members of so-called university Mensur clubs. Are you familiar with them?"

As it happened, we were. They were fencing schools in Germany where students showed their bravery with dueling scars on the left cheek or jaw. These groups were conservative and heavily nationalistic. One needn't hire an assassin when a teen would willingly do the work for free in order to be considered a hero.

"I have fought German imperialism since 1871 and they hate me for it. I wanted to work with England to curtail the imperial strategies of Germany, but until recently my entreaties fell on deaf ears. Richard, Lord Hargrave, was the first to suggest we come to terms."

"I must admit I had my doubts," Fraser admitted. "The French and English have been natural enemies for centuries. But now Bismarck has unified Germany and the kaiser wants more gunboats and as many territories around the globe as he can scoop up. A treaty between England and French makes sense in order to balance power."

"The colonel and I were just discussing this fellow outside," Gascoigne said.

"What is his game?" Colonel Fraser asked. "He shoots Lord Hargrave and kills Delacroix. Then for little or no reason, he stabs Richard's son, as if in retribution. Then he kills the lighthouse keeper and tries to poison everyone. There is no rhyme or reason to what he does."

"Oh, I disagree," Barker said, showing his square, white teeth. "He is choosing his targets very carefully. His Lordship was shot, Kerry was blown to bits. Mr. Flannan was speared in order to incapacitate the lighthouse. I suspect your friend Mr. Delacroix was a kind of test. Our intruder wanted to try his skills against a famous fighter."

"I cannot believe Antoine lost to anyone!" the ambassador said, pinching the bridge of his nose.

Barker and Fraser could only nod in sympathy. Anyone can hold a gun and pull a trigger, but to take on a fighter of Delacroix's caliber and win was another matter entirely.

"This fellow is strong," I said. "He is resourceful, intelligent, educated, clever, and tough. He's a very dangerous adversary."

"Now I wish you and Delacroix together could have gone after him," Gascoigne said wistfully.

"Perhaps that is why the man in the woods killed him when he did. Together you would have been formidable," Fraser said.

"Wishing won't save any of us, gentlemen. Tell me, Your Excellency, to your knowledge is there a bounty on your head? Has the German government offered any money that might attract a professional killer instead of the inept students that have come after you so far?"

"I don't know about inept. I have been nearly killed twice!"

"A bad choice of words. I apologize. The question stands."

"If there is, I have not heard of one. I think I know enough informants that if such an offer was made I should have heard about it. An anti-French assassination plot would attract attention."

"However," Colonel Fraser said. "If someone were to visit the German embassy with a plan that is in their best interest, they might encourage it and fund it afterward."

"That is so," the ambassador agreed. "If the plan failed there is nothing to connect it to the embassy. If it succeeded, they might or might not pay them."

"There is a hole in your logic, however," Barker said. "By shooting Lord Hargrave they drove you inside under stronger protection. It would have been far better to create conditions under which you felt safe enough to come out on the lawn, where you could be felled. If the assassin's sole purpose here were to shoot you, he is going about it the wrong way."

"So I am safe to go about my business?" Gascoigne asked.

"I wish I could tell you otherwise, but I still suspect you are a target, if not the target. It may even be possible that the targets are logjammed and by presenting yourself in public you will precipitate a slaughter. Needless to say, I would prefer to avoid that."

"I'm rather tired of sitting about cooped up in this house without fresh air and sunshine. It is too much like some conferences I have attended. But I can endure it for at least a few more days."

"Excuse me, Barker," the colonel said. "You say you are trying to decide if these killings are politically motivated, but what else could they be? Lord Hargrave was practically a saint. He'd never cheat on his wife, whom he loved. He adored his children. He was generous to a fault. He was a great master to work for and a fine man to work with. His death was either a political assassination or the work of a madman."

"He was no madman, sir," I put in. "I have seen him twice."

"Twice!" Gascoigne barked. "Under what circumstances?"

I told them about both encounters with the man in the woods.

"He was tanned and healthy looking. He looked rested and well fed. I got the impression he could go on for days."

"Was he a young man?" Colonel Fraser asked.

"Youngish. Early thirties, perhaps. Definitely English."

"Was he well set up and muscular?"

"Yes, I would say so."

"He sounds like a soldier of fortune."

I considered it, recalling his build, his posture, and his manner.

"He did have something of the soldier about him, I'll admit."

Gascoigne moved to the edge of his chair in excitement. "Then what else could it be? He is a professional soldier. He's being paid to come here and shoot, if not at all of us, then at least a list of individuals. It has to be politically motivated."

"I feel there is something else we don't know," Barker said. "Regardless, I suggest we keep His Excellency barricaded for a few more days until . . . Well, until something happens to make us change our minds. Agreed?"

Both older men nodded.

"You are both wiser and more experienced in political matters than I, sirs. I ask that you continue to turn over in your mind various scenarios that explain the situation we find ourselves in. In the meantime we shall continue to batten the hatches."

We all stood and shook hands formally, though the colonel had to shake with his uninjured hand.

"We may have gotten off on the wrong foot, Mr. Barker," said the ambassador. "Thank you for your willingness to help."

"Not at all, sir. We both want the same thing, a safe return to the mainland, and there is no reason we cannot work together."

Cyrus Barker had accomplished his objective, and it was through diplomacy. He didn't have to punch anyone or throw them over his shoulder. He merely had to lay aside several insults which Gascoigne had made. Was he reinstated as leader? Perhaps not, but he had the freedom to attempt whatever he thought might work, and could continue investigating, which amounted to the same thing.

"Why didn't you tell me you had researched Anglo-French relations on the day we were hired?" I asked, when we were on the stair.

"That is not the question, Mr. Llewelyn."

"What is it, then, sir?"

"You are the researcher. Why did you not think of it yourself?"

Still smarting from the remark, I dressed for dinner and went downstairs. Dinner was to be roast lamb and a hot curry. Mrs. Albans had even attempted a Cornwallian version of tandoori chicken. Unfortunately, the killer outside had grown restless. Halfway through dinner, he began shooting at the shuttered windows in the hall. We were all safe in the dining room, but it was stressing, especially to the ladies.

"He wants to remind us he is still outside and he cannot leave any more than we can," the ambassador said to us all.

"Does the fellow ever get tired of shooting at us?" I demanded.

"Be careful what you ask," the colonel said. "When he is resting he devises new weapons. He is liable to build a siege tower next."

Barker came down from dinner and surveyed the wreckage. Glass was being swept up by the footmen.

"Thomas, so far he has not shot you," Barker said.

"He tried on two occasions," I pointed out. "What do you want me to do?"

"I thought you might take out the horse and cart, and see if you can pry off several planks from the docks. We may need to barricade the lower windows, to keep the killer from coming in. You can employ the barrel beside you, as we did several days ago when we searched for Delacroix."

"Yes, sir."

It was my occupation. If an archer needed a target, I would hold an apple on my head. If Barker was teaching a lesson in his antagonistics classes, it was I who absorbed a kick across the room into a chair and over it. If we needed wood to cover the windows, then I was the logical person to go get it. Barker did the thinking and I did the legwork. It was a proper division of labor. I was a full enquiry agent now, however. Just once I'd like to sit about and cogitate brilliant strategies for some other bloke to implement.

I knew horses. In fact, I had one of my own, a bay mare named Juno who could run like the wind. The Percheron who pulled the cart was a big, gray dappled fellow named Apollo. I suspect that having a horse named after a Greek or Roman god showed that one had received a classical education. Unfortunately, it meant at least six Apollos in any one given square mile of London.

I tacked Apollo myself and let the stable hand lift the barrel up on the seat. When I was ready he opened the stable doors, and we clopped out into the drive. Immediately there was the sound of a shot, and Apollo reared up and bellowed. As I feared, the killer had shot at our horse. The bullet had passed into the thick flesh of the animal's neck.

I tightened the reins and bore down while Apollo protested his treatment. Then I began to click my tongue, encouraging him to go backward. The horse shook his head in pain or annoyance, but slowly began to obey.

He was being too slow, unfortunately. The barrel beside me bucked once, twice, thrice as bullets passed into it. I could actually hear them ricocheting around the interior. We reached the incline going up into the barn, and it was far easier to get the cart to go down than to go up backward. Meanwhile, the bullets kept coming in my direction, and Apollo continued to screech because of his wound. Finally I began to get some traction and the vehicle eased back into the barn. I thought the horse made too tempting a target and was sure he would be shot again, but I was glad to be wrong.

I jumped down and began unharnessing the gelding. I sent the boy with a note to Dr. Anstruther, asking if there were anything he might be able to do. The chances were small he would answer. Medical doctors do not work on animals. He came nonetheless, and after a full bottle of rubbing alcohol, a lot of straining, and a half hour, he was able to get the bullet out again. Apollo would live to pull his cart another day.

"You did the best you could, lad," Barker said.

Yes, that's it. It was my fault. The plan was sound, but I had somehow performed wrong. I received the official blame for the failure of the plan well enough, but I was not fit company for the rest of the night. I went to bed hearing bullets rattling around inside my skull.

CHAPTER TWENTY-NINE

Cyrus Barker is a sound sleeper. Something about a clear conscience, perhaps. As soon as he places his head on the pillow, the man is unconscious until the first birds in London awaken him shortly after five A.M. His senses are alert the rest of the day, but at night he sleeps well unless something occurs. Then he is instantly awake, having rested so well.

I, on the other hand, suffer from insomnia. I get up and read, I toss and turn, drink hot milk, and wait for dawn to appear. Sometimes I feel the world slowly revolving under me. Most of the time it is a curse, but every now and then something occurs that makes me, if not exactly happy, then at least useful.

"Sir. Sir!"

"What is it?" Barker demanded, sitting up immediately. He seized his dark spectacles and put them on.

"I hear voices shouting."

"Damn and blast!" Barker cried, pushing his covers back. "From now until we get off this island, we are sleeping in our street clothes!"

We pulled on trousers and braces, shoes and hose, and our jackets. The rest of our accoutrements were unnecessary. I was looking over the sill while tying my pumps.

"I think something is on fire. I see some kind of shimmering light outside."

"Back or front?" Barker asked.

"The back."

"That's good. There's the kitchen and a stout rain barrel back there. Come!"

We hurried down the staircase, then the back stair, coming out into a crowd of servants almost blocking it.

"Make way!" Barker bawled. Everyone quickly moved out of our way.

We ran into the area between the kitchen and the outbuildings. From what I could see, the bunkhouse was on fire. Partridge was pressing people in line to form a makeshift fire brigade, and we naturally joined in. The fire did not appear to come from within, but probably had been set. It was arson.

"I smell kerosene," Barker said in my ear as he handed me the first bucket of water to pass along. "Our assassin probably looted it from the lighthouse stores!"

I watched as the flames rose from the roof of the structure. The male servants who a week before had been so ill, now had black smudges and grim expressions on their faces.

It was maddening, waiting for the killer to make his move and then being powerless to stop him when he did. Colonel Fraser had instituted excursions, all the men hunting for him, but each time he had easily slipped through the net. All the advantage was on his side. He was making us look like amateurs.

"Keep an eye out for the French ambassador, and the Burrell family while you are at it," Barker ordered.

"Yes, sir. Cesar!"

Cesar was in the doorway, passing along a large soup pot full of water. "Si, Thomas?"

"Make sure none of the family or guests come into the yard. It isn't safe."

"They won't get by me."

The men opened the bunkhouse doors and began to apply water

both inside and out to the hungry fire. We were making headway. A few more buckets and it might be out. The young servants attacked the smoldering area with axes and hammers. Boards fell to the ground and there were showers of sparks flying upward in the night.

Just then I saw Percy Burrell coming between the main building and the bunkhouse. Having been thwarted in an attempt to come out the back door, he must have come around from the front. If what the Guv said was true, his life was in danger. I passed a bucket along, then came out of the fire line.

"Mr. Burrell, you shouldn't be here," I said. "It is too dangerous."

The heir began to say something. I had him by the shoulders when there was a sudden movement I couldn't account for. I looked down at him, puzzled, when I saw something protruding from his breast through the fabric of his jacket. It was an arrowhead. I turned him about and saw the arrow protruding from his back. With a groan, Percy collapsed into my arms. Barker hurried over and took one arm while I took the other and Cesar held the door for us to carry him into the house, to Partridge's office. Percy was half conscious, while I was merely incoherent.

"Where did . . . ? How did he . . . ? I mean, a bow and arrow?"

"It's a traditional weapon not too difficult to make from materials on the island," my employer explained.

"But he's got a rifle. What does he need a bow and arrow for?"

"Dr. Anstruther!" Barker called at the doctor, who was just coming down the stairs.

The doctor came in, assessed the damage as if he saw arrow wounds every day, and went to work.

"Hold him steady," Anstruther ordered.

He pulled a scalpel from his bag, and began cutting the jacket and shirt. The arrow protruded two inches from his chest and at least four from his back. The arrow was not pretty, but was effective.

Anstruther removed a pair of pliers from his bag, and without preamble, seized the arrow and broke off the shaft at the feathers with the pliers. Percy screamed.

"This will not be pleasant," the doctor continued, and began to work the arrow out from the front. The movement was too much for our acting friend, who promptly fainted.

The wound began to bleed. Barker pulled a clean handkerchief from his coat pocket and held it to the wound.

"Get Bella," the doctor told me. "She is a competent nurse. Tell her I need her here at once."

I turned, glancing in Barker's direction to see if he would contradict the order for any reason. He did not. I went upstairs in search of the dark-haired daughter, and found her on the landing with all the women, now fully dressed though it was three o'clock in the morning, and grouped around Lady Hargrave, who was crying. News ran quickly through this house.

Bella came forward quickly when she saw me.

"How is he?" she asked.

"It's hard to say. He has fainted from the pain. Your father has requested you."

She nodded as if such information were expected and hurried downstairs. I looked about. Philippa Ashleigh was comforting her old friend. Lady Alicia was standing by the window, looking alone and bereft. Her intended had died only a few days before, but already others had died since then.

Gwendolyn looked like someone who had been invited to a party but wasn't having a good time. My first impression of her had changed. She was a bauble and little else. Her less beautiful sister was worth twice what she was.

Then I saw Olivia in the far back of the room. Her arms were crossed and she was staring intently at me. Her eyes were on fire. She was no longer angry that I had turned her down. No, she was telling me that she was right. Someone was going after the family itself. She was quickly becoming the sole remaining heir of the Burrell family.

My quest was accomplished; I had alerted Bella. I nodded to Olivia and turned. Then I hurried downstairs to get word about Percy's condition.

The colonel was pacing below stairs, puffing an old briar between his false teeth like a firebox emitting steam. The kitchen was full of soot-covered menservants drinking tea. The fire was out. It had been a ruse to get at Burrell, I assumed. A bow and arrow. Somehow, I couldn't get my head around that. I couldn't make a bow and arrow from written plans and the finest wood. The killer had made his in the woods with almost no plans or tools at all. What sort of person can do that? But then what sort of person could shoot an arrow into another living human being and rejoice when it reaches its target?

A half hour later, the door opened, and Bella came out, the cuffs of her gown stained with blood. She tried to put a brave face on it, perhaps to please her father, but in the passage she broke into tears and then ran up the stairs to her room.

"Is he going to live?" Cesar asked, beside me.

Barker came out with a face like thunder, and shook his head. I didn't know if he even heard the question. The colonel smothered a curse.

I sagged against the wall. Some bodyguards we were, I thought. We might as well just line the family up to be executed. I don't generally doubt the Guv's abilities, but even I wondered what he was up to. There had to be some way to protect the guests and family from utter destruction. If and when news like this got out in London, provided we lived to return, could we ever hold up our heads again?

"There's nothing to see here," Barker said solemnly, and in unison we all turned and walked away. I was tired and needed to go to bed but I was certain sleep would elude me.

Cesar came forward, his eyes cast down to the ground. "Senhor, is there anything I can do? Do you need help moving him to the crypt?"

"No, Mr. Rojas. I believe we've got it this time. You can go to bed. But thank you."

He patted Cesar on the shoulder and the latter turned and went off to his room.

"We'll move the body in the morning," Barker said. "Let's return to our rooms."

We went upstairs again. The women had all gone to their rooms as well. A pall hung over the building. It was like the House of

Usher. Godolphin House was doomed. We were blind if we thought we could change fate.

Barker was not inclined to talk and for once in my life neither was I. We went to bed in our clothing, wondering if another crisis could possibly occur in the middle of the night. This killer was indefatigable. I tossed and turned the rest of the night.

Half asleep, I convinced myself that somehow we were responsible, that we had somehow imported this killer with us and wrought destruction on this unsuspecting family. But how? I wondered. What could we do that was different, without prior knowledge of what would happen? I cudgeled my brain to find a way to assess blame to myself or the agency, and fell into a fitful slumber.

I woke to the sound of a fulmar's cry and the sunlight shining into the room. It splashed scarlet rays of light against the wallpaper.

I got up and did my best to look presentable, while Barker slept. I tied my shoes and tie, and ran a comb through my unruly hair. Outside in the hall, I heard a sound. I crossed to the door and opened it. Philippa Ashleigh was just unlocking her door. She looked all in.

"Lady Celia was up all night," she said. "I finally convinced her to take some laudanum. This is a terrible thing, Thomas."

"Yes, ma'am."

"Cyrus will have to do something. We're running out of people on the island."

"He'll think of something," I said.

"Sometimes I envy you your disposition, Thomas."

"You should have heard it last night," I said. "You'd have had a hard time finding anything to envy then."

"How is Cyrus?"

"Asleep. Do you suppose he feels guilty about this?"

"I fear he does. He rarely blames anyone but himself. This must be killing him."

"He was wont to turn this case down, you know. Lord Hargrave insisted."

"Now you're making me feel bad. It was just that Celia wanted to meet him, to see how we were together. She had tried to play cupid for her sons and daughter. She wanted to do the same for us."

"What do you mean?" I asked. "The two of you are already a couple."

"Yes, but she thought she could convince him to . . . No, it was just a mistake."

"What? What was?"

"She wanted to convince Cyrus to propose, you see."

"Ah?" I said. "Really?"

"As I said, it was a stupid mistake. Now she is paying for it worst of all. I've got to go in. I'm completely exhausted."

She went into her room and I returned to Barker's. He was propped in bed with his dark-lensed spectacles on, and the covers pulled up to his chin. The scarlet sunlight was playing upon his sheets and counterpane, and he watched it morosely.

" 'Red sky at morning,' " he said. " 'Sailor, take warning.' We're in for a blow tonight."

CHAPTER THIRTY

I thought there was something ominous about the red light streaming in, tingeing everything bloodred. Fortunately, it burned off with the full arrival of the sun, and all was bathed in butter yellow again. It had none of us fooled, however. We all knew bloodred was the appropriate color and this benign sunniness an illusion. The breakfast table was all silence and gloom. Lady Hargrave did not come down that morning. Probably she was still sedated.

Seated were Colonel Fraser, his wife, Dr. Anstruther, his daughters, Olivia, Lady Alicia, the French ambassador, Barker, Philippa Ashleigh, and myself. Fully half of the table was now empty. As if that weren't enough, I was seated next to Millicent Fraser, not the most personable of women. A table of beautiful women, and I was seated next to . . . Well, I won't disparage the woman further. I'm certain Rebecca Mocatta would be very glad I was seated where I was.

Cesar was moving about with the tray of kippers, trying to interest the lackadaisical crowd in his wares. I think he felt it was his duty to try to jolly us up a little, so he was going about the table greeting us, though the meal was a buffet from a sideboard. Needless to say, it was an uphill battle, and he finally left in defeat.

"Funny little Spaniard," Mrs. Fraser sniffed.

"He is Brazilian, ma'am."

"Surely not," she said. "Venezuelan or Peruvian, perhaps."

"He is from Rio de Janeiro. He speaks Portuguese."

"Mr. Llewelyn, I was born and raised in Oporto. My family imports port wine to England. Portuguese is my native tongue. Your fellow speaks it, but with an atrocious accent. If he is a Brazilian, I'll eat my bonnet. It will be more palatable than this smoked fish he has foisted upon us."

I began to get a headache between my eyes. All this intrigue was making me ill. I begged my neighbors pardon and left the table. I decided to settle this matter right away.

Downstairs, they were setting the table for the servants' breakfast. The rest of the kippers were sitting in the middle of the table. Cesar was in the kitchen, preparing to take up some oatmeal that would probably be as unwanted as the kippers.

"Cesar!" I said.

"Thomas. Is something wrong with the food?"

"Cesar, come into the hall for a minute."

He followed me, with a curious expression on his face. "What is it?" he asked.

"Cesar, you told me you were from Rio. Mrs. Fraser is from Portugal and she just told me you barely speak a word of Portuguese."

"I speak South American Portuguese just fine! She is being a . . . , what is the word? A high-and-mighty?"

"A snob?"

"Si! A snob. Very well, I wasn't born in Rio. Mr. Kerry said to tell people that I was. It is more fashionable than the truth, which is that I was born in a hut in the jungle along the Venezuelan border. The war killed my family and I was displaced. I saved his life and he felt obligated to give me a situation, but he would not have a jungle boy working for him. He taught me himself how to be a proper servant. That is why I tolerated how he treated me."

"So, you weren't a bookkeeper either. I wish you had been honest with me," I said. "Lying when people are being murdered right and left looks highly suspicious."

"I am sorry. When he was alive, I knew Mr. Kerry would not let me tell you, and there seemed no need to tell you about it later."

"Well, try to be honest from now on, would you? It's hard enough trying to work out what's really going on here without having people lying to me."

I went back to my seat.

"You were right," I told Mrs. Fraser. "Venezuelan."

"I told you so."

I sipped my coffee. It had gone cold. I drank it anyway. Barker left the table with his chair under his arm. I met him in the hall.

"What should we do this morning?" I asked.

"I have a duty for you. Pray imagine a pair of invisible handcuffs. One link is around your wrist. The other is around Olivia Burrell's. Do not let her out of your sight. Whatever she wants to do, do it with her. If she wants to knit, hold her yarn. If she wants to play cards, you are her partner. Above all keep her away from any windows. There is one heir left in this family. Let us see if we can at least keep her alive."

"Yes, sir."

"And, Thomas, make sure you are armed. If it looks as if her life is in danger, don't hesitate to shoot someone. I'll accept the responsibility."

"Where are you going with the chair?" I asked.

"I'm overseeing the repair of that front window. All signs point to there being a gale coming in tonight. We'll try to use the glass from the burned-out bunkhouse."

I went. If I knew Olivia Burrell, she didn't want to knit or play cards. She was more interested in getting better acquainted.

I went upstairs and took my Webley from my suitcase, again. Mac had oiled it before we left. That seemed like months ago now, and a continent away.

Olivia proved elusive, but I finally found her in the library, trying to interest herself in a book. She was too near the shuttered window for my taste.

"Come away from there," I insisted, and drew the curtain.

"What's going on?" she asked.

"You got your wish. I am to be your personal bodyguard, and I am armed."

"Mr. Llewelyn, that wasn't my wish," she said. "My brothers are dead. Both of them. Father is dead. Algie is dead."

"You called him Algie?" I asked.

"Stop it. You're terrible."

"Forgive me. Barker says I'm not supposed to leave your side all day," I told her.

"The last of the heirs of Godolphin?"

"Something like that."

"Would you leap in the way of someone trying to kill me?"

"I would."

"That's romantic, in a way. Not that it matters much now, as I'm as good as dead. My only hope is that after I'm gone, the madman outside will be satisfied and go away without hurting anyone else."

"Mr. Barker believes the killer is after the French ambassador. He is shooting random people hoping to draw him out."

Very well, so Barker hadn't said that. The truth was, I had no idea what he believed, but I wanted this girl not to worry.

"So what shall we do?" I added.

"Read to me. Something romantic. Anything to get my mind off what's happening."

"Jane Austen, perhaps, or the Brontë sisters?"

"I've read them several times."

"Then choose a book. There's an entire library here."

"So I'm to be bored to death, then?"

"Choose one!"

She got up from the chair and looked among the shelves. After five minutes she returned with a yellow-backed novel.

"'The Rake's Deliverance,'" I read.

"My choice."

"Very well," I said. "Have a seat."

I began to read. The novel was about a young English lord, brought to his estate in Lancashire by his mother after debauching himself in London and running up a large debt. His mother, as it so happens, was trying to find him a wife. He was looking forward to inspecting the candidates. He also was interested in inspecting the new housemaid.

"Wait! This is improper!" I said. "Where did you get this?"

"It was Paul's. He kept it in the corner, up on the top shelf. You said it was my choice."

"I'm not going to read this."

"You have to. Your boss said so, did he not?"

"You're just tormenting me."

"I need to be distracted. I've read every book of interest in this library, save this one. Read it to me. Or will I have to speak to Barker?"

"That's blackmail."

"Call it what you will. Now, read!"

I continued. It wasn't as bad as I feared. When the actions became explicit, the terminology became so vague and quaint that one found oneself wanting to chuckle.

A short while later, Philippa came into the room. I immediately began a long discourse on eighteenth-century literature. Fortunately, Olivia did not start or look guilty in any way.

"I know what's going on, Thomas," she said, taking me aside. "You need not invent a lecture on my account."

I swallowed. "You do?"

"I suppose you must be about your duties and sometimes that involves being a bodyguard to young women."

"Oh, er, yes, ma'am."

"I propose a trade. I have a pistol in my reticule. I will watch Miss Burrell while you look after your employer. I cannot do a thing with him."

Barker had seemed perfectly normal when I left him, I thought.

"What seems to be the trouble?"

"First he took a chair out onto the lawn and tipped it against the building, daring the killer to shoot at him. Now he's sulking because his new friend has chosen not to come out and play."

"He gets that way, sometimes, when things do not go his way. It's as if he thinks any action is better than no action."

She pointed a finger at me. "That's it, precisely. Anyway, my nerves cannot take it another minute."

"Very well. I accept your trade. I'll see if I can get Mr. Barker out of the doldrums."

As I left, I saw Olivia Burrell cross her arms and push out her lower lip. Let Mrs. Ashleigh finish the story, I thought.

CHAPTER THIRTY-ONE

I found Barker sitting fully dressed on his pillows with his arms crossed and his feet straight out in front of him. I recognized the pose. Yes, he was brooding. Nobody ever talks about a brooding Pole or a brooding Chinaman, but Scotsmen are known for it. It was good that the weather was too warm for a fire to stare into or there would be no word from him all day.

"What's going on?" I asked.

"I thought you were guarding Miss Burrell."

"Mrs. Ashleigh took over for me. She was armed and I didn't want to argue with her."

"She sent you here, didn't she?"

"Sir, I am not going to be your Friar Lawrence. That's from *Romeo and Juliet*."

"I know where it's from."

"What seems to be the problem, sir?"

"I am thwarted. Lady Hargrave has not given me permission to view the contents of the safe, nor will she answer my questions."

"Can you move around her?" I asked.

"No, not from where I stand."

I considered the matter. I walked over to the window and dared move the curtain aside with one finger.

"In such circumstances, you generally tell me to go back to the beginning and start over."

Cyrus Barker sat for several seconds without moving.

"You're right," he said. "In fact, I need to interview someone right now."

"Who?" I asked, sitting down on my bed.

"You, Mr. Llewelyn."

"You want to interview me?"

"If you don't mind."

I lay down on my bed, as he had.

"Sure, ask any question you want," I said.

"That's no proper way to conduct an interview. Get out of bed and sit there in that chair."

I grumbled a bit. Perhaps more than a bit. I had just pummeled my pillow until it was comfortable. Not too cold or too hot, not lumpy or flat. Just right. Now with the greatest reluctance, I abandoned it.

I sat in the hard wooden chair he indicated. It seemed unnecessarily hard after the softness of the bed. He came forward and put the lit lamp on a table at my side. Right near my face. I could smell the hot metal and the oil.

"I'm ready, I suppose."

"This fellow that you alone have seen twice, when did you first see him?"

"In the hall by the kitchen."

"How was he dressed?"

"In a suit. Like a footman."

"Did it fit him?"

I screwed up my face in thought.

"Can't remember."

"Describe him. In detail."

"A little under six feet, well built, about thirty years of age, I'd say. His hair was light brown or perhaps dark blond. Light-colored eyes, blue or green. He had a mustache and a short beard. Very tanned."

"Did he act out of the ordinary?"

"Far from it. I took him for a member of the staff. He was carrying a piece of luggage on his shoulder."

"Was it a large piece?"

"I believe so. Is that important?"

"He may have been using it to conceal the rifle."

"Ah."

"What did he say to you?"

"I asked him where the housekeeper was and he pointed her out."

"So, he must have known her on sight."

"Yes, I suppose so."

"Interesting. Then what happened?"

"Nothing, really. Cesar and I went up to the housekeeper, and I didn't notice where he went."

I tried to get comfortable in the bottom-numbing chair. It was impossible.

"The second time you were outside, as I recall."

"Yes, I was coming from a dip and I spotted him among the rocks on the west side of the house."

"What was he doing there?"

"Just watching, I think. His hair was wet, too. He was sitting on a large rock with his feet dangling over the side."

"How was he dressed then?"

"Workman's clothes. He wore a singlet with braces. He had boots. Everything looked well-worn, from what I could see, and he held a rifle."

"What was his manner?"

"Very relaxed."

"He said hello to you?"

"Yes, after dropping a pebble on my head. That was disconcerting. With that rifle of his he could have shot me on the spot. He did not conceal who he was."

"Why do you suppose he spoke to you, lad?"

I considered the question for a few moments.

"Because he was bored and wanted to talk to someone. And I suppose it was to say he had complete power and could do whatever he liked. He told me he was having the time of his life."

I could barely make out Barker's face in the shadow but he nodded. He agreed with me.

"And you just walked into the house unmolested?"

"Yes, sir. Rather hurriedly," I said, thinking back to that moment. "I thought he could shoot me at any time."

"Is there anything you can recall that you have omitted to tell
me about this investigation?"

"There is something about Cesar."

"What about him?"

"He told me they had been in London before they arrived here.
I also found out he's not Brazilian. He's from Venezuela."

"How did you learn this?"

"Mrs. Fraser called him a Spaniard and he confirmed it.
Apparently she's from Oporto."

"Do you think it relevant?"

"To a Brazilian, perhaps. Not to me."

"Did he actually say he was Brazilian or did you infer it?"

"He may have said he came from Brazil. That doesn't mean
the same thing."

"True."

"He might have been more obvious if he had been speaking in
Spanish instead of English."

"Or Gaelic," Barker said.

"Or Welsh," I added.

"Hmmm."

"Any more questions?"

"I'm thinking."

"Can I lie in bed while you think?"

"No."

"Blast!"

"You haven't earned your rest yet. Talk to me. Tell me about
something."

"Something. Um . . . The library is nice here."

"I've seen it but I doubt I have the time to peruse it. Tell me
about it."

"It goes back a century or two, but the books appear to have
been read, not like some that you see that are just for show. There

are a lot of governmental journals and histories. Obviously, they are His Lordship's. Lady Hargrave tends to read more romantic fiction of the *Mary Barton* variety."

"Continue."

"What can I say? There are books of all sorts. No foreign editions. Modern, as well as antique. There are a lot of journals, which must be difficult to deliver, a big family Bible on a stand, collected editions of Dickens and Thackeray. The usual. All in all, a rather enviable library."

Barker raised a hand slowly and smoothed his mustache.

"All right, what have I done now?"

The Guv leaned forward so I saw his features lit one by one, like crags on a Scottish mountain awaiting the sun.

"Not you, lad. Me. It may have been staring me in the face this entire time."

"What?" I asked.

"The family Bible, with all the records of happenings within the Godolphin family. What a dunderhead I have been not to have seen it."

"Shall I bring it here?"

"No. A Bible that has survived for generations deserves its repose. Let's go visit it now, shall we?"

We slipped out into the hall and began to walk. Barker has two ways of walking. One involves a heavy tread in order to appear imposing. The other is near silent. Both look the same but he is careful in the second to let his foot down easily and more economically. He has trained me to do it but back then my stomping was not as loud, nor my gliding as silent. I followed him down to the library, where he put a boot up on the bottom edge of the lectern and perused the old family Bible. Philippa and Olivia had gone.

"An early edition of the King James Bible," the Guv said. "I must say I am impressed. This family is not nouveau riche. The Godolphins are one of the premier families of England."

"That's not proof against mischief," I said.

"Agreed."

He grunted. He was at the early pages of the book.

"Nothing out of the ordinary. I was expecting some sort of information or signs of a missing page. There's nothing here."

"Not everything is a clue to what we need."

"I'll take any kind of clue, no matter how small."

"You suspected some kind of written record?"

"Aye, I did, frankly."

The old book looked frail between his strong fingers. One shrug in irritation and the entire relic would be torn asunder. Cyrus Barker claimed to be able to keep his temper in check, but it was nearly as strong as he was.

"Sir," I said. "Perhaps there is something in the Bible. People use them to put all sorts of things in. Wedding announcements, birth announcements, and so on."

I didn't trust his temper yet. I went up and took over for him as gently as possible, and flipped through the book as carefully as I could. I finally found something several dozen pages in, a yellow cutting, years old. I opened it gingerly. It was a newspaper article at least thirty years old about a young man killed on this very island.

LOCAL LIFEGUARD'S BODY WASHES ASHORE

The body of Silas Hillary was found this morning on the beach of Godolphin Island, following a storm that occurred two nights ago. Hillary was last seen by several witnesses going out in a cutter to rescue fishermen trapped by the gale. There appeared to be no sign of foul play and it is believed that he drowned while attempting to save the stranded fishermen in the very teeth of the storm. Hillary is survived by his parents, Professor and Mrs. Hammond Hillary, and a younger sister, Charlotte. Services will be held at the Congregational Church on Bryher Isle this Tuesday.

"There," I said. "That's worth something, isn't it?"

"I suppose," Barker said.

CHAPTER THIRTY-TWO

Barker was still restless. I could see that from where I was seated in the library. The man had spent a good part of his life traveling or as a sea captain. Being trapped in a building for days on end did not suit his disposition. He was given to pacing, with his chin sunk upon his breast and his hands locked behind him. I was reminded of a lion in its cage, roaming from side to side continually, wanting to get out and run free on the savannah once more.

"Partridge," he said.

"Yes, sir?" a voice asked behind me. I had not heard him enter, but then that was how they were trained. Butlers don't stomp into rooms.

"Is Lady Hargrave herself again today, or has she been sedated?"

"She is awake, sir."

"Would you ask her if I may look over the papers her son was studying when he was killed?"

"Those are private papers of the family, Mr. Barker."

"I realize that. They may have some connection to this entire business, however. There is a lot of emotion in this case, but precious few cold, hard facts. Could you ask?"

"I shall try, sir. I make no promises."

"Understood."

Partridge evaporated, while Barker went back to pacing the floor, under my careful if slightly bored scrutiny. We should be doing something, I told myself, but I had no idea what that was. Looking at some stacks of old papers was better than nothing. At least it would pass the time.

Partridge returned in twenty minutes with his trusty set of keys. Lady Hargrave had reluctantly acquiesced to my employer's request. The Guv clapped his hands and rubbed them together.

"Come, Thomas," he said in my ear. "Let us see if we can rattle that skeleton."

We rose and followed the butler sedately down the hall and up the staircase to the study. I glanced at the door Kerry had tried to break down, and then the large library table where Paul Burrell had been seated when someone entered the room and jammed a knife into his heart. A carving knife, no less, which meant the blade was not brought here from off the island; he had palmed it in the kitchen at some point.

Under our close scrutiny, Partridge inserted the key into the lock of the old Chubb safe and turned it. We began to pull documents from inside, taking them to the very seat Paul had been sitting in when he was murdered.

"Financial matters here, papers related to His Lordship's work here, and family matters here," the Guv said, pointing to where each would go. "I shall sit and you bring the contents of the safe to me. Mr. Partridge, would you be so good as to count the monies? I require a reliable witness."

"Very good, sir," the old retainer said.

Barker sat while I brought envelopes and papers to him. I thought this part of the process deadly dull, but he looked excited.

"Might His Lordship actually have kept state secrets in the safe?" I asked.

"There is that possibility, yes, lad. Why?"

"Once you know one, you cannot unknow it."

"It won't be the first time I have stumbled across a secret that the government would prefer remain secret. We are enquiry agents. It is our duty to discover things under rocks."

Partridge cleared his throat. I'm sure he felt our going through the safe and the family private papers to be the height of impropriety. I wanted to ask if we were going to read everything, but I couldn't in front of the butler. Apparently, the time for secrets was over.

Barker began to go through the family accounts in the ledger book. Were there any curious expenditures or regular payments to some third party?

"Mr. Paul Burrell enjoyed a flutter at the track," Barker said. "It does not appear to have been a ruinous habit."

"I'm sure he wasn't the first elder son to do so."

"Lord Hargrave made regular contributions to the Catholic Church and his church sponsored charities, as well as local ones. We are fortunate that he was an orderly record keeper. One of the charities he gave to was the Bromley School."

"Really?"

"Did I not say this would be enlightening? And look here, he was on the board of directors at the home for pensioners where Mrs. Tisher died. So many charities."

"His Lordship was a respected member of the community," Partridge said. "He judged the sheep in the annual agricultural fair and opened the annual flower show."

"Did any of the children attend the Bromley School?"

"No, sir. A tutor lived here on the island, a seminary student. They had a traditional Catholic upbringing. His Lordship blamed him for encouraging the heirs to stay unwed. He'd have preferred his children be fruitful and multiply. He hoped he'd have grandchildren on the island again."

"No doubt. How are you coming along, lad?"

"I've been delving into some of the papers regarding the treaty, sir. It's all extremely long-winded. Better relations between our two countries—a spirit of peace and an end of hostilities going into the twentieth century—a bulwark against instability in Europe. Not very interesting, I'm afraid."

"Partridge, where were Lord Hargrave's people from? I forgot he was not from the island."

"Penzance, sir."

"Much closer than the school and the pensioners. Hmmm. Was His Lordship raised Catholic, as well?"

"Yes, sir. They were the two most prominent Catholic families in all Cornwall. It was natural that they should marry, though they were fortunate to be so well matched."

"How is Her Ladyship this morning, Partridge?"

"She's suffering, sir. We made sure the laudanum wasn't within reach, in case she did herself damage. Her husband and both sons in less than a week! I've only seen her this upset one other time."

"Oh, really?" Barker said, cradling one knee between his hands and leaning back. "What happened then?"

"It was when she was a youth and I was a footman. A young man she was sweet on was paying court rather aggressively, but he wasn't Catholic. The parents refused to sanction a marriage. It was a good thing, too, because he was a captain of the local coast guard. Drowned trying to save a vessel during a shipwreck. Washed up on that beach out there. Oh, it was terrible. She was screaming for days. There, sir, you've dragged a family secret out of me."

"What was the poor fellow's name?"

"I don't recall it, sir. He was not from one of the good families here on the isles."

I knew the name. Barker knew it. But we weren't going to tell Partridge that.

"How long was it before she met Lord Hargrave?"

"Two years. Perhaps three. They were both good for each other. Then the babies came, one after the other."

"He was in the army, as I recall?"

"The Coldstream Guards. A major, no less. He looked very

dashing in his uniform. The ladies can't resist a uniform, can they?"

"Apparently not."

A day or two ago we couldn't get a word out of Partridge, and now he was almost loquacious. What had changed? We must have begun prying open the case. There was no way to close it up again, so the butler had gone from a position of strength to one of weakness. He was seeking mercy, and I wasn't sure Barker would tender it.

The Guv sat back and folded up the papers in his hand. "That's all I need from you, I think," he said.

"I can stay if you have further questions."

"No, no, I'm sure you have many duties requiring your attention. Thank you for your trouble."

"Oh, it was no trouble, I assure you."

Partridge stood about for a moment or two trying to be helpful. Eventually he gave up and left the room for all the other duties he had.

"He is either certain we shall find something or he is afraid we shall," I said to my employer. "Which is it?"

"If he knew for certain a fact was in a particular document, he would attempt to take it away with him."

"Unless there is more than one fact he doesn't want uncovered."

"Nothing here appears very old or particularly damning. Even his will is only a few years old," Barker said.

"We'll soldier on, then," I told him.

Without the butler's interference, we delved deeper into the papers, making observations from time to time.

"His Lordship was generous with the people who sold goods in boats locally," the Guv said. "He bought flowers when he had a fine gardener, and vegetables when his own kitchen garden was adequate."

"It's a wonder a boat has not arrived over the last few days, hoping he would buy something. Have you noticed that everyone we've spoken to has a high opinion of Lord Hargrave except the killer?"

"I had noticed that. Granted, a man can't please everyone."

"Some don't even try."

Barker raised an eyebrow.

"Mr. Kerry, for example."

"Ah," he said, and went back to looking at papers.

"There are no legal disputes with anyone, nothing involving the coast guard or any local police constabulary. The family seems very law-abiding."

"You sound disappointed," I said.

"It means we have to dig deeper into the past of a family that does not deserve such attention."

"There must be some reason they have been targeted. The killer isn't moving from one island to another, wiping out the inhabitants."

"You don't know that for fact, lad. We are cut off from all local information."

"But it is unlikely."

"No less likely than someone plotting an entire island's inhabitants for destruction."

"True. What have you got there?"

"It is Lord Hargrave's will."

Barker opened an official-looking envelope.

" 'I, *Richard Allen Burrell, Lord Hargrave, being of sound mind and body . . .*' "

His voice trailed off. His mind was absorbed in the document. He did not speak for five minutes. I read over a handful of documents, none of much interest. Barker suddenly spoke again.

"In the event of His Lordship's death, the estate was split between the wife and eldest son, with a settlement upon Percy and a dowry for Olivia. In the event Paul died, his settlement and the title went to Percy. It was assumed that Olivia would marry into her fortune."

"And if they all die, are there charities?"

"In the event all of them died, the estate and all it entailed but not the title would go to a distant relative, a Mr. John Herbert Hillary."

"John Hillary. Could that mean Jack Hillary of the so-called Three Tigers, part owner of the Paititi Rubber Company?"

"It doesn't say."

"What kind of relation is he?"

"It doesn't say that, either."

"One doesn't just give an estate away, unless there is a title with it. Does it say if he is his relative or hers?"

"It appears to be in her line only."

"Presumably, his title goes to a cousin, the new Lord Hargrave. She has no family members for the estate to go to?"

"Not necessarily. This Hillary person could inherit after the children but instead of extended family members."

"So you're saying this Hillary could be a choice, rather than a natural successor. 'In the unlikely event that everyone dies, I choose etc., etc.' A very unlikely piece of legality."

"Aye."

"Would Lady Hargrave need to die for this Hillary person to inherit? Or could the estate be split?"

"It would be necessary for everyone to die before he got a farthing."

"That's not good."

Barker thought for a few minutes, shaking his head slowly. "No, there's only one thing to do."

"What's that?"

"We cannot speak with the solicitor in London who drafted this document, provided he's even alive."

"True."

"Therefore, the only person we can ask is Lady Celia herself."

I felt as if a weight had been lifted.

"Yes. Finally. But she is in heavy mourning. Her family has been decimated. She may not speak to us."

"We must do everything we can to force her. Perhaps we can trade information."

"What you mean?"

"I don't believe Lord Hargrave kept his wife informed about things. Between us we may know more about the family than anyone else on the island."

"We must talk to her, then," I said.

"Aye."

"When?"

"There is no time like the present. I'm afraid I cannot guarantee that all or even one of us shall be alive by the stroke of midnight."

CHAPTER THIRTY-THREE

B arker stopped in the hallway and knocked on Mrs. Ashleigh's
door. She and Olivia were no longer in the library. He could
have walked into his own room and called out to her through
the connecting door but for whatever reason he chose not to. There
was something very formal about the motion, as if he wanted it to
be on public record.

Philippa answered the door wearing a cream-colored dress and
matching pearl necklace and earrings. Having been childless her
entire life, and a woman of fashion, her waist was especially small.
I had the rare feeling that my employer was being thickheaded.
He needed to marry this woman before someone else did. One
might feel that he is some God-appointed sentinel to the capital
and that's all well and good, but to keep such a woman as Philippa
Ashleigh sitting on a shelf was a crime in and of itself.

"Where is Miss Burrell?" he asked.

"Locked in her room. I had to have a talk with her. Apparently,
she was trying to take advantage of Thomas's better nature. Has
something happened?"

"It is time for me to speak to Lady Hargrave. I thought you might be willing to accompany me."

She stepped forward, her dress sweeping the hardwood floor as she moved.

"Yes, I had better."

When we reached Her Ladyship's room, which was just opposite ours on the other side of the hall, Philippa stopped him with a hand on his broad chest, and went inside to speak with her alone. I could hear voices inside, but not actual words. Finally, the door opened and we were ushered inside by Mrs. Ashleigh.

It was a beautiful room. I still recall it now, years later. There were silvery stripes in the wallpaper, rose-patterned Axminster carpet, and Louis XVI furniture. The room might have been delivered here by boat piece by piece from Versailles. Every table was covered in ceramic bric-a-brac of shepherdesses and swains, sheep and castles. The paintings on the walls were landscapes, but sunny ones. All was beauty and light. They did not look like real places at all. She lives in a fairy-tale world, I told myself, created by her husband.

In the very center of a large bed she lay in a dressing gown of red and gold and white. Her hair had been perfectly coiffed. Only the puffiness of her eyes and the redness of her face told of some kind of tragedy.

She was only five or six years older than Mrs. Ashleigh, I thought, but her beauty had faded. Her features were soft and round. Her best feature was her eyes, blue as a robin's egg. She had been spoiled. Those were my observations, but what did they matter? She looked the way that pleased him, or else he might have strayed, but I don't think he did. The love between them seemed genuine.

"I have been dreading this," Lady Hargrave said.

"Consider me like a doctor, ma'am. We shall try to make this as brief as possible. My associate and I are trying to get at what is occurring here, knowing that you have only Olivia left alive. We understand that there is someone in your past. Specifically, a young man named Silas Hillary."

"Silas," she whispered to herself.

"I understand you formed an attachment with him, but that your family did not approve."

"He was not Catholic, you see. And he was poor. If he'd had one thing in his favor they might have accepted him, but, well. He didn't."

"Tell me about him, ma'am. I'm sure there are few that even remember him these days."

"Oh, he was a wonderful young man. So handsome and romantic. He wrote poetry to me. I've kept all his letters."

"May I see them?"

"No, Mr. Barker. They were intensely private, and of limited practical value."

"I shall not press you on the matter, then," he said. The Guv could be gentle and kind when he needed to be.

"The two of you formed an attachment."

"We were in love. I fell in love with Richard later, but I hope it is not wrong to state that I was in love before him, and in quite a different way. We were head over heels. That is the expression, isn't it?"

"I believe so, Lady Hargrave. And then he died."

"Twenty-ninth August 1855. He was captain of the coast guard. Some fishermen were trying to return in the middle of a storm. Their boat wrecked on the west end of the island and broke up on the rocks. Silas set out from the nearby island of Bryher. Hell Bay overturned several rescue boats. His foundered and he was tossed overboard by a wave and drowned. His body washed up on the shore two days later."

She was reliving it all in her head, remembering that day so long ago. A tear leaked down the side of her nose, but she did not have the strength to wipe it away.

"How long afterward did you learn you were with child?"

Her pale blue eyes went large.

"I do not judge you, madam. It is not my place. Nonetheless, it happened."

"It did," she finally answered. "I was only seventeen. I didn't understand what was going on. Of course, my family was scandalized and since my seducer was already dead, they blamed me. It was kept a secret, of course. After Jack was born, he was placed with a nice family in Land's End."

She sat for a full minute staring at the counterpane as if it were a conjurer's glass ball in which she could view the past.

"Then I met Richard at an estate ball in Penzance. He was dashing in his uniform and so clever. He was the smartest man I ever knew. My parents were so relieved, but before I could accept his proposal, I had to confess about Jack. He was as big-hearted as he was capable. He promised to take care of Jack for me and to see to his proper upbringing. Nothing was too good for Jack. I wanted him to bring my son home, but he pointed out that we would have children of our own and it wouldn't be fair to them. He was right, of course. Paul was born within the year, an heir between the two houses. It was as if Jack were never born. But we always exchanged letters at Christmas and Richard had photographs taken of him and where he was."

Lady Hargrave reached for her nightstand. Rummaging about in it, she produced a small blue book. Inside there were folded letters addressed to "Dear Mummy" from Jack and photographs of a towheaded boy in the yard of an attractive building. Another photograph was of the Bromley School looking majestic and successful.

"So, young Jack was in no doubt as to whom his parents were. How old was he when your husband took over his education?"

"When he was three."

Barker opened the first letter, read it, folded it again and placed it back where it had come from.

"One can follow his education."

"Yes. Jack was a clever boy. The headmaster, Mr. Throgmorton, said he was one of his best students. The letter is in there as well."

Barker retrieved it. I saw the stamp of the school on the letterhead. The note was typed on a typewriting machine, and then signed by the headmaster who had so recently been shot.

"So it is," the Guv stated.

He read through them all. When he got to the last one he stopped and looked up.

"So, Jack Hillary enlisted in the fusiliers when he was seventeen."

"Yes, he enlisted after he graduated. Richard told me he had offered to pay for university, but this was what Jack wanted. His regiment went to India. They were stationed in Calcutta."

Barker picked up the next letter. I saw some sort of military insignia embossed upon it. It was typed also.

"'*We regret to inform you . . .* '" he began.

Lady Celia broke down. Philippa came to her aid, of course, with a handkerchief and some smelling salts. She wailed. It was a cultured wail, produced by generations of breeding, but it was a wail nonetheless. A child had died. He would not be the last.

"This was written," Barker went on, over the muffled wailing, "in 1873. Can you tell me, ma'am, why your husband would make a young man who is officially dead the final beneficiary of his will?"

"What?" Lady Hargrave said, all at sea.

Barker pulled the folded will from his pocket and opened it before showing Her Ladyship. Over her shoulder Philippa stared, fascinated.

"Your husband wrote the will, which was witnessed by a solicitor in 1880, seven years after your son's supposed death."

"Is my son alive?"

"It would appear so, and as recently as nine years ago he was in contact with your husband."

"But why didn't Richard tell me?"

"I cannot speculate, Lady Hargrave."

"I can," Philippa said. "He could have been disfigured in the war or lost a limb. He might have considered himself unwelcome."

"He would always be welcome in this house!" Lady Hargrave cried.

"For whatever reason, Jack wished to be thought dead. He wished to be estranged from the family."

"Do you suppose he has married? Could he have children of his own?"

"He'd be in his thirties now. Most people marry and have children," Philippa stated.

Her voice sounded a trifle flat. She could not count herself among such people. Lady Hargrave pressed her hands against her mouth in wonder.

"Can such things be? I dare not allow myself to hope!"

"Perhaps you should not yet," Barker began.

"I lost three sons, but one of them may still be alive. Do you suppose he is in England?"

"It is a large world. He could be anywhere," I said.

Barker gave me a stern look. With Philippa I was encouraging hope where it might not actually be.

"Mr. Barker, you are a detective. When this is over, and you can travel back and forth again, would you undertake to track down my first son? I will pay you whatever you ask."

"We shall see, Lady Hargrave. Let us not put the cart before the horse."

She clapped her hands in joy.

"He has to be alive. And we shall bring him home. Olivia has an older brother she has never met!"

"May I borrow your commonplace book, Lady Hargrave? I promise to take extremely good care of it. Perhaps it can give me a clue as to where Jack is living now."

"Take it!" she insisted. "Oh, we've got to find him again!"

"Thank you."

"I was afraid what would happen when you came, Mr. Barker. I never suspected you would bring me such welcome news!"

Barker bowed and all of us left her to her happy contemplation. So why were all of us stone-faced, you might ask? The answer was none of us believed it in the least.

My employer sat down in the seating area on the first floor. It had become a waiting room, dining room, interviewing room, and now traveling office. Barker pulled the first photograph from the book that came to hand. It was from the Bromley School.

"This is not a photograph at all," he said, looking at the faded sepia image. "It is a print. More correctly, it is a postal card. One could purchase a copy in any post office or store in the area."

"But he's written a message."

"Rather, someone has."

Philippa looked through the letters. "The handwriting appears to be the same, counting for the change in age."

Barker lifted the earlier photograph, which was also a postal card. It showed a trim little farm with children playing with the sheep in the front yard.

"This is not the proper size of a card. A sliver of the bottom has been cut off. The portion which printed where this card was really produced."

"The card states it is the St. Ives School for Young Boarders," I insisted.

Barker shook his head. "You're not understanding me. The cards. The photographs. The letters. The book. They are all a forgery."

"Lady Hargrave created a fake book?"

"No, lad. Lord Hargrave did. He was fooling his wife. Jack Hillary never played in a yard like this, with the sheep capering about. He was raised in a mud pit more probably, and forced to do menial work to pay for his room and board."

"But the photographs of Jack," Philippa insisted. "They are actual photographs!"

"Yes, dear, but not of Jack! Don't you understand what Richard Burrell did for a living? He created false documents like school records and death notices all the time. He manipulated information. He manipulated his wife for what he supposed were the right reasons."

"Which were?" Philippa asked.

"She had an illegitimate child. Little Jack was a reminder of his father, of whom Lord Hargrave was jealous. It was he who sent the annual letters under controlled conditions. This rosy image of a boy growing up in an orphanage and being perfectly happy is codswallop. I've been to baby farms. Over half of the children do not survive beyond five years. Some caretakers are actually paid to get rid of the child. The care of illegitimate children is one of the worst secrets in our society. The child pays for the sins of the parent. I don't know which is worse, being killed outright as a child, or the long slow torture that extends to adulthood."

"Dickensian squalor," I piped up.

"That is an almost romantic literary euphemism for slavery and starvation. And that, Thomas, Philippa, is the first reason I have come across for blowing a man's head apart, and murdering his children one by one."

CHAPTER THIRTY-FOUR

The storm came shortly before dinner. As I changed, I peeked out of Barker's window and saw the wind tossing the trees to and fro. On an island, one is exposed to the elements from every direction. As I bided my time I heard the first drops of rain on the windowpane. It sounded like pins dropping on the tile floor.

I met Barker and Mrs. Ashleigh downstairs. Within a few minutes it seemed to go from midday to night. Angry clouds bunched and bumped across the sky, and thunder rumbled in the distance. The building shook with the rumbling. By then, of course, we had all grown a little tired of each other's company, and listening to the storm as it huffed and puffed at the Godolphin House of brick had novelty. Besides, we were snug and dry inside and it was satisfying to picture the assassin scrambling for shelter somewhere out there, slipping on rocks, wet to the bone, and miserable.

As it turned out, it was Mrs. Fraser's birthday, and there was an attempt at gaiety in spite of the rumbling that moved across the island and the unnerving bolts of lightning. They interrupted the conversation and turned it into a shouting match.

"I understand you went after that scoundrel the other night, Barker!" The colonel spoke in his strident, military way. I could picture him bawling at a squad of soldiers.

"Never got within a dozen feet of him," Barker grumbled.

"That fellow knows what he is about. A professional spy, you mark my words, sir! A German or possibly a Russian."

"We are currently at peace with both countries," Gascoigne said. "Such an act is unthinkable."

"It was unthinkable when Bismarck was the kaiser, but now he is in exile. That brat, Wilhelm, holds the reins. I don't trust the blighter. Either he will build up arms against us all, or break up Germany into a handful of unstable states. Neither will be useful to England."

This is what they did at the USRI, I assumed. They argued continuously over what might happen if the country did this or a ruler did that. It was still a time when some men ruled with full authority, and some were erratic or weak, or even mildly insane. England now governed a sizable portion of the world, and some countries and their rulers were jealous.

"Oh, come now, Colonel," Philippa Ashleigh said. "It's your wife's birthday. Why spoil it with talk of politics?"

The colonel grinned and embraced his wife beside him, who looked alarmed at the display of affection.

"You are right, my dear. Everyone, please, charge your glasses. I'd like to make a toast."

It turned out to be a speech. He talked about meeting her at an embassy ball, and learning she had many suitors for her hand. He charmed and pestered all his acquaintances, discovered his opponents' faults or weaknesses, and exploited them until he was the lone suitor. He was so good at it, in fact, that now he did that sort of thing with countries.

She was a faded rose, and I saw nothing in her to spark passion. But then, she was his rose. Once he must have seen her as exotic, bilingual, this scion of the English port-making industry. He had worked hard to get her, and he had kept her all these decades. Most everyone I knew was unwed. I was beginning to despair that marriage was going out of fashion.

He had false teeth and gray hair. She had pudgy fingers and bags under her eyes. They had been together, it transpired, for forty-eight years. They knew each other's secrets and loved them anyway. The truth was, I wanted to be an old man across from Rebecca Mocatta. Oh, not right away, of course, but someday. I wanted to get it right, you see. My first marriage had ended in disaster and even death. I was bound and determined not to make a mistake on the last.

We had agreed to marry, Rebecca and I, but it would be another couple of years. She was in mourning over the loss of her husband, though it had been a loveless marriage. I was not the kind of suitor her parents would have liked. I understand her mother called me "the criminal." That might have crushed me sometime in the past, but when it came to Rebecca, I was an immovable object. I was no longer afraid of her mother, dragon though she was, or her father, who preyed with soft words until he found one vulnerable spot. I wanted what Colonel Fraser and his wife had: a normal life together. Some men wanted money or power or fame. I wanted Rebecca and a long life, and the world could go to perdition as far as I was concerned.

A large trifle was brought out in a glass bowl and served. Champagne was opened and poured. Outside it still blew, but this house had endured centuries of such gales and shrugged them off.

"I don't like storms," Olivia Burrell said beside me.

"Why not?" I asked. "You are safe inside." I was guarding her again with those invisible bracelets.

"I have seen too many. Someone always gets hurt. Shipwrecks, drowning, or misadventures."

"I am sure no one is foolhardy enough to be out in weather such as this. They had all day to come into port."

"You do not know the islanders. One more haul of fish is almost worth the danger to them."

"Tell me, why has not anyone just pulled into the harbor? It has been days since the ambassador arrived."

"Father did not always appreciate locals using the harbor and bothering him with goods to sell. He was not always the easiest of men to get along with."

"Really?" I asked. "He seemed like a good fellow."

"Oh, he was if you were of use to him, but it was not wise to get in his way."

"Those are harsh words from a daughter."

"Oh, I loved him. Don't think I didn't. But I never fell into the belief of my brothers that he could do no wrong."

"I see."

Another rumble shook the building.

"I shall be glad when the morning comes," she said.

"I would think," I countered, "that with the dangers herein, you would not worry so much about something as mundane as the weather."

"You have not been out in a proper Scilly Isle gale, Mr. Llewelyn, or you would change your tune. Those brief showers you have on the mainland are hardly anything at all."

"I shall take your word for it, but we are not out in it, and I have no intention of going there. I will leave it alone if it will have the courtesy to do likewise."

Lady Hargrave was still absent from the festivities, mourning in private. Perhaps she was holding dreams of a lost son found again, clasped to her bosom. I didn't believe the story she was writing in her head about the prodigal son would come true. In her place, Olivia was overseeing the party, serving as hostess.

Olivia and I played whist against Dr. Anstruther and Gwendolyn. Bella was not at the table that evening, but I thought she might still be upset at Percy's death, and unable to come down. There was something vaguely bad form about playing cards in a house of mourning, but everyone needed distraction.

I dealt first and we were under way. The fact that partners were not able to communicate with each other in any way did not stop her from giving me a hard stare and warning. Luckily, she held the ace, and we took the first hand.

Whist is a pleasurable game, but I'm no great reader of card strategies, so I won't relate the game in any detail. Olivia played ruthlessly and we prospered. The good doctor should have stuck to surgery, and as for Gwendolyn, my opinion of her was not improved by her playing. Olivia played with an intensity that none of the rest of us shared, and I had a good run of cards.

Meanwhile, overhead, the gale did its best to rattle the windows and scrape the roof tiles. Under other circumstances, those not involving the death of a half-dozen people, I might have enjoyed the storm. It was not the fault of our hostess. The location was novel, the company interesting, the food well prepared. It was not her fault that a madman was killing off everyone one by one.

In deference to the card playing, the normal dinner had been replaced with a sideboard buffet that we all took advantage of after the first hour. There was a hot curry which I knew would please Barker, prawn sandwiches, a collection of sweetbreads and other cold courses. The rain from the west brought some warmth with it, which made it whole portions welcome. I longed to remove my jacket, and our guest of honor fanned herself as she chose which card to play next.

"I need to powder my nose," Olivia said.

"You look fine."

"It is hot in here and I am wilting. I need to freshen my face. You can stay here."

"No, I will go with you. Let me catch his eye," I said, referring to my employer.

"Does he even have eyes behind those spectacles of his? I thought perhaps the glass was painted over."

"I'll tell him you said so."

As if he heard us, Barker turned in his chair on the other side of the room and regarded us. I nodded as if to say we were leaving for a moment, and he nodded in return. We left the library and climbed the stair.

"I hope this is not a scheme to get us away from the others," I said.

"You had your one offer, Mr. Llewelyn, and you turned it down. You will not get a second. A gentleman would not have brought up the subject."

I stopped and bowed. "You are correct, Miss Burrell. I apologize."

"Thank you."

Barker had taught me that when caught out upon a question of manners, always be the first to apologize.

We went to her room, and I waited outside while she applied powder. As a man I knew that this was a euphemism and she could be doing any of a number of things, but women must be allowed their alchemical secrets. After what seemed like half an hour, she came out looking just as she had when she left though somewhat refreshed.

We went downstairs again into the hall. I was leading her toward the library when I stepped on something glittery underfoot. Someone had dropped a necklace, I thought to myself. Then I saw it was glass. Shattered window glass. Just then the wind whistled sharply overhead.

I stopped and looked up. There was a row of high ornamental windows, and one of the panes must have fallen out. That is what my mind was telling me anyway. But then there was a flash of lightning and it illuminated a form crouched at the window high above us. An arm protruded through the aperture, and there was a pistol in his hand.

Simultaneously I pulled her back out of harm's way with my left arm while reaching for my Webley with the other.

"Oh," Olivia said, as if she had thought of something. There was a red spot between her eyebrows. She sagged, sliding off my arm.

Vaguely, I remember pointing the revolver overhead and pulling the trigger again and again. Barker tells me I was roaring at the top of my lungs, but I do not recall. I was consumed with rage. The feelings of recrimination would occur later.

This was my fault. Had I been a second faster, she might have lived. If I had trained more diligently, if I had practiced shooting more often, if I had been just a little more professional, Olivia Burrell would probably be married now with children and grandchildren. Instead, she had died a virgin, just as she had feared. I had promised her I would protect her and I had broken that vow. To this day, I have not forgiven myself.

There was screaming and I was being jostled about, but I felt as if I were enveloped in cotton wadding. Someone took the empty pistol from my hand. I had been squeezing the empty chamber continuously as if it would change what had happened.

The shadow at the window was gone. I turned and ran out into the storm. The wind and rain buffeted me as I left the shelter of the house. I ran out into the rain and looked back, searching for someone on the roof. I was not thinking clearly. I was in a rage.

He was nowhere to be found, but I kept running around the front of the house hoping to see him. The alternative was to go inside, and if I did that I would look at her. I would look and I dared not. Eventually, I was as soaked through as anyone has ever been. There was nothing left to do but go inside.

Leaving puddles on the marble floor, I looked down at the body of Olivia Burrell. She had a look of faint disapproval on her face, as if I had made another boneheaded decision, which I suppose I had.

We were standing about looking at her the way one does at a dead body. Somehow the fact that she was female made moving her properly more important. Paul and Percy had been bundled away somehow, but moving her body required more respect. Partridge came out with a blanket and covered her completely.

Suddenly, we heard a scream from upstairs. My nerves were quaking and I nearly jumped from my skin. I was about to run up the staircase when Barker seized my shoulder and stopped me.

"Philippa is informing her mother of Miss Burrell's death," he explained.

"I think this may be the worst day of my life."

"It is not over yet, lad. Are you soaked through?"

"To the bone."

"Good. I have an assignment for you. Look over here."

He led me to a puddle of water made by the rain coming in the window.

"What do you see?"

"A puddle of rainwater, sir," I said, trying to hold my patience.

"And what else?"

"There is blood in it."

"Aye. You shot him, lad. Wounded him, at least."

"That's good," I said, though I did not feel it at the moment.

"That is very good, Thomas. I want you to go out and raise the flag on the pole."

"When?"

"Right now, lad. You could not possibly get any wetter."

CHAPTER THIRTY-FIVE

It was no small matter what Cyrus Barker was asking. I have watched grown men run from the assassin's withering fire. This request was tantamount to a death sentence. He was out there, wounded, though we knew not how badly. The Guv was pointing out that any attempt now would be unexpected. I would be screened in some manner by the rain, and there was a chance that the killer might already be dying or badly injured. Brought together, an attempt tonight to raise the flag seemed like the best opportunity to leave this accursed island.

The obvious question occurred to me, but I did not voice it: what made me a perfect candidate for this mission? My employer expected me to run through the woods on the heels of an assassin. Let him go, then, if he was so sanguine about our chances.

I was courting someone now. That had to make some difference. Unlike Barker, who seemed as if he had all the time in the world to marry Philippa Ashleigh, I wanted to marry soon. It seemed unfair that he was sending me to my doom.

"What about the flag?" I asked. "He destroyed it. I saw it in tatters."

"Miss Anstruther's maroon dress will suffice. You are re-sourceful, and I'm sure your knowledge of women's fashion will show you how to hook it to the pole."

He had saddled me with a totally erroneous expertise on the subject of women. If I know anything, it is my lack of knowledge on the subject. He developed some queer notions, sometimes.

"Yes, sir," I said.

"Unless you think the matter too dangerous."

I knew him rather well by then. He wasn't offering a way out. He was twisting the knife. Was I up to the challenge? Was I brave enough to see it through?

"Of course not."

"Because if you feel it is still dangerous, just speak out."

"I will do it, sir. Where is the dress?"

"It is folded it up there by the hat rack."

I hated when he did that. He had maneuvered both of us in such a way that he was trying to talk me out of it and I was insisting.

"As you said, I'm drenched anyway."

"No sense both of us getting wet."

That was it then. It was decided between us. I was going out to my death. There was no sense in both of us getting killed.

I crossed to the front door and opened it, looking out at the steady downpour. I hadn't heard before that the Scillys were subject to monsoons. Curtains of water cascaded down upon the lawn.

A minute before I was hot with anger, charging about and waving a pistol. Now I was cold, shivering, and sober as a judge. My will lay in a secure box at Cox & Co. in Whitehall Street beside our offices. I hadn't had the chance to change it since our understanding.

"If Mrs. Cowan should want any of my effects, I should like her to have them," I said.

"Oh, you do talk rot," he responded, and shoving the dress into my chest, pushed me out the door and shut it.

Within seconds the rain was pouring off my chin and working through my scalp. It was warm but sharp, coming down so hard it was like being poked with needlelike fingers.

I ran out into the storm, carrying the ridiculous red dress, which quickly became sodden and heavy, draping across my legs, hindering what I was trying to do. You work for a man for six years and then one day he hands you a death sentence. I recalled the Llewelyn luck: everything bad that can happen to one probably shall, and yet one will not die from it, as that would end the torment too quickly.

I ran, looking up into the roiling clouds overhead, spangled with lightning, and it must have been that I was overwrought or a trick of the light. I swore I saw Olivia Burrell's face and form projecting grandly against the storm like some fierce goddess. The rain was running into my eyes, however, and I didn't have time for fanciful images. Like it or not, the entire fate of the remaining few party guests had been placed in my hands.

My hair was plastered to my head and my clothing was like a wet tourniquet wrapped around my body. I had never seen such a storm in my life. It was as if the entire ocean were breaking over that one little island. Perhaps it wasn't I that was meant to drown, but the assassin, who was going against nature by killing so many of his own kind. I reckon it must have been around eight o'clock, and the sun would normally just be setting, but now everything was black on black. I could not see beyond the closest torrent of rain. I only guessed where the flagpole was from having seen it before at midday. If not for the flagpole I might have gone over the cliff, since the wall that encircled most of the island ended before this section of rocky coastline.

As I tried to tie the dress to the pole, the wind buffeting me to and fro. The wind from the west was powerful enough to knock me off my feet. One would prepare for a wall of wind coming in one direction and suddenly it would come from another direction.

I had grown up with gales but Gwent is a buttoned-down place. The rain battered our slate roofs, rolled down our brick walls, and disappeared into the drains of our cobblestoned streets. Here it had full sway. We were on an island and it could come from any direction, sometimes two at once. It attacked like a bird of prey, slashing you with its talons, pecking at your face with its beak. It did not help that there were but a few inches of soil before one met rock. The gale dragged you off your feet.

I saw things in the storm. A horse's oats bag flew about, opening and closing its maw as if it were alive. I ducked as it came at my head. I was pelted with small rocks, sticks, and debris. Whether it was from our island or someplace else was anyone's guess.

Logic told me that the easiest way to attach a dress to a flagpole was by the sleeves. The fabric fought me as I tied it into a knot, but after a brief struggle I managed a knot that no wind or rain could untie. Then I worked on the second sleeve. The wind took the bottom of the dress and began worrying it the way a dog does a trouser leg. Then something struck the flagpole loudly, setting it quivering, just whizzing by my cheek. I knew better than to think it was a mere rock or even an arrow.

I gauged from what direction it came and took what shelter there was behind the pole. I wasn't foolish enough to think a grown man, even a small one like myself, could shelter behind a pole no more than six inches in circumference. Looking for what direction he was shooting from was probably a useless endeavor, but then some might say my entire existence up to that point had been one long useless endeavor.

When lightning flashed, I finally saw him propped behind the beginning of the wall, using it to lean his rifle on. Idly I wondered if he still had one of those expanding bullets which would blow my head clean off my shoulders. If one cannot have a remarkable life, at least one might have a spectacular death, someone once said. It might have been me, come to think of it. Typical Tommy Llewelyn: he's on the verge of shuffling the mortal coil, and he's thinking up epigrams. I sucked in my breath, hoping to give the smallest target, just as another bullet struck the pole.

He wouldn't miss twice, even under these conditions. He was playing with me the way a terrier plays with a cornered rat. He had me right where he wanted me now. There wasn't anything to hide behind within ten feet, and he was an excellent shot. I imagine he was lining up his sight, taking his time, perhaps savoring the moment. The anticipation is sometimes more satisfying than the win itself. He was waiting for me to make a mistake, and so I obliged him.

The low shelter we had built days before was still a dozen feet away. If I did manage to get to it and lie down flat, he could not easily shoot me through the thick board. Once I thought it, it seemed the only alternative. Safety lay there and it certainly didn't here. And so I stepped out, preparing to run no more than five steps. That was where I stood when the bullet pierced the muscle of my bicep and passed through. I jumped back, and as I did there was a loud pop from the direction of the crude shelter. Looking back, I was just in time to see the form of the assassin clap his hands to his head and fall backward over the cliff.

Cyrus Barker stood in a glistening slicker and lowered the rifle, which still smoked from being fired. Bait, I told myself. He sent me out as bait, and all it cost me was an arm. Just that. Barker still had two, after all. The pain was intense, there were black spots moving around in front of my eyes. I'd been shot. I worry about it happening every morning I woke up, except on Sundays. Now it had finally happened. I could stop worrying now.

"How are ye, lad?" Barker rumbled.

"It passed right through my arm. I'm bleeding."

He came over to where I stood, pulling something from his pocket. It was his handkerchief, which he used to tie a tourniquet around my upper arm. Then together we walked to the edge of the cliff. It seemed impossible for a man to survive such a fall.

"I can't see the bottom," I called out over the wail of the storm.

"Nor I, Thomas!"

He turned and picked up the rifle lying on the wall. I recognized it as the missing Sharps that must have belonged to His Lordship. The Guv reached into the breech, and pulled out the spent cartridge. He handed it to me, as if by doing so he had returned the bullet to its origin, as if that made it all better. My arm would eventually heal and all would return to the way it should be. Funny thing about that cartridge. I still have it. It is sitting here on my desk as I write. My arm healed a long time ago, the only sign of what had happened being a slight twinge when the weather changes. The shell became a memento, a souvenir. Had that been on my employer's mind when he pulled it from the breech of the rifle and handed the hot metal to me? I rather hoped not. I wouldn't want to give him the satisfaction of being right.

Barker came over to me. His dark hair was plastered around his spectacles and his mustache was in tatters. Without warning me, he raised my arm. I cried out in pain. He looked at the rusty stains.

"Passed clean through," he said. He kneaded my injured arm with his thick fingers, feeling the tibia bone inside. The examination was by touch, as if he were blind. In the teeth of the gale with dark spectacles on his face, I'm certain it was close to it. "It'll heal well enough."

Barker in his early training had worked for a bonesetter in Canton named Wong. I do not know how much or how little he knew about medicine, but I assumed what he did know was little more than Chinese folk remedies. I would have preferred Dr. Anstruther's opinion.

Barker picked up a rucksack by the wall and began going through it. He pulled out a few papers and read them hungrily before the rain drenched them. They were identity papers in what I took to be Spanish.

"Captain Nigel Pelham of the Venezuelan Army," he said.

"Kerry's friend!" I cried. "Do you think they were working together?"

"Almost certainly."

"What does—" I began, but suddenly there was a loud booming sound from somewhere. It wasn't the rumble of thunder that we had experienced for half an hour, nor the crack of a rifle. It was deeper, more profound, like the explosion that had ended Kerry's life.

CHAPTER THIRTY-SIX

Now what?" I demanded as the sound reverberated across the rocky beach.

Barker turned, his bluntly chiseled features facing west. "Philippa!" he bellowed. Then he began to run toward the house.

I followed behind. The thought that Philippa might be in danger had not occurred to me, but it was true: no one was safe on this island.

One would think that after an hour of this, the storm would abate. Far from it, in fact. It was getting stronger. The sky was growing darker and darker, and it was becoming more difficult to see anything beyond arm's reach. Odd shapes came out of the gloom, requiring inspection with the fingers to ascertain whether animal, vegetable, or mineral. A stone swan became a sea serpent, a potted larch an ogre.

Barker saw neither of these things, of course, and it would have been no matter to him if he did. He was running as fast as his sodden limbs could carry him. My hose squelched in my shoes and I was miserable, but that didn't matter a jot. Philippa was in danger and we had to save her. A world without her now seemed impossible to me, so I could only imagine how Barker felt about her.

Something large and shaggy rose out of the gloom ahead of us. Barker shot past. Just as I came near a peal of lightning tore open the sky. I saw an eye the size of a tennis ball. It was the Percheron, Apollo, bolted from his stable. He neighed at me and shook his drenched mane as if he still found me responsible for his injury. Then I saw something that made me ignore the horse altogether.

In the middle of the drive, the old cannon stood, its barrel split open in long curls. Smoke rose from it in a desultory haze, as if in collusion with the rain. I came up behind it and sighted down its busted barrel. The big, stout door that had repelled the killer for all those days was torn asunder, like the Holy of Holies. Inside there was debris, and a broken beam on the hall floor. From where I stood in the rain, I looked in upon the lobby lit by candles and lamps. It was almost indecent, like seeing a woman's ankles on a tram.

Barker hadn't stopped, of course. His limbs were longer and his lady friend was in danger. He doesn't get these impressions that I do. He saw a horse, a cannon, and a hole. He accepted their meaning immediately. Someone had harnessed the horse to the cannon and wielded it here in the rain. Only I puzzled on how it was done. Cannons generally require dry conditions to fire. Perhaps he had loaded it earlier with the powder he had made and one of the cannonballs stacked by its wheel. A fresh fuse and a macintosh over everything might have done the trick. The metal had shattered. Finally, it had fulfilled its purpose after nearly a hundred years. The cannon had been built to attack a Frenchman, and now it had led a killer to his representative, Henri Gascoigne.

Had there been two of them out there in the woods all along, or had this been the work of the men or women in the house? Such powerful engines of destruction mankind has made and anyone can pull a trigger or light a fuse with a match. A sword at least required skill in order to survive. It has become too easy to kill these days.

I stepped over the sill and looked down at the debris. The rain

receded as I stepped into the house and began to drip and drib-
ble on the marble floor. My arm was throbbing and for the first
time I noticed my sleeve was soaked red. It was more than some
flesh wound I had sustained. I tried to retrieve my pistol, but it
seemed as if it weighed five stone. Switching to my left hand I
opened the breech and found the cartridges all spent. My precious
bullets I had discharged into the air over Olivia Burrell's death.
Had that really been no more than thirty minutes ago? I carried
the pistol with me. Perhaps I could distract the killer with it. I was
certain Barker still had plenty of ammunition.

I heard voices from somewhere deep within the house. I could
not make out what was being said so close to the gale. I stepped
forward and followed the voice, my pistol hanging awkwardly in
my right hand. I knew if I survived this ordeal I would start target practice with my left hand at once.

Coming closer, I could hear the voice now, but I didn't recognize it. A well-educated voice, English. Polite, even.

"Do set your gun gently on the rug, Mr. Barker. We don't want
it to accidentally go off, now do we? If it did, I promise you, this
lovely woman's brains will go all over the room."

No, no! I thought, willing Barker to read my mind. *Don't put
down the gun! You have the only bullets!*

"I declare, Mr. Barker, sir, you are even wetter than I, if such a
thing is possible," the man continued. "You shouldn't gad about
in weather like this. You'll catch your death. Or someone else's."

I crept forward. The voices were coming from the library. Raising my pistol, I prepared to spring in with a yell. I'd be shot dead in
all probability, but it might give the Guv time to dive for his Colt
and avenge my death. Did I really think I was going to marry someone and live happily ever after? Had I not paid attention at all these
last five years?

"Mr. Llewelyn! Is that you in the hall? Come in and put down
that silly pistol. I watched you empty it not half an hour ago. I took
the liberty of borrowing the other one from your luggage. There
is no need to lurk in the shadows."

Crestfallen, I stepped into the room. I couldn't do anything. I
was a liability. Who knows what Barker was thinking when he

hired me. I'd been nothing but a misery to him since then. As I stepped forward, my eye swept the room. Lady Celia and Philippa were both being menaced by a man with a pistol. Barker stood in the middle of the room, his arms raised and his hands resting on top of his head. Also in the room were Dr. Anstruther and his daughters, Lady Alicia, Mrs. Fraser, Partridge, and the housekeeper, Mrs. Tregowith. All of them were seated in chairs, even the servants. They must have been ordered to do so.

Cautiously, I looked about for some sign of the ambassador. I expected to see a boot sticking out from behind a chair, or splash of crimson on the wall. Dared I hope he had not proven the newest victim?

I stared hard at the killer, who leaned an elbow impudently against Mrs. Ashleigh's chair, dangling a pistol in his hand.

"Cesar, no," I said.

"Sorry, old man," he said. "Cesar Rojas was just an entry in the door."

He pointed the pistol at Barker, nearly upside down, as if he were enjoying using it for emphasis.

"Jack Hillary," Barker supplied. "You were named in the will, which is no doubt false."

"Not false, precisely. It merely had a sheet or two added, both here and in London. Not that I needed the money. My rubber plantation has done very well. No, I wanted this estate. Mr. Barker, keep your hands away from your pockets! I'm aware of your penchant for sharpened coins."

Barker raised his hands in the air again. "What do you intend to do with it, once you possess it?" he asked.

"I'll complete the work I have begun. Burn the buildings, tear them down, return this island to the bare rock it once was."

"A testament to your vengeance."

"I prefer to think of it as righteous wrath. It is her fault, you know."

He indicated Lady Hargrave by pointing my pistol at her, menacing her with it.

"How so?"

"We could have built a life together. This island could been my idyll, but no, she was too weak. She married that monster. Lovely little featherbrained mother who couldn't possibly make decisions for herself. I'm sure he was very accommodating. 'Let me take your son off your hands. I'll educate him, and send him to the finest places!' "

He was so angry, the gun quivered in his hand. I feared he could do anything. He could kill most of us, unless we got to him first.

"Mrs. Tisher's baby farm," Barker said, studying him.

"It had a reputation, you know," Jack replied. "Leave your child there and within a year he or she will be gone. Children get sick. Typhoid. Dysentery, whooping cough, measles. Actually they are all euphemisms for the true culprits: starvation and neglect. Mrs. Tisher spent all the money she brought in on herself and her family. We shivered in the winters without coal or wood and roasted in the summer. I tried to escape several times, but her sons always caught me and brought me back. I'd have been happier as a street urchin, begging or stealing, but no. They feared I might talk to someone about the conditions we were living under."

"Richard didn't know!" Lady Hargrave cried.

"Of course he knew! He is meticulous in his research. He wanted to get rid of his wife's illegitimate child before anyone found out. But I refused to die! I lived on potato peelings and gruel. I endured beatings and humiliation. Someday, I told myself, Mummy would come and rescue me and we would be a family again. I didn't know until years later that she had a new family to care for. There was no real communication from them from one year to the next."

He turned, focusing his attention on his mother.

"What is wrong with you, woman?" he screamed at her so that she cowered in her chair. "Have you no heart? Your child was starving, with rickets and scurvy! Did you forget you had a son? Did you think I was safe somewhere with another family? Did you even bother to find out?"

Lady Hargrave collapsed in tears. From the corner of my eye I saw Barker's arms go down but so did Jack Hillary. He trained the gun on Philippa.

"Stop right there, Mr. Barker. Pray, do not believe that I left

Nigel Pelham to do all of the killing. I had the greatest pleasure from wringing Mrs. Tisher's scrawny neck while she spat out curses in my ear. The sound of the bones breaking in her neck was the most satisfying sound in the world."

There were gasps from around the room.

"You were there," I spoke up, trying to buy time. "Every murder. Nearby, I mean. You were serving a drink to Lord Hargrave when he was shot. You caught Percy when the arrow hit him. You were nearby when Olivia was shot. And Paul—"

"Oh, Paul, I killed myself. I brought him some tea and stabbed him through the heart. It was a technique I learned in the jungles of Venezuela. Oh, I wasn't as successful a killer as Nigel, perhaps, but I've had my times."

"But why kill Algernon Kerry, then? He worked for you."

"His usefulness was over once we were set up here."

"You've spoken of Mrs. Tisher," my employer said. "What of the Bromley Boarding School and Mr. Throgmorton?"

"Oh, that? Well, when His Lordship was unsuccessful in starving me to death and I reached the age of twelve, he sent me along to Bromley. Mr. Throgmorton had a reputation for extreme discipline and not asking questions. If Lord Hargrave said I was a nuisance and a rotter, then that was what I must be. He caned me constantly. He tested new devices for punishment on me. He practiced each new caning paddle on my body. When Nigel informed me that the only way to kill him was with a high-powered rifle from a distance, I purchased bullets altered to become expanding ones. The sight of his brains spraying all over the window frame was the sweetest imaginable."

"What are you going to do?" his mother asked in a low voice.

He gave a wicked smile, and spoke as an adult to a child. "I'm going to kill you, Mother. If you didn't care the least about me, why should I care about you?"

Barker tried to keep the case on track.

"How came you to leave the Bromley School?"

"I escaped," he said. "I was fourteen. I'd been freshly assaulted, so his guard was down. I skipped over the roofs and made my way to the coast, stowing away on a vessel. It ended up in—"

"South America!" I interrupted.

"Yes. The vessel went to São Paolo. I lived on the streets. It was actually easier than my time at the baby farm."

Mrs. Fraser nodded. "I told you he wasn't Brazilian."

"Eventually, I heard of a war up north and enlisted. I was eighteen by then. I met two English adventurers down on their luck, Algie and Nigel. The war itself was brutal, and we developed a reputation for being brutal ourselves. At the end of it the war was lost, but we were considered heroes."

"What happened then?" Philippa asked.

I noticed that Barker, with his hands on his head, had stepped sideways at least a foot. There was a small circular table nearby, containing a box of cigars and a heavy glass ashtray full of cigars. If he could get his foot under it and kick it, we might both be able to jump on him. Of course, I had no idea how much good I would do with one arm. The other was throbbing from the wound and little circulation.

Jack Hillary hadn't noticed, and continued his story.

"After the war, we headed south. Algernon heard there was money to be made by desperate men in rubber. We made our way to Manaus. In the beginning, we tapped the gum ourselves, but Nigel found a way to exploit the local labor by raiding local tribes. One does what needs most. The venture succeeded beyond our wildest expectation. Bicycle tires. Who knew how profitable they would become? I have become what they call in America a 'millionaire.' I could have anything I wanted. Such as revenge on what had been stolen from me."

He suddenly turned and regarded my employer.

"Tell me, Mr. Barker, what has become of my associate?"

"I shot him," Barker rumbled. "He fell over the cliff."

"Poor Nigel," he said. "He was always good in battle, but not so much in peacetime. I suppose I should thank you. He was going to be a problem. Didn't expect him to go native on me. 'Just hide in the woods and shoot at various people now and then,' I said, but no. He had to be Chief Tecumseh and make spears and arrows. Mad as a March hare. A lunatic and a drug addict; that was what I had to work with."

"'A plague upon it when thieves cannot be true to one another,' as Falstaff said," I quoted.

"Spare me your university wit, Mr. Llewelyn. While you were at Oxford reading Horace, I was sweating in the Amazon, gutting natives with a machete."

"What do you intend to do with us, sir?" Barker asked. He had put his arms down again.

"Step away from the table, Mr. Barker. I'm not a child. What do I intend to do? That should be obvious. I cannot have any witnesses alive who have seen me here. I'm supposed to be in Manaus right now. Were I there, I could even produce witnesses. Paid ones, of course. Hands on top of your head, Mr. Barker! I'm not going to warn you a final time."

"And how do you plan to get off the island?"

"I've got some boys waiting for me on the other side of Hell Bay. All I have to do is light a signal fire."

"Not tonight," Barker said.

"That's very clever, Mr. Barker. No, I'll have to wait for the gale to stop. But by then all of you will be past caring."

"You horrid man," Philippa said.

He looked down at her, and put the muzzle of his pistol against her cheek.

"I assure you, madam, I don't give a damn about your opinion. I'd blow your brains out all over that pretty dress as easily as I'd swat a fly. I've never developed a taste for these pale, spotty, anemic English types. To me you're merely the waste of a bullet."

Barker suddenly kicked the table at him. Its trajectory had been perfect, and the ashtray holding cigars provided a diversion. All the same, Jack Hillary had ducked both the table and the ashtray and the cigars bounced harmlessly off him.

Jack Hillary lifted an arm and fired. The Guv had indeed lowered his arms in front of his chest, in the act of doing something. Perhaps he was about to draw his pistol from inside his jacket, or a handful of the sharpened coins he kept. The sound of the gun going off was especially loud in the quiet of the library. I heard and even fancied I felt the impact of the bullet.

Philippa screamed. The sounds traveled up and down my spine

as if it were a xylophone. I saw blood spatter across his white shirt. Across from me, Lady Alicia burst into hysterics. Her English reserve had finally been shattered.

The Guv teetered for a moment, then fell back full length on the carpet and stopped moving.

"Your Webley draws to the left, old man," Jack complained.

"Mine doesn't," said a voice behind me.

I turned. A man was standing in the doorway, rain and blood dripping off him. There was a gash in his head and his nose was broken. One arm hung unnaturally at his side. His face was covered with scratches and grime. But one doesn't forget the face of the man who shot at you.

CHAPTER THIRTY-SEVEN

Nigel Pelham stood in the doorway at the entrance to the library, freshly drenched in rain and blood. His head had been gashed open, then coated in sand. He was muddy from the knees down. His knuckles were burst from dragging himself up the side of the cliff in the middle of a rainstorm with an injured shoulder. He held a pistol in his hand.

"Hello, Jack," he said. "Remember me?"

"Of course I remember you, Nigel," Jack said, sounding irritated.

"Really?" he asked. "It doesn't quite look like it. Looks to me as if you were carrying on with your plan without me. Your precious plan. All this would be yours and you would finally get your revenge. As if you were the only bastard that ever lived."

"Not now, Nigel!"

"I've had my fill of this whole bloody mess, Jack. I've been living on seagulls and fish. I want a plate of beefsteaks and a pint of porter and a soft chair. I've been sitting on rocks for too long."

Perhaps he expected Jack Hillary to say something, but there was no reply. Nigel Pelham looked about as if realizing for the first time he and his partner were not alone. He grinned. His teeth were bloodied.

"So many pretty ladies. I'm sorry, I must look a sight. I'm Captain Pelham of the Venezuelan army. It's been some time since I've been in such genteel surroundings."

He looked up and glanced about the room with its cozy chairs and Oriental carpets, its rows and rows of books and its grand fireplace.

"Nice digs," he said. "It seems a shame to burn it. You do still plan to burn it, don't you?"

"To the ground," Hillary said with an edge to his voice.

"Heh, heh," the man from the woods said. "You never did do things by halves, Jack."

He was breathing shallowly. I could hear the wheeze in his throat. The man was practically dead. The only thing that was keeping him alive was hate.

"Sit down, Nige, before you fall down."

"Stop telling me what to do."

His pistol bucked in his hand. The bullet tore straight through Jack's vitals. There were no screams now. Everyone was deathly quiet. Jack's eyes started in his skull. Gut shot. It was the worst way to die. Stomach acid seeps into the wound, which festers quickly. He hunched over, literally holding himself together. He wobbled, then fell to his knees, and finally rolled over to the floor. It was a fatal wound, but not merciful. He would not die soon. And he would be in agony the entire time.

"Lad!" Barker growled. "Get Pelham! He's going after the ambassador!"

I turned again. Pelham was no longer in the doorway. I saw him climbing the stair, as dangerous as a wounded panther. I took a moment to pick up the loaded Webley and ran after him.

In the hall, rain and wind howled through the obliterated front door. I slipped momentarily, then forced myself to run after the captain. I stopped and fired at him, but my shot went wide. The pistol did pull to the left. Rounding the first floor, I was not more than a dozen feet behind him, but he burst into Gascoigne's room and locked the door behind him.

"No!" I cried, kicking the door and jiggling the handle frantically. It was a stout door, however, the kind one would expect on a near castle, such as Godolphin House. No amount of kicking would allow me entrance to that chamber. Then I heard it, that terrible pop that said someone's life had just ended.

Sometimes it seems to me that history should be divided, not into B.C. and A.D. but into before the gun was invented and after. It was the greatest change in history. The sword, the dagger, one has a fighting chance, and skill came into the equation. Now anyone, man, woman, or even child, can walk into a room with a loaded gun, tug on a little twist of metal, and open a giant hole in another human being. Whether it is for good or evil depends on a number of factors, the kind that cause a magistrate to stay up late at night and contemplate. But it is a change, a profound one, and there was no going back. The genie was out of the bottle and heaven help us all.

The door suddenly opened and the colonel stepped out. His old service revolver was open and he was retrieving a spent cartridge.

"Spot of bother, that," he said, as if he had just shot a pheasant on the moor and nearly missed.

I exhaled. I would have hugged the old gentleman if he hadn't had a gun in his hand.

The ambassador appeared, looking about cautiously. "Is it safe?"

"I believe it is, sir, but you had better let me talk to Mr. Barker to make certain."

I stepped inside the room and looked down. Captain Pelham lay crumpled against the wall, his pale eyes unseeing. He had been shot once by me in the shoulder, once by Barker in the ribs, and once by the colonel straight through the heart. He'd fallen off a cliff and crawled up again with broken limbs. He was about as tough a man as anyone would want to meet, but he wouldn't kill anyone ever again.

Going downstairs, I saw Mrs. Ashleigh was binding Barker's chest with what probably was far too much bandage, but no one was about to argue the point. I went into the library again. Lady Hargrave was kneeling on the floor, with Jack Hillary's head cradled in her lap. His face was rigid and he was perspiring with pain. She was comforting him as if he were a child in a pram and wiping his forehead with a cloth. She looked half mad to me.

"Sorry to trick you that way, Thomas," he said to me. "I thought you were a decent chap."

He had slaughtered close to ten people and here he was apologizing for lying to me.

"I'm sorry, Mother, about all the others. If your husband would have seen sense . . . ."

"Ssssh," she said, stroking his head and rocking him in her arms.

Dr. Anstruther returned with his medical bag. Without a word, he gave Hillary an injection of morphine. He opened Jack's shirt and examined the wound hastily before exchanging a glance with Barker. Jack Hillary did not have long to live.

"I did it, Mum," he said. "It's just you and me again."

The woman seemed to ignore the fact that this man had killed her entire family.

His eyes focused on Barker, who was now sitting up on one elbow.

"Dammit, man, you are a hard man to kill."

"I have people here who are depending on me," Barker rumbled.

"Where was I born, Mother?" Jack asked, looking at her. "In what room?"

"Upstairs, in my bedroom. It was a secret."

"I wish it hadn't been. I would have liked to be acknowledged. At Mrs. Tisher's I was told I mustn't say who my parents were. What did I do wrong?"

"Nothing, dear," she replied. Her face was ashen and she was barely holding on to her composure.

"You just want to live and have a mother you can write to."

"Of course."

"Thomas, you know what I mean," he said, weakly. "It's a cruel world out there, isn't it?"

"Yes, Jack," I answered. "Yes, it is."

"I knew you'd understand."

I noted there was blood at the corners of his lips. He was bleeding internally. It would not be long.

He tugged off his spectacles and blinked. It made his face look younger.

"Where's Nigel?" he asked.

"Dead," I told him.

"And Algie?"

"Also dead."

He knew that. His mind must be drafting.

"I was sitting with them in our offices in Manaus this year and I said, 'We're going to be rich. What have you always wanted to do?'"

Here he coughed and a drop of blood rolled down the side of his mouth to his chin.

"'I want to see home again,' Algernon said to me. 'I want to see my parents.' And I thought, I have all this money but no one will claim me. I realized I'd been thinking about it for years. And now I had all this money and two friends who might help me get what was due me."

It was slightly warm in the house, but the sweat was rolling down his cheeks. He grimaced as a wave of pain washed over him.

"Didn't know you were having a party. Homecoming party, I told Nigel. Where's Nigel?"

"He's upstairs," I answered.

"Oh. Nigel didn't care about coming back. All his family is dead. Had to pay him. God, that hurts!"

"You needn't talk if you don't want to, Jack," his mother said.

"I was a success, you know." Mum.

"Yes."

"Made something of myself."

"You did."

"Rubber baron."

"You're taller than I expected you to be. And handsome like your father. Your natural father."

"I came home," he said, as if proud of himself.

"Yes, you did, darling. You came home."

"Home," he murmured

"Yes, home."

"Godolphin House."

"Where you were born," Lady Hargrave said.

And then he died.

CHAPTER THIRTY-EIGHT

y entire family is dead," Celia Hargrave said, still cradling the head of her eldest son.

Then the tears came down her cheeks, cascading from her chin onto the still face of Jack Hillary. Lady Hargrave did not weep. She was totally silent but the tears continued to pour down like the rain outside.

"Lad," Barker's voice, much weakened, called to me from the floor.

I crossed to him and bent over his prostrate form.

"Yes, sir."

He raised himself slightly on one elbow.

"The butler's pantry," he muttered. "Knock twice."

I was out of the room like a shot. What did the Guv have up his sleeve? I wondered. There was but one way to find out. Down the back stairs I flew, and around the corner to Partridge's sanctum sanctorum. When I reached it, I stopped myself. Then I knocked once, twice. And waited.

The door opened. Bella Anstruther was there, eyeing me curiously. Now what? I asked myself. Think of something, I thought.

"It's time!" I blurted.

She turned and repeated the phrase to someone in the room. Who was in the room? I wanted to know. Then someone circled around her and appeared in the doorway.

"I'm coming," he said.

I followed him up the stair.

"There in the library. You look rather spry for a dead man."

"Thank you," Percy Burrell said. Like mine, his arm was bandaged to his chest in a sling, but he was well dressed and not a hair was out of place. He had been groomed for his entrance by Miss Anstruther, no doubt.

"Mother!" he called when we reached the room, running to her.

Barker was up on one arm, now being helped by Philippa.

"I hid him away," the Guv explained, "because I was sure there would be another attempt on his life. He has been in the butler's pantry this entire time, being watched over by Dr. Anstruther and his daughter Bella."

Percy came forward and gingerly hugged his astonished mother. My employer couldn't save them all; I don't believe anyone could. But he had saved one. The line would continue. I caught a glimpse of Bella Anstruther as she came into the room and noticed her cheeks were flushed. I sensed the line might continue sooner than anyone anticipated.

"Doctor!" Philippa called, kneeling down beside Barker. His face had gone pale.

Anstruther stood and began removing his jacket, while Bella unbuttoned Barker's shirt. I had thought when we first arrived that Gwendolyn was the better of the two sisters, but her sister was worth two of her. The doctor examined his chest.

"The bullet is right here," he said, indicating a small purplish lump along his left side ribs. "It passed along here, but it must have struck something to deflect in this direction."

In answer, Barker straightened his left arm and shook it. The knife he habitually kept up his sleeve, strapped to his forearm, rattled out and hit the carpeted floor with a thud. No self-respecting Scotsman would be without his *skean dhu*.

"That knife saved your life," Anstruther said.

"It wouldn't be the first time," Barker replied.

"I'll have to remove that bullet immediately."

"Do it, then."

"Not here. I'm not a military doctor. I prefer sanitary conditions. Your room, perhaps? Mr. Llewelyn and I will help you up the stairs."

I've had to carry him before. I was glad Anstruther was helping me. He moved slowly but he wasn't unsteady. We reached the first floor and walked him into the room.

The doctor began barking orders to housemaids while Bella arrived with the bag. Mrs. Ashleigh hovered nearby. It was the first time I had seen her nonplussed. She didn't know what to do. Bella would act as nurse during the operation, brief as it was. There was no need for her to be present, but it was difficult to make her leave.

"You should go to your room," I said. "I'll let you know immediately if there's a problem. As soon as the doctor gives word you may come back in."

She seized my hands.

"He gets injured all the time, but I always see him a few days later. This was so distressing. How do you do this?"

"It's what we're paid to do, ma'am. Go sit down. Drink tea. It shouldn't take long."

Reluctantly, she let go of my hands and went into her room.

Ether was becoming popular in operating theaters in those days, but Barker refused it, as he refused a snifter of brandy. He showed no sign he was in any discomfort. I'd have probably screamed like a banshee. The operation occurred about fifteen minutes later. It took less than ten minutes. Anstruther sterilized the entry wound and stitched it, then cut the skin and removed the bullet, depositing the lump of bloody metal into a small tin pan. He sterilized the wound with alcohol and stitched it up as well. Now Barker would have a nice new scar to go with all the old ones.

As promised, when it was over, I brought Mrs. Ashleigh back in. Her face was freshly powdered, but I could tell she had been crying. I imagined she would have a few things to say to him when we reached the mainland. If so, I didn't want to be a witness, either for the defense or the prosecution.

Barker was temporarily reprieved by a knock at the door. It was Colonel Fraser. There was something about the old man's tanned and homely face that gave one confidence that everything would be all right.

"Good shooting, Colonel," I said.

"Blasted pistol went off in my hand," he said, as if he had no part in it. "Hit the fellow dead center. How's the patient?"

"He won't stay down long enough to be one."

"How's the ambassador?" Barker asked, as if eager to return to work.

Philippa was seated beside him, watching him like a falcon about to pounce on a hare. I gathered he wanted a private conversation with Fraser, but that wasn't going to happen.

"Well enough. We have come to an agreement. It might have helped that I saved his life. A few more concessions on his part."

"Good," Barker said. "Now what is to become of Mr. Schroeder? Will you let him go free?"

"No. We have gathered enough evidence to charge him as a spy. That will be enough for now."

Barker nodded. This fellow was a member of the government, if an unofficial one. He was not to be argued with, although if I knew the Guv, he would see that Schroeder would be treated fairly.

"It's finished," Fraser said. "You cut it rather fine, I must say."

"How did you happen to be armed, Colonel?" I asked.

"Barker here suggested that I keep a loaded gun nearby. He was convinced an attempt would be made soon upon Gascoigne."

I pulled a face at my employer. It was he who had suggested to me that the killer was concerned with the family line, and there was no political element to the murders whatsoever.

"Barker, send a bill to the institute," the colonel said. "I understand Richard intended to pay for it himself, but we shall pay it instead."

"There shall be no bill," Barker said. "I have done nothing. Captain Pelham shot Jack Hillary, and you shot Captain Pelham."

Fraser chuckled. "Don't be an ass, man. Take the check. It will just cover both of your medical expenses."

"We'll take it, Colonel," Philippa said.

"Smart woman."

Barker looked at her. She looked back. He was the first to look away.

"How's your arm, young fellow-me-lad?" Fraser asked.

"Sore as the dickens," I said. "But the bullet passed through without hitting bone."

"That should heal up nicely, then."

Ross Fraser rose slowly from his chair. He patted my hand.

"I must get back to the ambassador before he realizes he's given away too many concessions. Take care of your two young patients, my lady! I don't envy you keeping them alive."

By then, it was near midnight. The storm had not yet abated, but it had turned into a steady downpour without wind or lightning.

Dr. Anstruther came into our room, examined and bound my arm, and offered us laudanum. We both refused. He seemed pleased with himself, having three living patients in the house, or was it because his daughter had bewitched the heir to Godolphin House?

I was too exhausted to check, but I was certain that Partridge himself was down below guarding the front door, just in case. Heirs had died to the right and to the left, but Godolphin House would go on.

Barker was still awake, immobile in his bed. I wanted to go to sleep, but he didn't look ready to turn down the lamp.

"What are you thinking, sir?"

"News of this will get out, of course. I believe the official line shall be that two ex-soldiers washed up on the beach and went on a rampage. Stress from battle. That happens sometimes."

"You don't believe the public is entitled to the truth?" I asked.

Barker reached up and turned down the lamp.

"Why start now?" he asked. "I believe the Burrell family has suffered enough."

We lay in the darkness for a few minutes. Then I turned up the lamp again.

"All right," I said. "Your turn."

"Damn and blast, I'm injured!"

"The chair!"

"Confound it," he said, but got up and seated himself in the hard chair. I put the lamp by his face.

"Why did you tell me the killings were due to family issues, and then warn Fraser to watch out for an assassin?"

"It seemed to me as soon as Lord Hargrave was killed that it was a political assassination. Later, I realized it was an illegitimate son angry over his treatment. But the killers didn't necessarily have the same opinions, so I thought it possible one wanted to have some money on the side. Killing the ambassador fit the bill."

"Speaking of money, didn't Cesar, I mean Jack Hillary, mention a sum he received for selling his rubber plantation?"

"A substantial amount, from what I can make out."

"So where is it?"

"I imagine it is stuffed into his prized possession."

It took me a moment to work that out. "The guitar."

"Very good."

"Why did Pelham go after more money if he were already wealthy?"

"He wasn't safely away with his share yet. You saw what happened to Algernon Kerry. They both knew only one would get away safely."

"Best of friends and mortal enemies."

"Something like that. Ouch! Another inch to the left and I'd have punctured a lung."

"No sympathies. So, why invent this entire Cesar persona in the first place?"

"It was simply to get Jack Hillary into the house to begin his mayhem. You see, this was planned for years but thrown together in the final moments. Hillary believed he was visiting the family with Kerry. They didn't know about the party until the last minute, or about the French ambassador coming. By then it was too late to put it off. Cesar, if I may call him that, recognized I had no normal function here and used you to tell him all you could about me."

"I should have kept my mouth shut. I'm sorry, sir."

"Just remember this lesson for next time," he said. He wasn't easy to cross-examine. The lamp reflected in his spectacles. He could not be intimidated.

"You hid Percy away because you knew Jack would stop at nothing to kill every heir."

"Aye, I did."

"Would he have killed his mother, if she didn't agree?"

"Oh, I have no doubt. He may have acted like the dutiful son, but he'd have cut her throat if he found it necessary."

"Coldhearted," I said.

"He was raised to be. Really, Lord Hargrave sent him away to die. It was due to his resilience and resolve that he survived into his teen years. His temperament was just what was necessary to survive in the Bromley School. At the earliest opportunity he escaped the school, worked his way to Land's End, and took the first freighter leaving. It happened to be going to South America."

"When did you first suspect Cesar was Jack?" I asked.

"He stayed close to you but avoided me."

"Sir," I informed him, "most of my friends avoid you. You terrify them."

"Have I not spent a week at a house party? I'm quite civilized."

"You do know, sir, that most house parties are not like this?"

"Spare me your witticisms, lad. I can't laugh with my side full of stitches."

He rose and shuffled over to the bed. I put out the lamp. Both of us were probably asleep within a minute. Being shot has that effect on one.

CHAPTER THIRTY-NINE

My throbbing wound woke me early the next morning. Getting out of bed, I crossed to the window in robe and slippers and looked out. The storm had abated, and the verdant lawn was bathed in sunshine. As I watched, the gardener passed slowly across my view with his wheelbarrow. Nothing that had happened this week had affected him save for the gale. People came and went, but the house and the gardens would go on forever.

I broke a cardinal rule that morning and did not shave. After we were up and about, Mrs. Ashleigh fastened a new sling for me in the landing on the first floor. She put my jacket over my shoulder. I went downstairs before breakfast and decided to see if the flag was still flying.

Before I could do so, however, I had to pass over the spot where Olivia Burrell had died. I shall never forget the look that passed between us. It was as though she were still standing, but the light in her eyes snuffed out. I had promised to protect her and failed. With other occupations, when someone fails, some project is pushed back or something is reorganized. People die in mine, and we don't forget them, ever.

I reached the front door and stepped between the makeshift boards. Partridge was off seeing to breakfast, presumably. As I stepped out from the porch, I stopped and looked about. Gulls wheeled and argued overhead in a blue sky. It was as if nothing had happened.

I walked slowly across the lawn, aware I was mourning a girl I didn't really know anything about. Off to my right, the gardener pushed a blade mower across the grass, making geometric patterns in it with practiced ease. Had last night even happened? I wondered. But I knew the truth.

The flag, or to be more precise, Gwendolyn Anstruther's dress, was still tied to the flagpole. The wind fluttered it unmercifully and there was no way it could ever be worn again, but as a flag it was beautiful. It stood proudly above my head and beckoned to the world: *Come save us.*

I crossed to the cliff and looked down over the spot where Nigel Pelham had fallen and then clawed his way back again. The rain had washed away all sign of him. He too had been here merely temporarily. To only a few of us survivors would he be remembered at all.

I looked up at the dark blue sea that seemed to stretch in every direction. How small and insignificant this rock was. Who had ever heard of Godolphin Isle? Who would remember it? Barker would move on to another case. Mrs. Ashleigh would do her best to help her friend begin her new life, and these incidents would eventually be forgotten. I alone was the one who would recall all that had happened to her last night, the sole custodian of the memory.

A sail. My God, it was a sail, out in the bay. Two sails! I turned and ran toward the house. As I reached the entrance, Partridge came out the door. It was as if he were a spider on a web and could feel every vibration that occurred.

"There are sails out there," I told him. "I'll bet they are rescue ships and the coast guard!"

"Thank you, sir," the butler said, as if he were humoring me and the information was of only passing interest. "Breakfast is ready."

I watched him walk toward the harbor. Did he hurry? Not a bit of it. He might have been moving through the house to replace a spoon someone had dropped.

When I entered, Barker and Mrs. Ashleigh were seated. Breakfast was corned beef hash and fried potatoes. We guests had eaten our way through the stores. The cook had made fresh biscuits and set out the last of several jams in small bowls. The tea was hot, but there was no more cream. In the midst of all the turmoil Mrs. Albans had fed us marvelously well meal after meal.

We did not linger. A ferry would be coming soon. I went back to the room and, upon seeing the luggage and Mrs. Ashleigh's familiar steamer trunk, felt blue. There was no Cesar to chat with while carting the luggage. I was still having a difficult time realizing that he had been Jack Hillary, the architect of this entire scheme. He had fooled me completely.

A boat finally arrived at the docks and was met by Partridge. He asked for everything: the police, the coast guard, a ferry, food supplies, lumber, carpenters, glaziers, and what have you. The island would be set to rights more quickly than I could imagine and the Burrells would stay on. There was a new heir, and there were family members to mourn and inter, including one that would receive no stone. His scheme did not work, but perhaps he would have taken comfort in being gathered quite literally to his forebears.

Soon we were out in front of the hall, and mounting the luggage on the dogcart. Apollo seemed to have recovered from his wound and hauling the cannon to the front door. I walked over and patted his huge gray muzzle. The party was preparing to leave, but they had little to say to one another. It was as if they were making a decision about what they would tell people about the event, and it required a lot of thought.

Philippa Ashleigh came out in an outfit of lace and yellow chiffon. Her hat was as white as a parasol. The night before she had been menaced with a pistol and she was determined to prove she was unbowed. She could have given the sun lessons in how to shine.

Cyrus Barker was equally resplendent. Beneath his black coat he wore a brown leather vest with a matching bowler. He held a wavering arm out to her and she took it, holding her skirt in her other hand. Some have called them mismatched, this aristocratic beauty and her rough-and-tumble swain, but just then, chatting as they walked toward the harbor, I thought them perfectly matched.

As soon as it arrived, we loaded the luggage aboard the ferry and without preamble it departed. The sea seemed frothy and insubstantial after nearly a fortnight on that rock. The boat rocked and kicked its heels like a lamb frolicking in a meadow. Or perhaps it was just me. But no. I saw it in everyone's eyes. Relief. We had lived, and life was so very, very precious.

I thought there might be recriminations. Barker had not contracted to protect Lord Hargrave but some might suppose he had failed in his duties. This case might tarnish his name a little. However, he had successfully outwitted two very canny and dangerous men. Three, if we counted Kerry. I doubted the case would haunt him professionally. I worried just the same, but that is just my temperament.

We arrived at the harbor in Land's End in time to catch the coach to Penzance and then the train to London. It was a hasty departure, and the luggage might have had reason to complain of its treatment, but we were all soon aboard. Later, I caught up with Barker in the smoking car, where he was filling a new pipe that he had purchased in the station. It was a simple briar but would serve until he bought another meerschaum.

"When did you first suspect Cesar?" I asked.

"That isn't how I work. I suspected everyone at first, then tried to remove them from my list one by one. Cesar refused to be removed. For example, when Paul Burrell was killed there was a fresh drink on the table. That meant one of the servants was the last to see him alive."

"But that could have been any servant," I said. "He might have brought the drink, killed him, and then locked the door. Then he'd get another drink and come across as innocent."

"That is what Cesar, or rather Jack Hillary, wanted you to think. Since there was no current suspect, it made the footman look suspicious. Remember, he had a lot of time to plan. Fifteen years or more."

"Did you believe his story about the war?"

"Some of it was true. Most likely, he met Kerry, then discovered later, in a conversation, his former connection to Godolphin House. If he were rehabilitated and invited back he would be Jack's entry into the house without arousing suspicion."

"And Pelham?"

"I believe he read Pelham's character correctly and offered him a unique opportunity: to visit an island and live on it, with no supplies, surviving while slaughtering the inhabitants. I don't believe one man in a thousand would consider such an offer, but Pelham did. It would be his biggest challenge."

"But what about the French ambassador?"

"I'll admit I was surprised when I saw Pelham run up the stair after the ambassador. I assumed he was a spy. More likely he was an opportunist. Having murdered the French ambassador, he could write to the German or Russian embassies in order to offer his services. Pelham was thinking of the future."

"He was a tough bird, I'll give him that."

"But the colonel had the skill to finish him off."

"Just coincidental that he happened to be in the room at the time."

"Well," Barker said, puffing on his pipe. "I may have suggested that Gascoigne was growing tired of being cooped in his room, and the details of the treaty had not yet been fully fleshed out."

"Yes, but most treaties don't involve having one party fully armed."

Barker shrugged his broad shoulders.

"That's the best answer I'm going to get?"

"Never reveal your full hand until the game is over, lad."

"Not even to me?"

"Especially not to you. If I spoon-feed you the answers, however shall you learn?"

"I had worked out that there was a bastard son, and that he was killing off the family line in order to inherit, but I assumed it was Pelham. If there was anyone with him, I thought it was likely he was working for him, not running the entire scheme."

Again, Barker shrugged as if to say "I'm not responsible for what you thought."

"If successful, would he really have killed us all?"

"By then we had become witnesses. The only way to inherit would be to have Pelham kill us all, and then get back to Brazil quickly, leaving the impression he had never left. Hunting trip, perhaps? Exploring the jungles for more rubber?"

"Why kill Kerry, then? I mean, he did get him in the door."

"He had become a liability. He was hopped up on cocaine and garrulous. These men were ruthless, even with each other."

"So I assume Pelham killed Jack for the same reason, that he could implicate Pelham in the scheme. Do you suppose Jack offered him a lot of money to do this?"

"Oh, Pelham didn't care about the money. He wanted to test his mettle against an island full of people. A siege."

"He hadn't realized Cyrus Barker would be there." I had said too much. My employer changed the subject.

"Sir! The pistol! Where did Pelham get hold of a pistol."

"Ah. It was Kerry's. I saw it in his luggage when I examined it. Hillary must have smuggled it to him. The irony is that by doing so, he sealed his own destruction."

"How is your arm?"

"It hurts. I'll have it looked at in London. Anstruther offered me laudanum again, but I prefer to avoid it. How is your chest?"

"It will heal well enough in time."

"No doubt."

"You must see to your Webley when we get back to London. That sight must be readjusted."

"To be truthful, I've never used the sight. I just point and squeeze and hope for the best."

Barker sat quietly for a moment, then a chuckle rumbled from inside his depth. It became a full laugh. I turned red, which only made him laugh harder. He groaned from the pain of laughing.

After he finished, he mopped his eyes under his spectacles with his pocket handkerchief.

"I must get back to Philippa," he said, and left me alone.

"'I must get back to Philippa,'" I repeated to myself. Then I fell into a brown study that lasted a good hour at least. Some things fell into place and not merely about the case. Something had to be done.

We arrived late in London and saw Mrs. Ashleigh to her elegant town house in Kensington. Then we took a hansom to our house in Newington. Mac and Harm seemed glad to see us, well, Barker, anyway.

The next morning I awoke to the sound of sparrows twittering in the trees outside my window. I much preferred them to seagulls. It was eight thirty, and Barker had gone into the office and left me to rest and recover. I had to see to my arm, but first I had another appointment to make. I picked up the receiver on the telephone set.

"Operator, Aldgate two-one-four-seven, please."

I was connected through.

"Cowan residence," a male servant answered.

"I wish to speak with Mrs. Cowan. My name is Llewelyn. I shall wait."

"Very good, sir," he murmured. "Hold the line."

Anticipation thrummed in my veins. I danced a jig on the linoleum, under the disapproving stare of Jacob Maccabee, who was adjusting the standing clock in our hall, the better to hear me with.

"Good morning, Thomas!" a voice from heaven said in my ear. A perfect voice. A musical one.

"Rebecca! Good morning."

"Safely back in London, then?"

"In a manner of speaking, yes."

"To what do I owe the pleasure of your call?"

"I was wondering what you have on for today."

"Just a few social calls. Why?"

"Would you like to have lunch with me?"

"Oh, Thomas, it's a trifle early to be seen together in public."

290 • WILL THOMAS

"A park, then. Battersea or Hyde Park, it doesn't matter. Your choice."

She laughed. It was the most beautiful sound in the world. "Impatient man! Whatever is this about?"

"Oh, not much," I said. "I just wanted to ask you a question."

Then time stopped. I heard nothing but the beating of my heart. Nearby, Jacob craned his neck and glared at me over his cheater spectacles. Not much gets by him. His eyes were like saucers.